DISC

MW01639760

cult

Other Books by Warren Adler

The War of the Roses
Random Hearts
Trans-Siberian Express
Mourning Glory
The Casanova Embrace
Blood Ties
Natural Enemies
Banquet Before Dawn
The Housewife Blues
Madeline's Miracles
We Are Holding the President Hostage
Private Lies
Twilight Child
The Henderson Equation
Undertow

Short Stories

The Sunset Gang
Never Too Late for Love
Jackson Hole, Uneasy Eden

The Fiona Mysteries

American Quartet
American Sextet
Senator Love
Immaculate Deception
The Witch of Watergate
The Ties That Bind

Available in all formats as e-books and Print on Demand wherever books are sold online and off.

Visit www.WarrenAdler.com and join the Warren Adler Book Club

cult

a novel of brainwashing and death

warren adler

STONEHOUSE
PRESS

STONEHOUSE PRESS

ISBN: 0-9717049-6-1 Trade Paperback
ISBN: 0-9717049-0-2 Hardcover

Inquiries: www. warrenadler.com

For Daphne Greene

Introduction

The horrible events of September 11th, 2001 are yet another example of the power of the cult experience. Those deluded young suicide bombers had been brainwashed into believing that their action would somehow buy them a ticket to some imagined afterlife where they would spend their days frolicking with more than seventy odd young virgins provided for their pleasure by some divine entity.

Worse, they had been persuaded, beyond reason and logic, that by killing themselves and thousands of others these dubious and utterly ridiculous rewards would be assured. How can any sane person subscribe to such an incredibly bizarre idea? Unfortunately they can and they do.

Obviously, there is some flaw in the human psyche, perhaps in the brain itself, which causes ordinary people to ingest and absorb such views and be controlled by them. And there are ruthless people who have discovered the process and are willing to use this flaw to enslave and gain power over others and exploit them for their own sinister purposes.

Because the process is such a mystery, it is difficult to comprehend, although the evidence of its power is overwhelming. It is indisputable that people can be brainwashed. Destructive ideas can be implanted in people's mind and they can be programmed to carry them out.

The fictional cult described in this novel is one of many that are in existence today all over the world. While they are different in focus and objectives, they have one thing in common. They brainwash people, program them and send them out into the world to do the bidding of the so-called Guru or "Messiah" who runs the cult as absolute ruler.

Hard to believe? Visit Ground Zero in New York City. Or Auschwitz, or Jonestown, or Waco and on and on.

In *modern usage, the term "cult" is often used to describe any religious group or sect viewed as strange or dangerous, unorthodox or extremist, with members often living outside of conventional society under the direction of a charismatic leader. These organizations often employ abusive, manipulative, or illegal means to gain control over their followers' lives.*

cult

1

"Barney Harrigan!"

The name, the voice, the memory stunned her. Her fingers shook and she steadied the instrument against her ear.

"Is this Naomi Forman?" the voice inquired, still tentative and uncertain. The red numbers on the digital clock read three a.m. The hour of desperation. Would the voice of Barney Harrigan announce disaster? No call could come at that moment without a reason. Barney Harrigan! She shivered at the ancient memory, the old painful love, her own awful guilt. From the beating pulse in her throat and the sudden emptiness in the pit of herself, she knew it still lingered. Hadn't she killed it for good years ago? Five. Nearly six.

"I can't believe it."

"I'm sorry." He offered the obligatory apology.

Kicking off the comforter, she sat cross-legged on the bed.

"Where are you?" she asked.

"Fort Lauderdale."

"I didn't know you moved out of Manhattan."

Had he moved since she had last looked up his name in the Manhattan directory, a guilty whim? The address had changed. It was not the place in SoHo they had once shared, in which they had once loved. The flame had burned hard and hot, ending finally, the reasons blurred by time.

"I'm at my parents' place in Lauderdale. I dropped off Kev."

"Kev?"

"My son."

"Son?"

"I married a few years ago. He's four."

A brief pause, a mite too long.

"Congratulations." Her tone was sarcastic, and she was embarrassed by her reaction. He ignored it.

"Why I called . . ." He hesitated, clearing his throat. ". . . At this ungodly hour. But you see, I just found out. And you were the only person I could talk to in Washington."

So it was Washington he needed. For a fleeting moment, she had allowed a part of herself to yearn for something more. He had her at a distinct disadvantage. He had found someone else to love. She had not. As if he had won and she had lost.

"It's very complicated," he said. "But it boils down to this."

So he was boiling down again. He had once called it the bottom line. How bitterly she had reacted to that phrase. The bottom line, he had ranted, is that I cannot live a life that is totally political. Not everything is politics and causes, there is home and hearth. Family. Sharing.

Their old one-note argument. She hadn't been ready for surrender. Not then.

"Charlotte." He coughed. "My wife." A bark of hoarseness quickly cleared. "She has been captured by the Glories." He paused, obviously waiting for a reaction.

In her mind, the Glories were merely a vague collection of information. Rich, powerful, right-wing, espousing a totalitarian view of the world, a dubious religious sect. Some called it a cult with political pretensions. Their leader was Father Glory, an Indian businessman, who believed he was the Messiah. She thought of Jim Jones, the People's Temple Guru who commanded 900 people to die in Guyana; David Koresh, who created a standoff with the government, then ordered his band of crazies to head for Armageddon; Marshall Applewhite, who talked his followers into believing that suicide would buy them a UFO to trip to a "higher level," wherever that was. Other images came to mind, shaven-headed Krishnas chanting on street corners; neatly dressed Glories selling candy, knickknacks, flowers on street corners; stories of frantic parents chasing lost adult children.

And of course, there was Bin Laden and all those associated crazies who believed, really believed, that paradise awaited them, paradise being an eternity with 72 virgins. An eternity? Yuck. Sounds like a headache to me. She remembered her own clumsy and painful deflowering. It was equally horrendous for what was his name. She had forgotten, only that his "thing" stabbed mercilessly and the whole experience was appalling. But a cult was a cult, and fools who believed such things were just that, fools and worse. Seventy-two, no less. The "thing" would have to be made of wrought iron.

Besides, this only happened to other people. Unless, of course, you were caught in the crosshairs of their horror, like on September 11th. The date stirred her disgust, and she shook it away and recalled what Barney had said about the Glories.

"How awful," she said, shrugging. It seemed an appropriate response.

"I just found out."

"How ..." she asked, but he was already off, explaining in a choppy narrative. As she listened, she wondered, Why me? What has this got to do with me?

"She had gone to Seattle to visit her sister," he explained. His voice conveyed a touch of hysteria and she forced herself to listen respectfully, patiently, although her interest in the subject of his pain was marginal. "She has this sister, Susan. Both their parents are dead. I said fine. She hadn't seen her in two years. Why not? She worked pretty hard with Kevin. What's one lousy week? We both knew Susie was involved with something. But we didn't know it was that. Not the Glories. Sure, go ahead, I told her. I encouraged her. So she went." Out of the cage, Naomi thought, pulling together a picture of Charlotte and her life, hoping it would bring back the old image of her own rebellion. It didn't.

"She called every day from the coast. Spoke to Kevin and me. Told us how much she missed us. Said she had gone with Susie to some kind of farm, had met fabulous, really caring, loving people. Wonderful, I said. Just wonderful. Then she called and said she'd like to spend some more time out there." He was talking at her, not to her, compulsive, slightly hysterical. She let it happen, trapped by the old tie.

"Charlotte is 25. That's the age in their target range. They zeroed in and got her. Just like that. Imagine." She heard him swallow, picturing his bobbing Adam's apple.

A ten-year difference, Naomi calculated. From her vantage point, he had robbed the cradle. She was his age, 35.

"She seemed happy." State of mind was another. "We have this big apartment, a co-op on 74th and Fifth." Financial status. "And she loved the kid. Loved him." He paused. "Me, too. We were all very close." Family ties. Naomi winced, resisting the gnawing envy.

"Then she called two days ago." His voice broke, and the panic slid into the dark room, raising involuntary goose bumps on her thighs and arms. She waited until he cleared his throat, her ears clogged with the pounding pulse of her heart. For some reason, she felt his fear now. Was this voice really Barney's? Or some disembodied bleat that had splintered loose from an old fantasy? Keep your distance, fella, she begged. This mess is on your plate, not mine.

"She said ..." His voice steadied. "She said she was not coming home. Never. That she loved me and Kevin. That she had found something important, a new way of life, something spiritual. That someday we would understand. It wasn't Charlotte talking. Not her at all. Not my Charlotte. She was different, sounded different. I couldn't understand it. First I thought she was drugged or hypnotized. But then I thought ... hell, the son of a bitches brainwashed her." His voice had risen. "Am I making sense?" he said quickly, his tone lowering. "I'm just so fucking mad."

"Easy, Barney," she whispered.

"I'm really sorry for throwing this shit on your doorstep, Nay. I have no right." So the issue was rights now, she thought. Rights, after all, were her business. She was assistant director of the Human Rights Council, a group that monitored rights in countries with repressive policies, a growing menace. Did he know that? Of course. She had just started with them as they approached the exit door of their relationship. So now, invoking the word "rights," he was subliminally appealing to her sense of compassion? This might explain his motive for calling her. But the word had other meanings, in different contexts. Actually, despite his assertion, he did have the right. There was the right of past relationships, of old friendships, of shared experiences, of loving. They had once touched each other deeply. Often she had felt his mark on her, like fingerprints on her body, tangible and telling, and on her heart and soul, intangible and abstract.

"You have every right," she told him with conviction.

"The thing is," he said, his courage hardening. "I'm not going to just accept this without a fight. There has got to be some channel of official help. The FBI. Congressmen. They can't just take people, tear them away from their families, from the people who love them. This is America, dammit."

Torn away? Suppose it had been Charlotte's conscious decision. Like herself. Perhaps, she, too, had had enough. But to tear a mother from a living child, that was unnatural, wrong. Nobody can make someone do this.

"So I'm going to fight this," Barney said. "I have no set plan. But I'm going to fight. That's why I called, Nay. I need your help."

She hesitated. Help? What could she do? But at this hour who could deny a willingness ...

"But how can I help?" she asked, hoping he would sense the negative spin, that she could not help. He had, indeed, the right to ask her, but not the right to enmesh her. Guilt, the eternal enemy, prodded her. The dead fetus they had created bonded them. Their baby. She had never told him, never would. Ever.

Despite her political convictions that she had the right to make this choice, she could not totally shake the guilt of the action. For a long time she had put it in back of her mind. With his call, the discomfort came raging back.

"I ... I don't know if I'm the one, Barney. I mean, I know about human rights and I do have some connections in Washington. But this, the Glories. I don't know much about so-called cults."

"I need you, Nay."

"I'll grant you that you need something, Barney." She paused, hesitated. "I may be the wrong ticket. The rights I monitor deal with another dimension ... governments mostly...."

"Rights are rights," Barney said. This time it was he who paused. "I'm invoking ... well ... what we once were to each other. I know. I know. It's bizarre. I'm pushing the envelope. Hell, we have history, Nay. History counts. And you have this heightened sense of justice and compassion."

"You're conning me, Barney," she said.

"I hope so."

"I've toughened up even more so," she said. "I don't guilt so easily." She lied. Guilt would make her comply and she knew it.

"Yes or no, Nay. I'm begging and you know from experience that's not my style."

"Shit, Barney. Why me? Why now?"

"Yes or no, Nay?"

"It's not fair, Barney."

"Is that a yes?"

"I don't want this."

Of course not, she cried within herself. He must have divined her tacit consent.

"Please, Nay. Do it."

"I'll disappoint you. I haven't got the connections you need."

"We'll see. I'll be in Washington tomorrow." He giggled incongruously while she groaned. "Today just call around, so you'll be able to point me in the right direction. Maybe that's all I'll get from you. A road map. Who to see. What to do. Where to start. What's your office number?" She gave it to him. "I'll get Kevin set with the folks. Poor kid. He's all confused. Where's Mommy? You tell me how to explain that to a four-year-old kid."

"I wouldn't know," she said thinking suddenly of their own lost baby, bitterness welling up, her gut cramping.

"God, Nay, I'm grateful," he said. She heard the click and the connection went dead.

In the stony silence of the dark room, she was shivering, but only partly from the cold. His presence had descended like a tornado, leaving a trail of destruction—her tranquility, her courage, her sense of self, her carefully erected barriers. It had taken her years to construct the protective dikes. The tornado had shaken loose her underpinnings.

She could clearly remember the beginning and the end. Between was not exactly a middle. More like revved-up images on a projector gone awry, leaving impressions, but no continuity. She smelled his presence in the room, an amalgam of his aftershave and man scent. Yet it came from memory like a flood. He had never lived with her in this place. But that fact did not stop the memory from coming.

"I loved you instantly," he had said.

"Pshaw," she mimicked the word seen frequently in a cartoon character's balloon, meant to be humorous incredulity. They had known each other nearly three hours.

"A hundred and seventy minutes, actually," he said, looking at his watch. They had been sitting at a window table in the Oak Room of the Plaza Hotel, drinking white wine and looking into each other's eyes. Hers were hazel, flecked with yellow, and it seemed as if he were counting the yellow specks. His were blue gray, heightened by the outside brightness of the late afternoon on 59th Street and the green from Central Park across the way. They both knew that something momentous had happened. "Not pshaw," he said. "Egad."

Of course, she didn't trust it. Nothing happens that fast. "It's the wine," she said.

"It's the heart."

She was working for this organization involved with women's rights in Africa. He was selling computers and her group was in the market to buy a few.

"I'm not the person to see," she had told him.

"You're the person I see," he had said, brash, flirtatious, self-confident. It was true.

"How do you feel about our cause?" she had asked, full of the idea and the outrage.

"I'm for it. How can anyone be against it? Besides, I'd be for anything you're for. That's why I'm making this call. Computers will enhance that cause, speed the victory."

"You don't sound sincere," she had countered, noting his good looks.

"I can prove my sincerity," he said.

"How?"

"Over drinks. It might take time. You look like a hard case to convince."

She had laughed. It was a Friday and it had been a terrible week. The cause exhausted the mind and senses, left everyone ravaged with intensity, frustration, horror and commitment. There were so many injustices, so many terrible stories about the lives of women in Africa, a daily diet of despair. There were times when she needed a respite. Something without tales of injustice and pain. Barney

Harrigan was a perfect choice for such a respite. She could tell he couldn't really care less about the suffering of anyone thousands of miles away. When he invited her out for a drink, she consented.

"Sure, I'm all for the cause. Mostly I like the messenger," he said, watching her sipping the wine. She felt the intensity of his focus. She wondered exactly how casual an encounter this was.

"I don't believe it," she had said, laughing.

"I am a great believer in women. I worship them."

"Don't you have any real convictions?" she said.

"You. You're my conviction. Put me in a cell with you and I'll take the rap."

"You're making fun of me," she had said. "I'm a very serious woman."

"That's my favorite flavor."

It was banter, pure blarney. He had the kind of Irish charm that could protect his real self. She had a mind that probed and reasoned. Men sensed she searched too hard, too fiercely. People had told her often that her compassion gave off too much heat, her love for mankind in general was too intense, which left little room for attention to an individual person. They had a point, and she tried to correct this trait in herself, bank the fire. Her record was spotty on this point. She couldn't, after all, help what she was. "Don't think and analyze so much," her mother told her frequently. "It doesn't make you sexy."

Then, suddenly, far out of context of the moment, as if to prove her seriousness, she had begun to tell him all about, of all things, the practice of female circumcision.

"Bad timing," he said, winking.

"That's obvious," she said with a snicker. She had caught his drift. He was right. She retreated.

He lifted both hands.

"Okay. I buy it. You are a serious woman. But I'm a serious, very serious man. And I'm very serious about you."

"Blarney." She giggled foolishly, enjoying the fun of their repartee. It was fun to be silly. Just what she needed. His persona wrapped her in a warm bath. I know it's just a line, she told herself. A salesman's line. He took her hand in his and raised it to his lips.

"It doesn't happen like this," she said, growing dangerously comfortable.

"Who said?"

He had the Irish look as well, his skin colored like fine sand, a good long straight nose, a chin with a cleft, large teeth, although one eyetooth was crooked. His hair curled and waved, covering his ears up to his lobes. An Adam's apple bobbed in his neck, tightly wrapped in a high starched collar. A gold pin held the edges together over a tight knot. Her mother, a slave to Jewish chauvinism, would have called him a scutch and worried about his not being circumcised. That again. The thought had made her blush blood red.

"Is it hot in here?"

"It's me," he said.

Actually, it was quite cool. Outside, which she saw through the high windows looking out to 59th Street, the setting sun threw long shadows along the pavement. People changed their pace and clothes to greet the night. It was September. Summer was fading. There was a chill in the air and a sharp breeze, which made people who walked against it squint oddly, nodding their heads.

"They're changing now," he said.

"What?"

"Your eyes. The yellows are fading. The greens are getting bluish."

She had begun to wonder how long they could sit like this. Not that she wanted it to end. But she felt obliged to act, a compulsion to pull herself out of limbo, into action. It was another quirk of hers, and she felt the guilt of time passing unproductively. She tore her eyes away from him to look at her watch.

"I had planned to go back to work."

He snapped his fingers and took a little notebook from the inside pocket of his suit jacket. He was, as he told her later, an addicted note taker. Then he looked at his watch. "Damn. I was going to the beach. See? You made me forget. Made me forget everything. The point of writing things down is to never forget to look at your notes." He peered outside. "Too cold anyway." He looked at her and sighed. "Your sun is a thousand times brighter."

"Come on, Harrigan." She mocked him finally. He shrugged but did not seem insulted.

"I know what I feel."

Her mother had taught her what thin ice was. Never make a step unless you know it's solid. She had learned that attraction often lied. Anyway, she had no time for "relationships." She was involved in a cause and that took precedence

"It's purely hormonal," she told him honestly, feeling her own attraction.

"You got that right."

"I know your type, trying to book your weekend."

"Even your insults are like sweet nectar."

"You're being a silly romantic," she chided. "It's called weekend panic. Fear of being alone, without a girl, for two whole days." No substance here, she decided, gratuitously. It doesn't happen like this.

She was still on that tack, long after dinner in an Italian place in the Village where he told her he had an expense account.

"See. It's just been business," she told him. By then, of course they had exchanged lives, at least the surface narratives.

"I want to make money," he said. "I don't want to be a schlep. I believe in the golden rule: He who has the gold rules."

"That is crass and insensitive," she told him, one of the first of many rebukes.

"Neither," he said seriously. He spent some time, justifying his sales career, calling himself a peddler. He had chosen sales, he told her, because it meant a quicker route to the pot of gold. "The world belongs to the salesman. My father was a goddamned bookkeeper. A butt-kisser." A generation of bitterness excreted. She knew he was talking from his interior now. He was Irish to the core, and she saw a black gloomy streak. She sensed he had sharp mood swings. "I want money, a family, loving, luxury, fun, trust, goodness. A private nest to rest my weary brain and bones."

"What about ideals, making a better world?" He looked at her, not certain of her seriousness.

"I'm more your bread-and-potatoes man. Let the world take care of itself."

"You can't close you eyes to bad things. It can happen to you."

"I'm not a fool, Naomi. Shit happens. I just don't want to step in it. I'm on the money trail. When I make it give I'll give it away. Hell, you can help me spend it."

"And in the meantime?"

"I'll concentrate on numero uno."

"Most people do. But my ship is on a different tack."

"Helping to save the world, right?"

"Mostly. Fighting for good over evil. Helping mankind."

"Mankind?" He laughed. "I'm mankind."

"I mean generically. People."

"A true liberal," he sighed.

"Jewish and flaming."

"I'm with the Pragmatic Party. It has one constituent: me."

"And its party platform?"

"The golden rule."

"Which one?"

"The only one that counts."

So the curse had been on it from the beginning, but she hadn't let herself dwell on it then. People changed, compromised, grew together. Besides, by then, reason had surrendered to love.

"It's happened," he told her later that same night, standing in the doorway of his small apartment in Greenwich Village. "I've been betrayed by amour."

Her legs had floated her there, and now he pressed against her in the semi-darkness of the dusky corridor where the faint smell of provolone cheese drifted up from the Italian restaurant on the ground floor. All the time-honored clichés rushed through her consciousness.

"This is dumb. I'm not that sort of girl."

But bells were going off. Cannons exploding. The earth moving. She would never forget the moment.

They spent the entire weekend in his bed, barely getting enough of each other, trying to understand why it had happened.

"I never really saw one like that," she said. "I guess I lived in a ghetto. My mother would be rabid."

She was, but then his charm won her. She would have loved to have him for a son-in-law.

She remembered, too, that he had tried to describe what he was really feeling, to show her that under all the salesman blarney was a sensitive and loving heart.

"It's like an incompleteness trying to find its completeness. A half of a thing looking for the other half. We've found it, Naomi. Don't you see what this means?"

"Trouble," she said, pecking his ear.

"Nay," he said, chuckling. "That's what I'll call you from now on ... Nay. As in naysayer."

"Stupid mick," she whispered.

"I found it, the other half. I love you, Nay."

"Too fast. Don't trust it."

For some inexplicable reason, she started to cry. Tears bathed her cheeks and he licked them with his tongue, tear by tear.

"You see," he said, "we're like blood brothers now." He had chuckled at the reference. "Like Indians that transfer the blood of their cut veins. I drank your tears."

A month later, she had moved in with him to a SoHo loft that he had just bought. He spent a great deal of time designing the space. Working on blue graph paper, he drew and redrew lines for rooms, pressing her for opinions about sizes, flow, asking for a sense of her own concept of space.

"It's yours, too," he assured her. Yet she resisted the idea. It smacked of materialism.

More important to her were her causes, not only women's rights but minority rights, animal rights, equal justice, lifting people out of poverty, strengthening civil rights, prison reform, the preservation of endangered species, the smorgasbord of goodness and, to her, the only real diet for a concerned contemporary citizen, the only aspirations worth pursuing.

"And when all was said and done, what have you?" he asked.

"A better world."

"Ha."

"You mock me," she cried.

"I love you."

Through it all, he maintained, to her mind, his worship of the material. Attention must be paid to things, to space, to comfort. He pressed her continually on how the loft was to be done.

"Any way you design it is fine with me," she told him.

"But two people live here."

Her indifference exasperated him.

"I'm trying to make you part of everything in my life."

"I know."

"I'm building our nest, Nay." It was his brand on her now. "Look how the birds do it. Bit by bit. Relentlessly. Every strand has its place."

"Any way is okay," she told him repeatedly. To be with him then was all that mattered, to touch and love. Why this obsession with space, with things? He kept bringing home gadgets.

"The way space is allocated is important," he persisted.

"Allocate it any way you want. I'll fit in."

She did not fully develop hard doubt until a year had run out. She needed a bigger stage for her causes—the nation's capital, the center of the world. She had made connections and was being pressed to join the action. Washington was the place she needed to be. There were jobs to be had. Because she vacillated, she lost one at the Civil Rights Commission and another at HUD. It wasn't that he had the power of veto. Their being together was their most precious priority. She got a job with the mayor in the cultural affairs area, which did not satisfy her.

"The action is in Washington," she told him.

"Am I holding you back?" he said, pouting.

"Of course you are."

"It's all in your imagination."

She felt the unmistakable pull of his denial. Also her growing subservience. Love was making her a vassal, and she hated it.

She met his family. "Black Irish, the lot of them," he had warned her, mimicking a brogue, although they were all-American Brooklyn. Still, they harbored a mass of hard-line prejudices and stereotypes. He hadn't bothered to warn his family about her being Jewish, and at their first dinner together, his father rambled on about "Reds and the damned sheenies. It's them that got the niggers all riled up."

He kept her calm with amused winks. At the table were two pimply sisters and a corpulent mother who scrutinized her and burrowed in with pointed speculation.

They had begun the evening in the living room, which they called the parlor, a mismatched collection of worn upholstered velvet chairs and a sofa, all decorated with doilies, like Band-Aids. The radio was on, some right-wing talk show. Somebody mentioned Hillary.

"Goddamned pinko," his father sneered.

"Christ," she had hissed, looking at Barney.

Barney lifted his eyes in exasperation and shrugged, a gesture urging her to remain silent. With effort, she did.

"Damned libs. I nearly lost my ass for them."

There was a picture of the father in uniform, World War II. What had he fought for, she remembered thinking.

By the time they went to dinner in the shabby dining room, the hostility had expanded.

"Just a good old Irish homecoming," he had whispered.

"They express their love with meanness."

"Well, I don't," she responded.

By dessert, the family knew the worst of it. Jewish. Liberal. Living in sin. They grew so cold and silent, she excused herself to go to the john just to warm up. From behind the thin walls, she heard Barney's rebuking voice, certain that it was for her benefit as well.

"She's my girl, a part of me. I'll have no nonsense about it. Keep your narrowness to yourselves. Any offense against her is an offense against me."

"You'll bring no kikes in this house."

"Then I won't bring me as well."

"You shut your mouth, John!" his mother shouted to his father.

"Comes of leaving the church," the father muttered.

"Look who's talking." It was one of his sisters.

She flushed the water twice and turned on all the faucets to drown them out. But when she same out, after further stalls, she could see that the parents had surrendered. There was no point in banishing him. He had already banished himself.

"I'm sorry," he said later. "They're awful, but they're mine. Suffer them," he pleaded. "They've been beaten."

"By what?"

"Depressions. The old ways of the church. The old world just collapsed around them."

"But it was full of ugly prejudices that hurt other people."

"Just ugly thoughts. They never really harmed anyone."

She kept silent, although it bothered her. Later, after they had made love, the troubled thoughts broke through the calm between them.

"That's exactly the problem. They're bigots. Bigots are harmful to all of us. It's just wrong and it can be very hurtful. People must be judged as individuals. Hating groups is wrong and dangerous."

"What goes on in their heads is their business," he sighed, obviously upset to have it thrown back at him. "The important thing is that it made no dent on me."

"But you don't even question it. You let it pass. Indifference. That's the real culprit."

"But I do question it. I told them off."

He rose on one elbow and looked into her eyes. A stray bead of light caught his own. They flashed back like burning agates, emphasizing his anger.

"The fact is, Nay, I never cared what they thought. Or paid any attention to them. But they're still my family. My blood. You can't disown your family and can't make other people think right thoughts. In their world, it was the norm to hate by group. Hell, they hate the Irish most of all."

"Well, that's wrong, too."

"Listen, Nay," he said. His head shook from side to side. "I don't give a flying fuck about how other people see things as long as they leave me out of it. I couldn't care less."

"But I care."

"That's exactly the problem. Let's just love each other. Who cares about the starving Patagonians?" She knew what that meant; everyone who was powerless, helpless, hated, ignored, weak, sick, suffering.

"They could be you," she said, tasting her own self-righteousness.

"I'm sorry, Nay," he said, searching the ceiling with his eyes. "I feel only for the people I love. For you the most. I would have more compassion for your hurt pinky than all those poor bleeding souls. I wish I had your compassion, but only because I want to be inside of you, like you, to prove I am part of you, to be you."

"I don't want you to be me to prove your love. I want you to be you." And I want to be me, she had added silently.

Yet he seemed to be growing fearful of the differences between them. He, the Irish blarney salesman. She, the probing neurotic Jew. Different worlds. It was then that she discovered that it was at the heart of her fear as well, the death knell of their love, which they both heard in the distance.

Seeing the difference between them so starkly slapped her mind free of euphoria, causing her to think in terms of consequences. Marriage was becoming a serious issue by then.

Her mother, too, emphasized their differences. A widow, she had been left fairly comfortable by her father's insurance policy.

"She'll call you a scutch to your face," Naomi warned. "But it's all right. The battle has been fought."

"But who won?"

"No one ever wins a generational war. Like with your parents. It's a standoff. Besides, she lives vicariously through me. Her modus operandi is to be funny about it. That's the way she copes."

Her mother was all bouffant and gold chains when they met in her Flatbush house in her French Provincial living room with the gold-trimmed mirrors and tchotchkes everywhere. Two art nouveau prints depicting stylized females and Greek columns dominated the room. She served Danish and coffee, pouring it out of a sterling silver teapot.

"I missed all the revolutions," she said, "especially the sexual one."

"You didn't miss it, Mother. You never let it happen." Naomi turned to Barney. "My father has been dead since 1983."

"I had enough of men from him."

She inspected Barney blatantly. He seemed amused by it.

"He looks like an advertisement for shirts," her mother said.

"Isn't he handsome?" Naomi had chirped with pride.

"For a scutch," her mother said, smiling.

"And he's a good provider," Naomi mocked. This introduction had its own conventions. Only one thing was truly important to her mother. Safety. Her little girl must be safe.

"She wants to save the world, Benny." Her mother sighed.

"Barney," Naomi corrected.

"Barney," she mused. "Sounds Jewish."

"Not with Harrigan."

"He's circumcised?"

Barney laughed so hard he nearly fell off the chair.

In the end, of course, he won her.

Naomi giggled compulsively, stopping suddenly when she remembered what the reference had caused. The rush of these old memories unnerved her and she got out of bed and roamed her apartment, dipping into the papier-mâché cigarette box and lighting up. She had given up smoking, but one stale cigarette remained. The drag of smoke choked her and she doubled up coughing. When she quieted, she punched out the cigarette and sat on the floor with her head against the couch's edge and continued to remember.

It was because the Washington issue had risen again. A black friend from the African women wars wanted a bright young woman to join her group in Washington. An important rights group, well funded. Out of the blue, Naomi had been offered a job. If it had been a single isolated issue, she might have weighed it differently. But it came at a time when another issue gnawed at her. They had become careless about birth control and she had not told him she was pregnant, although she knew it was dishonest to keep it from him. The knowledge would have made him ecstatic. It was exactly what he wanted. Home. Hearth. Family.

"Marry me. I'll do anything. Be anything." He pleaded, cajoled, nagged. When she put it off, gently, he would probe her for days.

"Is it because I'm not a big bleeding heart? I swear, I'll become one. I'll stand at your side."

"No."

"Because I'm just a salesman. I haven't got the prestige."

"Don't, Barney. It's wrong ..."

"But it must be true. Why then? Don't you love me enough?"

"I love you deeply."

"Then why? Because I'm a scutch?"

"That is ridiculous."

"Why then? Why?"

In their hearts, they both knew why.

He had been away a week at a convention in Los Angeles, and with computers booming, he was beginning to make wads of money. She had decided not to go with him, more as a test of separation than out of real reluctance. She had it in her mind to accept the Washington job and offer a split residence deal. A weekend in Washington. A weekend in New York. It would be a test of the endurance of their relationship, a challenge. Caring also meant compromise. Didn't it?

Unfortunately, her pregnancy had complicated matters and she had to decide whether to keep the baby or not. It was one thing to be pro-choice for other people, but something else when it happened to you. In his absence, she agonized over it. Years later, she was still agonizing.

He returned home filled with tales of personal success. He had impressed so-and-so. His bosses had hinted that he was going places. He was becoming a real corporate man.

"It's a game," he told her, like politics. He had to tickle the right buttons, kiss the right butts. The goal was getting ahead.

"In politics, you have to have some ideology," she told him.

"Liberals always say that."

"At least if you were a conservative, I could understand," she berated. "You're nothing."

"Not nothing. A man without a label."

"A hired gun."

"Right. I'll fight under any flag that pays enough."

The memory of that night had taken on deep colors in her mind. Sometimes they became so bright they nearly blinded her and she had to kill the lights of remembering.

She decided to tell him about her decision to accept the Washington job. His reaction would determine the future of the baby. The coming baby meant marriage. Permanence. The job in Washington meant satisfaction for her. She wanted it all. As he talked about his convention success, she waited for the right moment to tell him.

"I have a surprise," he said, coming into the bathroom. She was sweet smelling and powdered after her bath. He was wearing a paisley robe, bare beneath. Sitting at the foot of the bed, he looked at her.

"I wanted to buy you something," he said, speaking slowly. It was always a sign of something deeply serious to come, something worked out carefully in his mind. "But what would it mean? Hell, I can buy you anything. It wouldn't mean a thing." He was right, of course. She never believed in gifts like that, much to his disappointment. As Emerson wrote, she had told him, a gift must be a piece of one's persona, the essence of one's self. Often she had written him a poem or given him a flower. Her biggest present would be their baby.

"I searched my mind for something so special that it would mean a bond, a part of both of us."

She had sat up, reached out her hand, but he had, oddly, moved away.

"I know we have some basic differences," he had continued. His tone worried her. Was he going to give her the change in himself that she craved, that alliance with her causes?

"I just hope you won't think it's crazy. To anyone else, it might seem crazy."

"Crazy?"

"All right, symbolic."

Symbols? It was more the way her mind worked than his. He was being murky, unintelligible.

"Just an idea," he said with oddly boyish embarrassment, as if he had regretted whatever it was.

"For God's sakes, Barney."

"Close your eyes."

The whole process worried her, brought her to the edge of a hidden panic. But she obeyed him, closing her eyes.

"Now," he whispered.

When she opened her eyes, nothing seemed to have changed except that he had cast aside his robe and stood naked before her, his long lean muscular body, with its thin coat of gilded hair, picking up the light. Then she saw what he had done.

"It's still a little sore. It was nothing. Took ten minutes. Not ready for action yet. A few more days."

Even in her memory, the flash of hostility could still burn. It was an act of futility, ludicrous and impotent. Indeed, it was a symbol and it crushed her with the force of its realization. She did not want that kind of proof and sacrifice of his love. It was a total misinterpretation, revealing the terrible gulf, the difference, between them. It frightened her to the core. Such a stupid act could not bridge the gap. It was a superficial act, a grandstander, pathetic. It was merely her mother's joke. If this was what he meant by getting inside of her, she recoiled. In the giant burst of epiphany, she saw their life together, an endless series of misinterpretations. Whatever his love meant, it would strangle her.

It was absolutely the last clear image she had of him, standing there, naked, the circumcision scar still unhealed, her love and respect for him diminished beyond repair. You can't become someone else, she wanted to cry out at him, knowing that she would now have generated enough anger to do what she should have done from the beginning: save herself.

And she had, leaving him standing there in her mind, an image now suffused with the glow of her regrets. She had killed the baby as well.

2

Holding the stem of her glass to quiet her nervous fingers, she watched him come toward her in the crowded restaurant, the same sandy-haired advertisement, the eyes bright with a watery mist that could not disguise the pain. She had tried to chase away her doubts through the fury of her investigation. It hadn't worked, not completely.

He fell awkwardly into a chair, obviously exhausted with anguish, kissing her perfunctorily, as if he had expunged the real memory of their relationship. Their parting had been soft. No harsh words, like a candle being snuffed. She packed and left while he was at work. There were tears, of course, but finally her persona absorbed her mind's revolt. She hated the inference but accepted the reason. He was simply "beneath her." The awfulness of this conclusion plagued her to this day. But the old ashes just couldn't expire. Something deep inside of her had been moved, the core of her female self still smoldered. Nothing she had done to exorcise him had ever worked.

"You're looking good, Nay," he said, putting a spiral notebook he had been carrying on the table between them. It was the kind with a plastic cover that students used.

"You too, Barney."

In the awkwardness of the moment, they began to speak simultaneously. There were still preliminaries to breach.

"I appreciate your doing this." He watched her, showing a flash of the old Barney. "Bet you have a direct pipeline to the White House by now." He offered his old salesman's wink, but it had lost spontaneity. It hurt to see the mechanics of his charm show through.

"I'm a Democrat, remember?"

"I thought all you guys worked together hand in glove."

"With them? Never."

She felt the old resentment, the black Irish cynicism. Hell, it was irrelevant. They were dancing around a cold bonfire.

"Anyway," she said hoping to put a halt to the clumsy small talk, "I'm glad to help. But don't put too much faith in what I can really do."

"When you're desperate, you reach out ...," he began haltingly, forcing her eyes to turn away in embarrassment. Odd how they had returned immediately to the most corrosive issue of their relationship. She shrugged it off.

"What I have is not encouraging ..."

The past just wouldn't do. Not now. Or ever.

"I can imagine. I've done a little homework on my own."

Reaching for his notebook, he opened it and flipped the pages. "I've written it all down. To whom I spoke so far. What they said. It's a very consistent story."

She had been looking at the notebook as he spoke.

"I don't want to miss a beat. Want it all down on paper. Bearing witness, so to speak. I guess it's a salesman's habit, writing down reactions, noting possibilities. I've got one helluva problem on my hands."

"I know," she replied. She had talked to lawyer friends and to a number of congressmen that she knew. She had also contacted a friend at the FBI. She had personally gone through the back files of the Washington Post and New York Times and had her assistant plug in to every data service available. She needed to know whom he perceived as his enemy, the people who had taken his wife. By now, she had lots of facts, but no real conclusion as to a course of action for him.

"It boils down to this," she said. "The Glories are a religion, bona fide in the eyes of the law. Their status has been challenged by various people—mostly ex-Glories, by the way—but on the point of being a legally sanctioned religion, they emerge victorious. Apparently they have a huge cadre of prestigious law firms on their payroll. They are very, very rich. The fact is that all you need is 50 names and an application to the Internal Revenue Service to declare yourself a religion. If the IRS says it's okay, presto, you're a religion."

She thought she was presenting what was obvious. His reaction was passionate and swift.

"Legal or not, they're a fraud, a scam. They have these businesses. And their followers work for them, literally, as slaves. Oh, they're very clever. They know how to slip just under the legal radar. They'll have Charlotte doing their bidding in the name of their all-holy idiot guru. Working for nothing in their various businesses, selling their products, health foods, candy, toys, whatever. They're into everything, ubiquitous and powerful. And they're one of many. They challenge our vulnerability. Sure, they're rich. They're also in real estate, media, big-time business. It's big, big moneymaking. Tax free. All religions are tax free. How dumb can our government be not to see through this scam?" He shook his head. "But then how the hell did they allow September 11th to happen? How come we didn't fight back earlier? We knew the score. Hell, we've always known the score about the Glories and all these other cults. So what the fuck are we doing about it?"

He shook his head in disgust. He had ordered a scotch for himself while she settled for white wine. He brought the glass to his lips to sip. His fingers shook. A few drops fell on the notebook. She stayed silent, letting him vent. There was no point in offering counterarguments just yet, raising issues like civil rights, free society, separation of church and state. He was listening only to his own inner drummer.

"They've been sued by parents over and over again," he continued. "They win most of the time. They're also litigious. People are intimidated by their gaggle of smart lawyers."

She nodded, refusing to be baited.

"Money talks and bullshit walks," he said. "Religion!" He shook his head. "Makes them untouchable."

"Part of the price of freedom," she muttered, unable to resist.

"Yeah. Freedom to exploit others. And Charlotte is paying that price big time. And me. And our boy. And thousands of other families. You know how many cults there are in this country?"

"Many?" she sighed. Her research had not provided a pretty picture. Yet she retained what she liked to think was a healthy skepticism. Where was the line between a cult and a religion? She shrugged. It wasn't the moment to wax philosophical.

"And no one is doing a fucking thing about it," he cried, slapping the table. People turned to stare. He threw up his hands and shook his head. "It's not only in this country, Nay. It's worldwide. These people are no different from those Bin Laden assholes. Their followers are brainwashed into doing anything the boss orders them to do, even if it means blowing themselves up for some stupid idea of paradise in the next life. Do I have to cite chapter and verse?" Again he raised his voice. "Waco, Jonestown and on and on. They're everywhere. Lice. Shits." He was unstoppable, angry, fulminating. His eyes misted and he slapped the table with the flat of his hand. "Fuck!" Again people turned around to look at them. "It is beyond people's ability to comprehend. Nobody fucking understands!" he cried. "And what the fuck do they want with my Charlotte? She was an innocent, for crying out loud. Just a wife and mother, a good loving ordinary wife and mother."

She listened patiently, respecting his anger. She could understand his hurt, his sense of loss and frustration. He was entitled to his hysteria. She vowed to remain rational, arguing silently. Why had Charlotte chosen them?

"I read their so-called bible," he continued. "Oh, they all have something like that. Words. They all have words. Call it what you want, Koran, Old Testament, New Testament, Book of Mormon, words, words, words. The Glories bill their so-called bible as the divine revelation of some mythical heavenly father. Another pipeline to the alleged almighty. Shit. I hate that man's dark, craggy, evil face. It's been posted on enough billboards to make you want to puke. I used to laugh at it. Who the hell is that dopey-looking man? I know who he is now, all right. He's a greedy wog bastard who's gone and taken my wife away from me, that's who he is."

Wog? Good God, she thought, he's into bigot range.

"Easy, Barney," she said gently. "Not that."

She felt the eyes of other patrons watching them. He was not the Barney she remembered, more an echo of his father. Barney had never been a bigot. Also, he would never make a public scene. Outwardly, he always observed the proprieties. She was beginning to feel quite uncomfortable. Lifting his hand, he seemed to wave away her consternation, showing more outward calm.

"I even read their fucking bible. It's gobbledygook. The Power and the Glory. I read it on the plane. Something about Christ having failed, and this little prick being the new Messiah, appointed by you know who. It's a religion of obedience, not love or peace. You know what I'm saying? Just listen to me, folks. I got the force. Do what I command. Don't question. I tell you to walk into a fire, you fucking better do it or you won't go to paradise or wherever. Not any religion we were taught."

Here goes, she told herself, unable to keep her silence any longer.

"All religions look stupid to people who aren't true believers." She was instantly sorry she had said it. His expression darkened. "Look," she said, trying to prove her alliance with him. Hadn't she made that determination? "I have no truck with these so-called cults. Tell you the truth, I'm not sure I understand them, the Glories included." she said. "Despite what I've read—and I do acknowledge the pain they have caused you, but don't get offended—I'm still hung up on the idea of freedom of religion. Oh, I've read the horror stories. And they do have their various agendas. I know all that. But I'm speaking as an American. Okay, a liberal. What they all seem to want is for everyone to accept their own version of the way they believe things are." She felt suddenly inarticulate and confused, but she pressed on. "What Father Glory wants ... what is it? Power." She mimed quotation marks with her fingers. "Yes, power. From what I can gather, he believes that he has received some revelation and been anointed to run the whole show. That's his schtick. Believe him or not. Your free choice. Take your pick. Is he a megalomaniac? Probably. Nevertheless, his views are protected by our Constitution. You don't have to buy in. That's the beauty of America."

I'm making a political speech, she admonished herself, forgetting his pain. She was discovering that any counterargument, like his, led nowhere. In this instance, there were only questions, no answers.

"There are also laws against coercion," he muttered, retreating. He had calmed. Thankfully, she had not set him off again.

"They've been tested," she said, with knee-jerk persistence, "The Glories win every time."

He sucked in a deep breath.

"That's because the system is out of whack. These people know every trick of the trade. Hell, in some quarters in this country, they're even respectable. Nay, this bastard's organization brainwashes people. They've done it to Charlotte. That's what they do. That's what they all do."

She held up her hand.

"Okay, Barney, I surrender. I understand your pain and I want to help. Really I do. But I'm a skeptic. You know that. Just don't force me to buy in. I'll help, but strictly for auld lang syne. I've got my views. You have yours. Leave it at that. I'm here to help if I can."

His fingers gripped the glass, the knuckles whitening. She wondered if it would break. "They have no right to take away her mind, to take her away from me and Kevin." He looked at her for a long moment and shook his head.

"You just don't get it. Not really, Nay. Am I right?"

"Be patient with me, Barney. I have to understand all this logically. But I'm open to education. You know me. I'm literal, I guess. So humor me. I'm helping, aren't I?"

"Okay, Nay. I'll back off. When I spout this stuff people look at me like a deer caught in the headlights. I'll take it slow."

"Good. My mind is open. I promise you. If I have questions be easy on me." She paused, swallowed hard. "You think she's been drugged?"

He shook his head.

"They don't need drugs. It's a process."

"Is she being forcibly detained?"

"Yes."

"You mean she's literally imprisoned, locked in a cell, unable to communicate with the outside world."

"Her prison is her mind. Don't you see that, Nay? They've taken away her will. They control her. Telling anyone about this is like reinventing the wheel. Shit." He paused for a long moment as he studied her. "God, Nay, I know this hard to believe."

"I know. Just bear with me. The fact is that brainwashing is a controversial subject that has not been legally defined. She hasn't been drugged, right? Or physically confined or shackled? As far as the authorities are concerned she is a follower of a legitimate religion. When she says she has her rights ... well, she's right. She has them."

"Dammit, Nay. Not you too. I've been hearing that crap everywhere I turn." He sucked in a deep breath. "I want her home is all," he said. "I don't give a flying fuck about what they believe or their goddamned agenda. They have no right messing with my Charlotte."

She did not want to add to his anguish. What she really wanted now, after observing and listening to him, was for him to go, get out of her life. Quickly. He should never have called. Nor did he have the right to stir things up in her. She was learning the meaning of being on the horns of a dilemma. She was torn. She wanted to help. She had done the research. But her commitment was crumbling.

"There's no point in going over the what and whyfors," she said. "Bottom line as I see it at this moment. Despite all you've said. Don't get angry. I'm listening, trying to make head or tail out of this. So far what I get is that the Glories are indeed a religion, protected by the Fifth Amendment. Sacrosanct in the eyes of the law. Charlotte has been proselytized. She's over 21. In the law's eyes, quite in command of her will. Forget about the organization, its theology, its bizarre philosophies. Call it whatever your want. Wrongheaded. Evil. Weird. None of it matters. It's protected turf, protected by the Constitution." She caught herself being brutally officious and repetitive, but she could not stop herself.

"She's been brainwashed. That's all I know," he interrupted. "All the rest is bullshit." He shook his head, his face flushing. His exasperation was palpable.

"There's stuff in the law books and the libraries as long as your arm. There's all sorts of data telling stories like yours ad infinitum. I really researched this, Barney. Anguished parents, grandparents, husbands, wives, brothers, sisters, friends, telling the story of their search for a loved one caught up in these, as you put it, cults. Some get out." She paused. "Some don't."

She could tell he was fighting for control. He bit his lip and his Adam's apple bobbed as he swallowed deeply, working hard to calm himself. "I know it's hard to understand. I've read all kinds of studies on the whole subject of brainwashing, the methods employed by these groups, theories on how the brain works, stories by ex-Glories, ex-Moonies, ex-Hare Krishnas, ex-Scientologists, ex-anything, stories to curl your hair."

"But that doesn't impact on the bottom line, which is, call it a cult or a religion, it's still within the protection of the law."

"What about Jonestown and Waco?" he interrupted again. "One self-appointed guru orders more than 900 people to take the big dive. We just ignore that, right? And this fucking Waco thing? Who do they blame on that one? Not the idiot that caused the standoff, then ordered his disciples to resist and burn themselves up. They blame the authorities. The people charged with enforcing the law. And I'm not even citing the big enchilada, the World Trade Center. Imagine that nightmare—a bunch of assholes kill thousands of people, thousands just vanish into thin air. For what? Why? And for this act, these lousy fucks think, really believe, they are going up to paradise. Paradise? What do you think is going on? Why do people want to do away with themselves? Because they have been brainwashed, their ability to think by themselves destroyed." He blew out a big sigh. "Over and over again. People just don't get it, Nay. They just don't get it. You don't get it."

"The criteria for criminal action are clear. Frankly, Barney, I don't know what you can do. You can't forcibly kidnap her. You can't break the law."

"That guy in Waco broke the law. He stockpiled arms illegally and then when they came to apprehend him, he said fuck you to the law and burned up his people. Now he's a damned folk hero for standing up to the authorities. Worse, they blame law enforcement guys for killing his people. Dumb. Dumb. Dumb. He killed them himself, told them they're all going to heaven. They were brainwashed, for crying out loud."

"Brainwashing, as presently interpreted, is not ..."

"It's so fucking hard to get this message across."

"I know you're exasperated Barney, but ..." She paused and went over what she was about to say. It was the one point that troubled her above all the others. "Brainwashing is still only a theory. It doesn't wash, not legally. Persuasion is not illegal if it is carried out in a manner that is not illegal. Psychological coercion is not illegal, especially if it is accomplished without physically harmful methods. That's what I really found out, Barney. Some people do believe in the possibility of brainwashing, but few believe it is illegal to persuade. And most people are convinced it can't happen to them. Not if they don't want it to happen.

Also the concept comes close to what might be thought of as religious conversion, and religious conversion is protected by the First Amendment. Every person in this country has the right to believe in a supreme being or a thousand different supreme beings or in one God or many, living or dead, human or not, fish, fowl or animal. No proof required, thank you. The Constitution protects your right to believe anything you damned well please in the name of religion." Her eyes roved his face. "You can declare yourself God, Barney or create another idea of God or worship the stars, the sun and the moon. Or you don't have to believe in a damned thing. Now there I go. I talked too damned much." She looked at his sky blue eyes, glazed now with his pain. It's not me saying this, Barney, she wanted to cry out at him. It's what all the others say. The law. The authorities. The system.

"Three cheers for freedom," he said.

She had not expected her challenge to his position to be so adamant. That wasn't the role he had given her at all or the one she wanted. All morning, as she talked to others and read material, hungry for answers, but she wasn't ready to abandon her own value system. It wasn't fair, wasn't her battle or her choice.

"Hear, hear," she said, trying to lighten the effect of her response.

"Does that mean you won't help?"

"Who said that? All I can do Barney is, as you suggested, point you in the right direction. Not that there is a right direction. It's the best I can do."

His eyes darted away. Had he expected a blind alliance? He sipped his drink and shrugged with resignation.

"I made appointments," she said gently. "Hal Phillips. He's with the FBI. As a general rule, they're not my favorite outfit, but he's a very good friend, a great guy." Had he caught the implication? Hal was an old lover, but hardly in a class with Barney, who was defined by her as an old love, perhaps her only real love.

The affair with Hal had been brief. Like all the others, it had ended with Barney's image between them. The memory of Barney was always the spoiler. Even with men with whom she shared passionate affinities, men who were intellectually and socially superior to Barney. All had come a cropper in terms of a real relationship.

"I also made an appointment for you with a woman who got her son out of the Glories, a Mrs. Prococino."

He nodded. "I appreciate that, Nay. That's all could ask for." She knew he wanted more, but she had no idea what more was.

Obviously, he plucked at hope, like a fish jumps at bait. But she knew he was disappointed. As information, what she had found out that morning was factual, not hopeful. Deliberately, she had tried to avoid any visceral emotional involvement. He was trying to bring his wife home, dammit. Staying uninvolved was getting harder every minute.

"You've been terrific," Barney said, as he might have said to a salesgirl showing him a collection of ties. It wasn't, she knew, what he really meant. Outside, he put out his hand. She took it and their eyes met.

"I could tag along," she said, her throat constricting. She had debated that question all morning, her instincts opting for the negative. But seeing him now, forlorn, unhappy, confused, she broke her own caveat.

"Really, Nay ... haven't I imposed enough ..."

"Hell, Barney, don't get maudlin. What are old friends for?"

Their eyes met and she felt the old spark. Extinguish that, she admonished herself.

"I won't forget this, Nay," he mumbled.

"Might be an educational experience," she said, hoping it took the emotional sting out of the moment.

3

Phillips worked at the main FBI building on 10th Street. They obediently went through elaborate security checks, clipped on badges and eventually followed a prim secretary down a long corridor to Phillips' office. On the way over, Barney said nothing more than was necessary. The reunion had been a disappointment. She had been a fool to even let herself think otherwise, admitting a secret speculation that something might rekindle their old relationship, then dismissing it with embarrassment. Any feeling for her had died in him, she concluded. What stupidity to even entertain such thoughts! The man wanted his wife back. He had come to her for that purpose only. Would he have come searching for Naomi? The fact was ... he didn't. He had let her go without a fight.

But hadn't she left him that long apologia, which precluded any recourse? Wrong man. Wrong time. I'm sorry. She hadn't mentioned the baby. Baby? Fetus? It had no life, was barely five weeks from conception. On many a cold night, she had remonstrated with herself, forcing the distinction on her conscience. Perhaps that was why she still felt somehow connected to him.

"Naomi filled me in," Phillips said. He had the scrubbed typical look of the quintessential J. Edgar soldier, despite efforts by later FBI chiefs to exorcise the type. He was an executive now, in charge of others. He made a practiced effort to keep Barney at ease. Under shaggy dark eyebrows, he looked kindly. He had been a kindly lover, as well, Naomi recalled. Lots of warmth but no fire. Naomi had begged him to see Barney, begged hard.

"Just see him, Hal. Please. He has nowhere to turn."

"Is he a relative?"

"Sort of." For some reason she resisted explaining their relationship. "He's at his wit's end."

"I don't think I can help him. I've been down that road. You can't make a case."

"Just see him. Hear him out."

It was enough of an explanation for the FBI man to be persuaded, as Naomi knew he would. Their affair, unfortunately, had never been over for him.

"It's not against the law," Phillips said after Barney had outlined the situation. They were seated around a small conference table. The prim secretary, despite caveats to the contrary, had brought them coffee. There was a picture of the President on one wall. A flag stood in a corner of the room.

"No one gives up a home, a child, a husband, in two damned weeks," Barney said. "It's not normal." He looked briefly at Naomi and shrugged. His look seemed incongruously accusing. Although Phillips tried to mask it, the interview was a transparent courtesy, a bureaucratic shuffle. Nothing useful for Barney would come of it. Naomi saw that immediately. But Barney, a trained salesman, had a certain tenacity. She had always admired that quality about him. He would never give up, never admit defeat was possible. Hadn't his last desperate effort years ago told her that?

"Could it be drugs?" Barney asked Phillips, despite his previous denial to Naomi.

"Not in the case of the Glories. We would know."

"She crossed state lines," he said with fading hope.

"Of her own volition."

"It wasn't her own volition. She was lured by her sister," Barney persisted.

"But it was her decision, Barney," Naomi said gently. She owed Hal that.

"How did you first find out about it?" Phillips asked, crisply professional. It was a question that she had not thought to ask.

Barney coughed, his body squirming, as if he hurt. In the harsh office light, she could see heavy puffs under his eyes, a sagging of his jaw. There were even specks of gray in the gilded hair. He seemed ravaged by life, yet a few weeks ago he might have been smug, self-satisfied. She became conscious of her scrutiny of him and flushed, lowering her eyes.

"I called my sister-in-law's old boyfriend. Both their parents are dead. There's only two of them. Charlotte is older. Twenty-five."

Robbing the cradle, Naomi thought again, not without a pang of jealousy. She had just turned 35 and felt old, slightly jaded, very single, missing being paired and very sorry for herself.

"He told me Suzie had been a Glory for six months. It was Suzie who brought her in." He swallowed hard. "The bitch," he muttered.

"You didn't know this?" Phillips asked.

"If I did, would I let her go?"

"You know, Mr. Harrigan, it's not an FBI matter. Not now."

Did that imply that one day it would be, Naomi thought. They were always burrowing into organizations, paying informers, working undercover. Everything she detested. Pigs in dark suits, she thought. And they had failed to root out the bastards that wrecked the World Trade Center. Phillips looked at Naomi, then at the anguished Barney. His kindly mien had disappeared. He was all business now.

"We've been in these cases," Phillips said. "Kidnapping. That's part of our mission."

"Kidnapping?" Barney asked, but it was strictly rhetorical. She could see his interest. Obviously, the idea had crossed his mind.

"Parents. Brothers. Friends. In desperation, they pull a snatch, then turn the subject over to a deprogrammer who attempts to reverse the process. We have laws against such activity."

"But these people practice brainwashing," Barney interrupted.

"We don't call it that, Mr. Harrigan. Kidnapping is a federal offense. Deprogramming is an industry. The objective, as I understand it, is to pressure the subjects out of their beliefs. Sometimes it works. When it doesn't, it becomes either a kidnapping, a very dire criminal act or a civil suit, depending on the circumstances. It has pretty severe consequences for all perpetrators."

There could be no mistaking his meaning. It was a warning.

"It's a heavy offense. We get involved."

"So I have no recourse," Barney said suddenly, slapping his thighs and standing up.

"Not here, I'm afraid."

He exchanged glances with Naomi. Hal had done his duty. No small talk, quick, brief, to the point. The interview was in its last gasp.

"You might try to talk with her," Phillips said.

"I'd love to," Barney said bitterly. "I've tried. Boy, have I tried. They won't let me. I don't even think they'll let me see her. They have these camps ..." He cleared his throat and his lips trembled. "You guys just don't know. I mean, what good is the FBI if they can't protect people from this."

"I'm really sorry," Phillips said. "It's not in our jurisdiction. But that doesn't mean I don't empathize." He looked toward Naomi and shrugged.

"Empathy is not what I came here for," Barney said.

"I understand," Phillips said.

"That's exactly what I'm up against. Nobody really understands."

"I hope your wife comes home, Mr. Harrigan." Phillips said. "Give it time."

He stood up and held out his hand. Barney, in a typical salesman's reflex, took it heartily. In a salesman's eyes, Naomi had learned, no potential sale was ever completely dead, no bridge ever burned.

"Don't do anything foolish," Phillips said, with a glance at Naomi.

"Foolish?" He forced a wry chuckle. "Have I ever, Nay?"

An answer seemed superfluous.

In the cab on their way to Mrs. Prococino, Barney came out of his silence to mumble, "Dead ends. It all leads to dead ends."

"I'm sorry, Barney."

He patted her arm.

"Not your fault. You shouldn't even be in this, Nay. Phillips was.... by the book. I didn't expect much."

"He did it as a favor, Barney."

"I appreciate your calling in your chits."

She wondered if he knew about Phillips and her. Or if it mattered. It was soon obvious that his mind was elsewhere, far from speculating about her personal life.

"They take people from their homes," he said, "capture their minds, and we who are left behind have no recourse."

"It's tough, Barney. I see what you're going through and I can see how much it hurts."

"They all say that. In the end, you're alone."

"Not quite," she whispered.

She felt his eyes on her, but she did not raise hers to meet them. It wasn't fair to judge him now, she decided. Not in the midst of this crisis in his life. Poor Barney. He could not transfer his outrage.

Mrs. Prococino lived in a quiet street in Silver Spring, a split-level suburban home, typical of those built in the '50s, the complacent Eisenhower years. Naomi had found her through a newspaper story she had discovered online.

Four years ago, the Prococino's son, Paul, was recruited by the Glories in Seattle. The Prococinos, who, according to the clipping, originally came from Brooklyn, would not accept their son's fate. The Glories had picked him up on a street corner and brainwashed him. The Prococinos had found him, and by grit and subterfuge got him home and deprogrammed him successfully. For a time, they were Washington media heroes of sorts, a condition often measured in mini-seconds of notoriety.

"Why not?" Mrs. Prococino told her when Naomi had called for an appointment. At first, the woman had been reluctant, but Naomi had been forceful. It seemed a logical way to deflect Barney's attention from official Washington, from which he could expect no help. At least Mrs. Prococino would offer him the succor of a common experience.

"For a while that's all I did," Mrs. Prococino told them. "Help other people who got caught up in this ... this horror."

They sat at a marble table on a screened porch looking out on a garden heavy with plantings of flowers and vegetables. At its edge was an arbor, and the smell of sweetish grapes floated through an open window. She had set out iced tea and those Italian cookies in colorful wrappers. Behind the static sanitized facade of the split-level, she had somehow put her stamp of ethnic preference. The atmosphere was indisputably Italian.

Mrs. Prococino's olive skin had drained of color, but her eyes dominated the fleshiness in her face. They were large, dark and expressive, ringed by still thick black lashes under heavy, unplucked eyebrows. There was a tough earthiness about her, a determination that had come through even in the reporters' stories.

"Finally, I couldn't take all this emotionalism, especially after Vinnie died. Vinnie was my husband. I think it killed him. No, I don't think. It killed him."

"It's my wife, Mrs. Prococino," Barney said.

"I feel for you." She shook her head. "You're dealing with the most ruthless bastards in the world."

As they listened to the bits and pieces of her story, anger flared up in her. Barney had read her story in the printouts that Naomi had provided, but the sound of her voice, her expression and emotion, gave it another dimension. Her son had gone on a skiing trip. Unfortunately, he had stopped first in Chicago, met two beautiful girls, who took him to one of the Glory houses in downtown Seattle. Somehow, they persuaded the young man to go with them to their camp in a nearby rural area. All very harmless. No mention of the Glory Church. They worked behind the facade of some do-gooder front group. Little Vinnie was an innocent, an idealist. Not a New York street kid like Big Vinnie and herself. They would have smelled a rat within ten seconds. But this suburban life weakened kids, didn't expose them to the hustle, the con game. Surely she had told the story many, many times. Yet it came out of her fresh, raw, with all the vitriol and bitterness intact.

"Once they lure you into isolation, it's a slam dunk. They control your environment. Your time. Your information. Your diet. They lock you in."

"But how ..." Naomi heard her voice, then retreated when it was ignored. She had been asking that question since Barney's call the night before. How can they make someone believe, commit their lives, so quickly? It was a stone wall against her reason. The boy must have been weak, ready for it, vulnerable, she decided.

"They withdraw protein. Sugar you up. Makes you logy, loses your alertness. They crash in on your sleep. Cut it down to three or four hours. They sardinize you. Put you in with others your own age, crowd you in, surround you with themselves. They wake you up with familiar songs, with restructured lyrics that float into your subconscious. And all this time, they have big sister watching you. For the girls it's big brother. Anyway, big sister is with you at all times, controlling you by eye contact, a kind of hypnosis.

There's no newspapers, no television, no conversation unless it's controlled by them. It's all titillation at first to draw you in, but no sex. Control! That's what they want. Control! And every time you say you want to go home, they lean on you, push you to stay. For your spiritual health. That's a laugh. Besides, it's not easy to find your way back to civilization. Their camp is far away from any means of public transportation. They've got you cornered. Now they start to fill your mind with the Father Glory pitch. You're ready, you're exhausted, you have been subtly prepared, you're not thinking clearly, you're starved of protein, you've been love-bombed, your ego inflated to its furthest limit. Everything you do is declared marvelous by them. You're Mr. Wonderful. When you fart it's like you sang the "Star Spangled Banner." You're back in the womb, in a warm bath of manufactured admiration. You are never alone. They take you to the bathroom, to your meals, to the lectures. And they push you to call home, telling you exactly what to say, listening in when you talk. It's a critical time. They don't want interference. The subject isn't quite cooked, but he's in the oven, trapped."

"I spoke to her at the beginning," Barney interrupted. "It was like you said. I knew something was wrong."

"Sorry about that," Mrs. Prococino said. "Bet she told you she'd met these fantastic, wonderful, caring, loving people, that she was having a fabulous spiritual experience."

"Yes. Exactly that."

"And she was going to stay just a little while longer."

"Yes."

"And when you finally inquire where she is or get suspicious, she wouldn't tell you where she was. Not exactly. Not enough for you to hop a plane to find her."

He nodded, trembling with anger.

"Finally, it's too late. Big Vinnie would scream at him when he called. I would get hysterical. We had no idea. No idea." For a brief moment, Mrs. Prococino's large eyes misted and her voice broke. The emotion, Naomi sensed, despite the number of times she had told this story, would never go away.

"We're ordinary people, Mr. Harrigan. Second-generation Italians. Not good Catholics. Not bad Catholics. Vinnie worked for the Post Office in New York and was transferred to Washington.

He had a good administrative job. Young Vinnie had just graduated from college. We got his medical school acceptance while he was in their hands. Imagine that kind of explosion in a family that lives on dreams for our children. He was going to be a doctor. You know what that means to a family like ours. A doctor. It tore our hearts out to get that acceptance letter. He was giving that up for some two-bit religious fraud. Oh, we read this Father Glory's so-called bible. Bullshit. All bullshit. We researched. We did all the things you're doing now." She paused. "He was our child. Our hopes were locked into him. Finally, we flew out there and went through hell to get to see him. They had this lawyer you had to go through. Real Ivy League. Pompous. An obvious phony." Her anger peaked and ebbed. "By some miracle, we finally got to see our boy. He was zonked out, a zombie, glassy-eyed, unable to make an independent decision. He called us Satan's people. Imagine that. And he was always with this girl. His spiritual sister, he called her. Before he could answer a question, he had to look at her. She had him under control through eye contact, like hypnosis. We couldn't do a damn thing about it. All the laws and traditions of this country, all its concepts of freedom and liberty seemed ranged against us. The law. The goddamned law. The law was with them ... the enemy. There was nobody to turn to for help. No one. We were ..." She paused. "Up shit creek without a paddle."

As she talked, Mr. Prococino explored Barney's face, as if she were gauging the effects of her words on him, testing, prodding.

"Talk about a private hell. All Big Vinnie and I could think about is what we'd done wrong, where we made our mistake. At night ..." She seemed to be debating whether or not to tell it. Then she nodded and went on. "We just lay there in bed, the two of us, two kids from Italian immigrants, Depression babies, who came up the hard way, two-fisted tough, and they had reduced us to two quivering jellyfish. It was a completely foreign experience. Nobody ever told us how to handle this. Nobody. In the camp, these smug bastards would tell us: 'Withdraw. Withdraw.' And call us Satan. Big Vinnie would shout back: 'Fuck you, monsters. Fuck you.' That only made it worse. You should have seen my big beautiful son, Vincent Peter Prococino, Jr., who was about to become a medical student, our investment of a lifetime of love and care." She seemed to have forgotten that there were others present, and

Naomi understood her earlier reluctance. "They had taken away my boy, not only from me and Vinnie, but from himself. And the worst part was that I hated him for it. My own flesh and blood." She held back tears to the limit of her control, then they came gushing out of her eyes. Turning away, she wiped them, embarrassed. When they saw her face again, she was smiling thinly.

"No one should have to go through this." She sighed, then remembering, as she looked at Barney. "I'm sorry. I didn't mean ..." Her eyes widened and she shrugged. "Listen. It has a happy ending. We went through six months of hell, trying to figure out ways to get at him. We tried everything, letters to our congressman, to the FBI, even the CIA. We contacted others who had lost loved ones to the group, spoke to ex-members. Nothing. Just like you. I'm sorry, Mr. Harrigan. You're not unique."

"What do they want?" Naomi asked suddenly. It was a recurring question in her mind. That, and another. "Why your son?"

"It starts with control. They want numbers. People they can turn into moneymakers. People are money. Money is power. They have an apparatus. They're a force. They're something now, like this dopey kid Koresh in Waco. He had his numbers on a small scale. He was something, right? Suddenly he was a big shot. Spoke to Jesus. The idiots believed him. He made the government the guilty party. The Glories are a million times worse, because they're a million times bigger." She shook her head and sucked in a deep breath.

"But how did they start?"

"Who knows? They're very totalitarian. They're very political. It may sound nuts, but they want to take over the world. God help us. Father Glory as the great one, leader of the world. The living Jesus. What does it matter? They took our son. This Father Glory took our son."

"Amazing," Naomi said. She had wanted to say: "But how?" She kept her silence.

"Bastard," Barney muttered.

"Father Glory," Mrs. Prococino said contemptuously. "He lives like a potentate. He's a front within a front within a front. He's got worldwide business interests; they send these kids out to raise money. That's all they do once they're completely under control. Raise money and get other kids in ... to raise money. His principal expertise is manipulating others. He needs numbers, believers, because religion offers an easy way to power. So he brainwashes. That's the scam. He's an evil bastard and he's got absolute power over the kids who fall into his trap."

Naomi's mind filled with other questions. Mrs. Prococino was letting her hate get in the way, she thought. Reason was disappearing. It was as if she were in a hospital ward with a hangnail, while the person in the next bed was dying. She just couldn't relate to it. What had it got to do with her? On the other hand, she could see that Barney had no doubts on that score.

"The meek don't inherit the earth," Mrs. Prococino said suddenly, and a sour bitterness filled the room. The acid had eaten away some part of her.

"And your son?" Barney prodded. "How did you get him out?"

It was, of course, the central issue for Barney. He asked the question with frantic anticipation.

"Kidnapped him. That's the truth of it. Call it want you want. We told the press 'subterfuge.' Sure it was illegal, but who gave a rat's ass. Pure and simple. Kidnapping. We picked him up selling candy. He was on one of their fund-raising teams. Imagine that. They either raise money or do things to gain credibility and acceptance so they can raise more money." She checked herself. "To do all this cost us plenty."

She had started off again on the well-rutted path, stopping suddenly when she realized that she had continued to stray. "We hired a guy to kidnap him, a deprogrammer. It was, believe me, the only way. It was like planning the snatching of a President. All cloak-and-dagger. It cost us every cent we had. We got him into a van and raced away as fast as we could. Then we holed up in a deserted place and the deprogrammer went to work. It wasn't much fun to watch. As a matter of fact, it was awful. He was kicking and screaming all the way. It was heartbreaking ..." She laughed, but it was not with joy. "Heartbreaking. It ruined my husband's heart in the end. Anyway, we had to lock him in a room. We were lucky. If it hadn't worked, we would have been sued by our own son. Maybe even worse. It's against the law to kidnap, remember. Or haven't you heard?" Her tone was mocking, tinged with bitterness. Phillips hadn't been far from the truth.

"This deprogramming. What is it?"

"They reverse the process. You see, the Glories stopped his ability to think, to make decisions on his own. Something to do with the brain."

Naomi had heard about the process but it was always cloaked in some unsavory connotation, a violation of sorts. She had read somewhere that certain of them had been convicted and jailed.

"What did he, this deprogrammer, do to him?" Barney asked. He had been fidgeting with his fingers, now he locked them together to keep them from shaking.

"Talk. Talk. Talk. I told you. I don't really understand it. The fact is that the Glories had terrorized him, had led him to believe that he would rot in some eternal hell if he wasn't true to Father Glory. It's a real active, vicious fear, and they never let him forget it. In fact it is reiterated over and over again, like a mantra. The mind absorbs it like a sponge. I'm told it clogs all receptors. No dissent can get through. Hard to believe, but that's what experts have told me. The deprogrammer has to break down the fear that's been stuffed into the victim's head, wash away all the garbage. It's fighting fire with fire."

"And it works?"

"Not all the time. It worked with Vinnie. He came down like a rock dropped from a high place, complete with hysterics. They really did a number on his head."

"How long did it take?"

"Three days. Sometimes longer. Depends, I suppose, on the person."

"It's incredible," Naomi said, hiding her doubts. In her mind, it was difficult to sort out what was worse, the Glories or the deprogrammer. Above all, a mind is free, she told herself militantly. She had not wanted this involvement and she did not want it now. She wanted to get away, to run as far from here as she could.

"So he's fine?" Barney asked. Telling the story had drained Mrs. Prococino. She looked exhausted, pausing now to sip her tea.

"It took 11 months for him to be really fine. He was afraid to go to sleep in the dark, jumpy, totally uninterested. He had no desire to do anything. Mostly he slept. It was another nightmare. We were perpetually afraid that he would wander back, or they would come and get him. They do that, as well. You don't know these people." The flume of her hate revived her. "They finished Big Vinnie off. He had been through the Brooklyn streets, wars, the Depression. But this finished him off. The old ticker gave."

"You can't blame ..." Naomi swallowed the question, but it was too late.

"Yes, I can. I went through it. I saw it with my own eyes. They put us through hell."

"And Vinnie? Your boy?" Barney asked.

"Vinnie's great. He lost two years is all." She sighed and smiled, calm now. She had salvaged her boy. "He's in his third year of medical school."

"And does he remember?"

"Not if he can help it. It embarrasses him."

"Why?"

"He blames himself for letting it happen."

"Why did it happen?" Naomi asked. It had come on her too fast, like a tornado. She watched as Mrs. Prococino shook her head, then sipped her tea. Naomi watched the tendons in her neck work as she swallowed, unable to understand the long pause. Finally, she leveled her eyes at Naomi, seeming to search her. Naomi felt the twinge of discomfort and the sudden realization that she was being looked upon as a potential enemy.

"It can happen to you, lady," she said. "To any one of us."

No! She would not express her doubts. Then, Mrs. Prococino appeared to retreat, as if accepting the realization that, despite all she had said, she could not transfer her outrage completely. The interview was over. Barney stood up and held out his hand.

"I appreciate this," he said gently. "And I'm sorry if I stirred it all up again."

She walked them to the front door, opened it, as if she wanted to shunt them out of the house, like a bouncer getting rid of unruly customers. Naomi left first, starting down the stone steps edged with blooming mums. But when she turned, Barney was not behind her. He was framed in the doorway, clinging to Mrs. Prococino. They were locked in an embrace, rocking back and forth, lost in private consolation, two poor souls mourning a dead loved one. Embarrassed, Naomi turned away and got into the car.

4

When he slid in beside her, his eyes were still moist. Without looking at him, she handed him some tissues. The exclusion had, inexplicably, angered her. What did it matter, she told herself bravely? Barney did not "belong" to her. Not now. Not ever. If he had, he would have pursued her, brought her back.

"Amazing," Barney said as she headed the car into Washington. Time had slipped away and it had grown dark. She flicked on her headlights. "I've heard this all before," he continued. "Hell, I've seen it on television, read it all in the papers. Other names. Other faces. It meant nothing. Nothing! It's what happens to other people. Boring to read about after you've read it once or twice."

"Barney ..."

She needed to punch a fresh breeze into this vacuum of emotion. Into herself as well. She detested the old feelings that his presence had resurrected. Her new isolation from him had, she told herself, brought her back to reality. They were different people, living on different planets. They felt different things, thought different thoughts. She had to make that perfectly clear, to separate herself.

"I don't believe it can happen to everyone," she said, remembering what Mrs. Prococino had told her: "It can happen to you, lady."

He shrugged, lost in his own thoughts. She hadn't made any impact.

"Where are you staying?" she asked.

"Oh." He reached into his pocket and pulled out a key.

"The Marriott. Near the Pentagon."

Heading the car through traffic on 16th Street, she realized she was taking the longest way, stalling. For what reason, she wondered. Then she knew. She had to find out. Why did Charlotte do this to him?

"Was there any hint? Any sign?" she said suddenly, glancing toward him. She watched him raise his eyes. "I mean in Charlotte's ... attitude ... before she left to visit her sister."

His wife's name seemed to recall his sense of the present.

"None."

"No arguments? Nothing ..." She felt a tight clutch in her chest. "Nothing between you?"

"We had arguments, sure," he said, growing restless. His foot tapped on the car floor. "Nothing cataclysmic. We have plenty of money. She had everything she needed."

"Everything?" She was probing now, the stiletto in her mind sharpening, the old curiosity exploding. Often in her work, she had to burrow in this way to get at the truth. "But why are these people missing? Why haven't they been accounted for? Surely, the next of kin had the right to know. Are they dead or alive?" Recently she had probed a government official in Rwanda in this way, showing no mercy, deflecting his obfuscations. I'm speaking for the dead and missing, she assured herself. Bleeding for them. Was she bleeding for Charlotte now? Identifying with her?

"Not everything is measured in material things, Barney," she lectured, an echo of the past. He bit his lip. She was surprised at his concurrence in the interrogation, surprised that he was lending himself so readily. It encouraged her to probe deeper. She suspected he had asked or was asking himself the same questions.

"She had Kevin." A nerve began to palpitate in his jaw.

"And you."

"That makes us a family, right?" he seemed suddenly belligerent.

"But was she happy?"

"Happy? Why not?" He seemed to be probing deeply within himself now, the flare-up of belligerence subsiding. "Nay. I swear to you. I saw nothing. Nothing that would make her do this. It was out of the blue."

"Was she religious? What was her denomination?"

She felt his gaze, but she did not turn her eyes from watching the road.

"A Catholic. Moderate. Not a fanatic. She went to church a few times a year."

"Confession? Did she take confession?"

He hesitated.

"Apparently not. She said she didn't need that. We were married in a church. Religion wasn't a dominant factor in our lives."

"Was she Irish?"

"She was of Irish extraction, as a matter of fact." He showed some irritation. She knew his sudden testiness was directed at her. His parents must have been happy, she thought, remembering them, not with fondness. Obviously, Charlotte had been acceptable to them.

"Had she ever visited her sister before?"

Barney reflected for a moment, then shook his head.

"No. Seattle is a long trip. She thought Kevin was too young to leave. Besides, she and her sister weren't that close, not during the years of our marriage. Oh, they called, spoke. But it was always brief."

"Then why this visit all of a sudden?"

"It wasn't all of a sudden. She had planned for it for months. It was her sister's birthday."

"A sort of reconciliation?"

"I thought so. She did not enjoy their being distant. There was guilt in it for her. It bothered her. I thought it might be a good thing. Fat lot I knew."

"You think the sister ... well ... helped get her involved."

"I have no doubt about it. She was involved. She probably got brownie points for bringing in a sibling."

"So you think Charlotte was set up?"

"I'd bet the barn on it. I'm sure it wasn't what Charlotte wanted to happen. Leave Kevin and me. No way."

His continuing forbearance encouraged her to proceed.

"Nothing you can think of? Nothing set her off?" Then she said what stirred beneath the surface. "She was younger."

"Ten years. Not a lifetime."

"I mean when you married her." It had been in her mind from the beginning, and she had calculated it. "Kevin is four. What was she 18, 19? That's pretty young."

"She was young. No question." He looked at her. "Okay, so I robbed the cradle."

It was a couple of years after they had split, Naomi calculated—her Pyrrhic victory. At least it was not a rebound. Perhaps he had pined for her. It took all her will not to call him after they had gone their separate ways. Finally, years later, she had dialed his number. It was a weak moment, a lonely time. As soon as the ring began, she remembered, she had hung up. The irony galled her now. It wouldn't have mattered. He was involved with Charlotte. So much for everlasting love.

She marveled at his patience as he surrendered to her questions. Throughout, he had been only mildly defensive. She tried to recall him as he was, but couldn't draw a true bead. Time did change people—some people—she decided, wondering if it had changed her.

"I think I know what you're getting at, Nay."

"Do you? I wish I knew."

"I think you're trying to come up with a valid, logical reason for what happened to Charlotte. It doesn't work that way. Did she think she had missed something by getting married so young?" He said it calmly. Obviously, he had been over this ground before. He answered his own question.

"Probably. I won't deny it. I can't say she ever expressed it that way. Doesn't everybody think they missed something now and again?" He kept his eyes averted from her face. Nevertheless, she felt the rhetorical question was directed at her. She had to stop, she rebuked herself, before it got too painful for her. Despite this, she continued.

"You never know about people," Naomi pressed. "You think you're communicating, but you're not." Her present conclusion was that men and women never truly communicated, not on every level. It was something, a flaw perhaps, or some protective mechanism built genetically into the genders.

"Maybe so," he sighed. Was he comparing, remembering? Had he smothered Charlotte with his willingness to do anything to win her, to become what she wanted him to be? Had he become that, whatever it might have been? She remembered what he had done to win her, Naomi.

Possible explanations began to spin in her head, engaging her mind against all conscious design. Charlotte had married too young. Barney had prodded her, Naomi speculated, rushed her.

Hadn't she experienced at first hand his anxiety to build his nest, his infernal nest? Perhaps he was panicked by, up to then, his missing out on finding a mate, a family maker.

After all, six years had gone by since her, since Naomi. Kevin was four. Barney had given Charlotte, say, a year of grace. Then Kevin had come. Charlotte hadn't seen much of anything. She might have been a virgin, known no other men. She had been trapped by love, that irrational and inhibiting emotion.

But why not another child, or more? For true companionship, she speculated, siblings needed to be spaced closer, perhaps two years apart at most. Had she refused to propagate? The explanation spun forward, throwing more images onto her mind's screen. Charlotte was uneasy, unfulfilled, beginning to wonder if this was all there was. Perhaps the first flush of blind love had receded. She felt cheated. She needed more of life's experiences under her belt. To visit her sister was certainly a chance for reconciliation. But she was going alone, leaving her family, perhaps for the first time since her marriage. Perhaps Charlotte might have pondered. It could open doors, show her a way to escape.

Through her sister and the Glories, she had found the exit she craved from her present life. From Barney. From Kevin. From the old narrow, stultifying, crippling, preprogrammed life. Was this wishful thinking on Naomi's part? Which was worse for Charlotte? Naomi wondered, admonishing herself for the thought.

"Nothing will convince me that she wanted this to happen. Nothing. They did it to her. She was the victim," Barney said as if he had read her mind.

"You don't think she was vulnerable?" Naomi pressed.

"Vulnerable?" he mused. "No more than anyone else. We were, by any measure, a happy family," he sighed.

It was, she decided, the wrong tack. He must have sailed those choppy waters over the past sleepless nights. It can happen to anyone, Mrs. Prococino had said. "It can happen to you, lady." No, it can't, she protested. Not if you didn't want it to happen. She was not rejecting Barney's and Mrs. Prococino's pain. That was quite real. It was the rationalization that troubled her. They are trying to justify themselves. Why had it happened to their loved ones?

"What kind of a person is Charlotte?" she asked suddenly. In this context it was harmless, almost.

"She's like a piece of fine china. I'm not saying she's a mental giant. She's smart, but not an intellectual. Not into ... you know." Naomi knew. Not into politics, causes, compassion, all the rest. "She was just a decent, good, loving young woman. Her life was her family. Just like me. We had a co-op on 76th and Broadway. Cost a mint. We traveled. Last year I made nearly $500,000. She had everything she could want."

"How come you didn't have another child?" She had deliberately hit him obliquely with that.

"We were planning another, but not just yet. We wanted to stay in the city," he said, "It's okay for one child, but for any more, you have to think suburbs. We both loved Manhattan."

"Did she like your parents?"

"She tolerated them. As you know, they're not exactly charming. But they loved Kevin. They've moved to Lauderdale. I helped get them this condo. My father's still the great black Irish hater."

"I remember," she said.

"The worst part of all this, Nay," he said finally. "Like Mrs. Prococino said, you blame yourself." He retreated for a long moment. "When she hugged me back there, she said it again. It's not your fault. It's them. She said no one would understand that unless it happened to them."

"And you believe that?"

"I want to. If I thought it was my fault ..." He let the thought drift away.

So, in his mind, it is everybody's fault but his, Naomi thought, wondering if she was reaching at last into the heart of the matter. His fault? Naomi wondered, going over the ground again. Then she tried to put herself in Charlotte's place. Charlotte had to talk to someone. What better confidante than a sister? Their marriage was becoming intolerable. She had simply taken the first exit that was available. There just was no other way to judge these circumstances. The cult was merely a device. They opened their arms and she walked right in.

Now it was her turn to remain silent.

In the absence of her question assault, Barney descended into his own brooding reflection. A black Irish funk, he had once called that mood. Watching the outline of his face, she saw the silhouette of the only man who had ever moved her, the one she had thrown away. She, too, had looked for her exit, finding his version of a smothering, traditional middle-class life intolerable.

The car crawled into the rush-hour traffic. What was the point of all this interrogation? What did it mean to her? His personal travail had no relevance to her life. Even admitting the old attraction made no difference. He hadn't come to see her. To him she represented Washington. Despite knowing that, she had done her best to help him. What more could she have done.

As she pulled up in front of the Marriott, she braced for the goodbyes. Not once had he referred to their life together as if it had happened to other people. Probably didn't even think about it much. She giggled suddenly, remembering the display of his denuded organ, that ludicrous symbol of his "sacrifice."

She felt ashamed of the thought. It was not the first time she had thought about it in the years since she had left him. The image had lingered in her mind. Sometimes it seemed to sum up his persona and her obscene attraction to him. It had become a memory that could trigger sexual fantasy as if somehow it signified her own incompleteness. There were times when she longed for, lusted for it. God, she was thinking of it now, picturing it. What had he done to it? Shame, Naomi, she admonished herself.

"You've been wonderful, Nay," he said, turning to her, taking her hand. His was cold and moist. Or was it hers? Yet he continued to hold it, searching her face, until his eyes drifted away. The memory of loss surged back and with it the prospects of more loneliness and longing.

She let her hand slip through his, as he got out the far side. She rolled down her window.

"Come have a drink," he said, bending low to see her face.

She looked at her watch, probably to give her consent with dignity. There would be nothing to do but go back to her apartment. The office was closed by now, she remembered, and she had left her briefcase of take-home work beside her desk.

"Why not?"

Getting back in her car, she followed his directions to that section where his room was. She hadn't quite expected that, feeling a ripple of expectation that tensed her foot on the accelerator and made her park badly.

Following him up the single flight of stairs, she waited until he turned the key, opening the door into the familiar commercial aura. Inside, he put his notebook on the dresser.

Odd, she thought suddenly, a computer salesman with an old-fashioned notebook. She noted that there was a laptop, open on the desk.

Her threw his jacket on the bed and brought out two glasses wrapped in plastic that he ripped off, pouring out equal amounts from an opened bottle of scotch.

"I can get water and ice."

"It's all right," she said.

"Sure?"

"Sure."

Kicking off his shoes, he stretched heavily on the bed, puffing pillows for a backrest, while she took a chair opposite. Upending his glass, she watched his Adam's apple slide and bob in his throat. Often in bed, she recalled, she had traced it with her fingers, traced everything.

"Do you really think it was my fault?" he asked. A light from a lamp on the dresser put his face in shadows. Only his eyes glowed, like cups of molten lead.

"How did you know I was thinking that?"

"We have history, Nay. I did know something about the way your mind works."

"I'll concede that."

But how could she possibly know what went on between him and his wife.

"I did everything I knew how to keep her happy. Everything."

He drank again. "The truth of it was, I was happy. Happy as a pig in shit."

So he was facing up to it at last. Drinking, she felt the scotch burn its way down her throat.

"Who knows better than you, Nay. All I ever wanted was the happy, secure life. Home and hearth. That's me. A wife, kids, money. The American dream. I'm successful, Nay. I'm one of the hottest computer salesmen in Manhattan. I've got my bosses terrorized that I'll go elsewhere. Maybe I oversold Charlotte." He took a deep sip. "Hell, I couldn't sell you."

"I'm a hard nut, Barney."

"It wasn't me," he whispered. She avoided any response, changing the subject. It was futile to pursue it.

"She had to be vulnerable. Otherwise, why?"

"Nobody changes that fast," he sighed.

"That's the point," Naomi agreed.

"They did it to her, Nay. They know how."

From the shadows, she saw him watching her surreptitiously studying her for the first time that day.

"When we split ... You shattered me, Nay. You really did."

"You seem to have recovered." She hadn't meant to be bitchy.

"I did. I really did. Took years. But don't think I ever forgot the hurt. God. I nearly went crazy." He got up and, for a moment, she thought he was coming toward her. But he had risen only to pour another drink. She declined with a shake of her head and he went back to the bed, bashing the pillows again.

"I shouldn't be laying this on your doorstep." He paused and drank. "A mother doesn't give up her child. No matter what. It's against nature. Everything that is happening is against nature. I can see her giving me up. But not her child, not our baby. Not Kevin. Christ. He's an innocent."

She felt her body begin to tremble, forcing the memory of her own dead fetus. Baby! The word was being jammed into her mind. Against nature? How dare he say that. Thankfully, he had turned his face away, burying it in the smashed pillows, his shoulders shaking. She resisted getting up to comfort him, afraid that her legs would not work. Thinking it would shut him away, she closed her eyes and, for a moment, she lost all sense of time and place. When she opened her eyes again, he was blinking away tears. A large moist spot had formed on the pillowcase.

"Those sons of bitches." He got off the bed and poured another drink, slopping whiskey over his fingers. He began to pace the floor.

"They have no right to come into people's lives. No right to take her away. Glories. Father Glory. He's a pariah, a scavenger. No one can promise anyone salvation. That's bullshit. At least give her time to doubt, to choose. They gave her none of that. They just took her away, like a prisoner without a trial. It's wrong, not fair, inhuman. Mrs. Prococino is right. You are alone. There is no one to turn to." Suddenly, he came toward her now, kneeling beside her.

"Come on, Nay. What do you really think?"

Think? Was it possible for her to think?

"You think it was them or me?"

When she did not answer, his head toppled in her lap, and she felt the heat of him in the center of her, then the moisture of more tears soaking through her dress. Reaching out, she slid her fingers through his hair, caressing the tight softness of it, pressing him against her. Great sobs convulsed him and she buried her lips in his hair.

"I'm afraid," he whispered when the quake within him ended. Still, she held him. Another woman's man. Gently, she lifted his head.

"She's not dead," she whispered, wondering if it sounded harsh. Inexplicably, he forced a smile as he rubbed his face dry.

"One of the people I visited had lost a daughter to the Glories," he said, his voice hoarse, then clearing. "Never got her out. I went to their house and spoke to both the mother and the father. They were devastated. Couldn't even muster a brave front. They had pictures of the daughter everywhere. I had to see them all. They even showed me her room and a ruler nailed to the wall that marked how high she had grown from time to time. It was awful. I don't know why, but I opened a drawer in that room. It was empty." He shook his head. "You discover you're only a tiny link in a long chain of terror. You know what the mother said?" He didn't wait for an answer. " 'Mourn her.' "

He stood up, taking deep breaths.

"I will not mourn her," he cried. "She is not dead. I'm going to get her. I don't know how. But I'm going to get her." Again he faltered, struggling for control. She sensed that he was searching inside of himself for all the courage he could find there. "I'm going to get my wife back. No matter what. I'm going to get her back." He raised his eyes to hers and found them. She felt the old deep magnetic mystery pulling at her, drawing her in. She saw his fear, his pleading. "I don't know how I can do it alone," he whispered.

She wanted to hesitate, to mull over the idea in her mind, to think, to reason, to find the sense and logic of it. But she knew he had engaged her, sucked her in.

"You won't be alone, Barney." She heard a woman's voice and wondered if it really belonged to her.

5

Sheriff T. Clausen Moore tapped the warm plastic phone still moist with his palm print. He had been thankful for the interruption. Exposure to this kind of anguish had a near-toxic effect on him, turning his stomach to acid.

The man before him looked slightly yellow, soiled by desperation. He knew the look. He had seen it many times before, especially back in Appalachia, from where he and Gladys had fled years ago. It still lived inside of him, the memory of those mountain people, cast into hopelessness by events beyond their forgotten world. He had also seen it in the faces of these crushed and grieving people searching for their lost loved ones. Beside the glum man sat a woman. She appeared cooler, more in control. Looking down at the pad on his desk, he refreshed his mind with the man's name.

"It's private property, Mr. Harrigan. You can't enter it without an invitation. And you can't break in, forcibly enter and bring anyone out. Could be a hostage rap, a kidnapping rap. Be surprised what these guys can cook up. The people must come out only of their own free will."

In the long pause of uncertainty that always followed, he sighed and pictured in his mind what he had seen many times in the camp, hoping it would not trigger the depressing images stored in his mind. Glassy-eyed young people, exhausted, some barely coherent, herded like sheep. Actually, he was sparing loved ones the pain of it. He knew the scam, but there wasn't anything he could do about it except warn people to keep away. Hell, he'd fought them as hard as he knew how. And had lost. Sometimes he felt he would drown in the ocean of tears that had been shed at the other side of his desk. It wouldn't matter. His words would have to be the same.

"It's a bona fide tax exempt religion, approved by the high offices of the United States government. I do not represent anyone but the people of this county. The law is the law."

He was not able to tell them that he had tangled with their lawyers, with the so-called officials of the Glory Church, with the bastard who ran the camp. Jeremiah! What was his real name? Billy Perkins from St. Joseph, Missouri. Jeremiah now, the great prophet. Nothing but a ruthless son of a bitch. Also, he couldn't tell them of the deal that he had finally made with Jeremiah to keep the peace. Hell, wasn't that his job?

He'd agreed to do his best to keep troublemakers away. Parents, brothers, sisters. Sometimes to salve his much-abused conscience he'd go in and slap them with sanitation violations. They were always filling up their outhouse pits too damned high with shit. And there had been two suspicious drownings in the river that ran through the camp. Slipping along the bank was always the reason, and nothing he had tried could break that assumption. He still had his doubts, but left it alone. Too much hassle involved. It was, he often snickered bitterly to his wife, like shoveling shit against the tide.

"But how do they do it to those kids, Tee?" Gladys had asked, maybe a thousand times since the Glories had come in with their permit for the 300-acre Bobson place. The records showed that they had bought the farm from the widow Bobson fair and square for three times its value, a fact that had a profound effect on local landowners.

In the beginning, the locals had fought it, but in the end it was money talking. "Hell, that price raised the value of our property," they told him, quietly at first, then louder, taking the wind out of the sails of the opposition. How many years had they been there now? Ten? Eleven? God knew how they did it. Sometimes he laughed at these questions. It wasn't anything he knew about. Nor wanted to.

He had seen the busloads of young people come in from Seattle, about 50 miles west. They were a mixed bag, clean-cut, scrubbed and brushed, some with long hair and guitars. Coming in, they looked like ordinary young people. Soon they were trapped, neat little dolls. More like sheep. And Jeremiah was the shepherd.

Often, hysterical parents would get to the camp. It wasn't hard. There were no gates. They didn't need gates. The gates were in the kids' heads. When they got too obstreperous they had to be forcibly removed by his men, locked in jail until they cooled down, then sent away with a tough warning. This tactic hadn't really satisfied Jeremiah and that oily lawyer Holmes, who always pressed charges. But then, parents rarely came back to face them, and other jurisdictions were reluctant to go through extradition procedures. The law! In this case, it seemed he was on the wrong side of it.

"You go near that camp, I'll break your ass," he had told his own boys. Two were away at college, and the oldest, T. Junior, was working back east. Hell, if it was ever his kids in there, he'd have gone in, guns blazing.

"Not us, Pop," his kids had laughed at his warnings. "You think we're dummies?"

"Don't be smart-asses. It can happen to anyone. I see it every day."

It had bewildered him at first. Even when he saw the scam in action. A kid, usually in his early twenties, would be picked up on the city streets by members of the opposite sex. They'd invite the kid to any one of the various houses they owned in the city, give him the old love-bombing routine, then cart him or her off to the camp, inducing expectations of a three-day hang-loose adventure in the country. The kids must have thought they'd get laid a lot. Or discover some new kind of thrill. Only natural that kids that age looked for thrills and adventures. Hadn't he been the same? What they got instead was a good dose of brainwash. Some thrill.

The Glories had built this complex. It looked like a summer camp, with wooden barracks, a mess hall, meeting rooms and cabins for administration and other uses. They'd usually bring the kids in during the night and hand them sleeping bags, lining the boys up on one side, the girls on the other. They slept all right. Too tired to do anything else.

In the morning, just before dawn, they'd be awakened by a brace of guitars strumming out familiar songs but strange lyrics with words like "centering" and "glory." Innocent words. There was always lots of stuff about Glory. The kids didn't understand a word of it, not then. Father Glory and the Glories happened to other people. Not them. Hell, they didn't even know the Glories were behind it.

That first morning they were split into groups of 12. Six were Glories, only the new kids didn't know that. Each kid had his own Glory watchdog, a girl for a boy and a boy for a girl. They didn't know that, either. They called them spiritual brothers and sisters. No sex. They were with them all their waking hours, even when they went to pee.

They used eye contact as a kind of hypnotic control. Eyes! Powerful instruments, eyes. They'd start off the day by marching them around to the head, a quick shit, a wash, then off to breakfast. There, they'd get sugared up. Cereal with sugar; Kool-Aid, sugared up; coffee, sugared up. Once he had come there early and they had offered him breakfast and he had tasted it. He nearly threw up. He had never really understood the power of sugar.

After breakfast, the groups of 12 would sit around and talk about their lives. They had never let him in on that, although he knew they used hidden tape recorders. He'd seen them lined up in their storehouses ready for use. What did they tell each other? Whatever it was they had the goods on them. When would they use it? Who knows?

Some parents told him that the kids revealed their innermost secrets, real heavy personal stuff, whatever imagined sins against themselves and society they had imagined or actually committed, all to great applause. It was called getting out the garbage. Hell, everybody had garbage. Like Catholic confession. The Glories liked to tell him they were just like Catholics, but he knew better. He had never seen a desperate parent ready to kill to get his kid away from the priests.

Then they'd play crazy little games, like dodgeball. The idea was to get them always to think "center." They chanted things about "centering" and "Glory." More confessions. More love bombing. More sugaring up.

By sundown, the kids were so tired they fell into their sacks, exhausted, only to repeat the cycle the next day. This went on for three days. Sometimes he'd get a call from some kid who said he had to get away, but usually by the time he got there, the kid had changed his mind. Except if he got really sick. They didn't much believe in medical care, except for minor things like bee stings and sunburn. But when a kid got really sick, they let him go. Lucky bastard, he always said when he'd visit the kid in the county hospital. Of course, he never dared say that publicly. Wouldn't do to rock the boat. Not as long as the voters tolerated it.

The voters! He snickered. The Glories had become voters. With so many establishing their legal residences at the camp, they were becoming a formidable political force. Soon they would tip the balance. Hell, he thought, T. Clausen Moore could count.

By the third day, they'd start the head-pounding lectures. Some guy would talk for hours, writing with chalk on a blackboard, rattling on about this mumbo-jumbo religion based on the teachings of Father Glory. They had them fully under control by then.

Hell, the kids had never been left alone, had been leaned on pretty heavy. There was no television, no newspapers, no outside influence. There was only one phone, and they made the kids call their parents or spouse or sister so they wouldn't get wise too early. Of course they were never allowed to make the phone call alone. Always, they had their spiritual brother or sister beside them. Sometimes two at a time. In a week, the Glories had them, lock, stock and barrel. Brains and all. If they had possessions, or control of money, down Father Glory's gullet they would go.

When they were sure the kid was theirs, they'd give him this weird amulet or charm that the kid was to wear around his neck for the rest of his life. It was a plastic likeness of Father Glory's head, complete with that wide smile and scary eyes. The charm was transparent and inside was this liquid that the Messiah had blessed. Moore was always suspicious of this liquid. Probably poison. Maybe one day the whole lot would take it, like in Jonestown. He hated the idea, of course. All those innocent kids … but it did cross his mind from time to time.

In the early days, Father Glory himself would come regularly and they would have these ceremonies. Now that he had become a big-time religious star, grown fat with the good life, he came about once every two years. It was always a pain in the ass, dealing with his bodyguards and security arrangements.

It was a mystery to him how they did it. That was the part he would never understand. Nor did he want to. He only knew that whatever they did to those kids, it worked and it was legal and there was nothing in the damned world that he or anyone else could do about it. Nothing!

Actually, in the beginning, he had tried to do something about it. Hadn't he told Gladys that something suspicious and wrong was going down at the camp? Something damned sinister.

"You mean voodoo?" she had asked.

"Maybe," he had answered.

Then when the first parents started to troop in, he had gone with them to the camp, genuinely on the parents' side. Nobody had the right to take away another person's kid. Okay, they were in the twenties, but to him they were still kids. What he got from all this was some real lessons about the law, about what can and cannot be done when these kids were over 21. Occasionally, he got one out when they were underage, but they had become pretty careful about that in the last few years.

When he tried to explain what was going on to other folks, they just shrugged. None of their business. It wasn't their kid.

"They're raising a whole fucking army of zombies," he would tell Gladys. "If Father Glory said go kill your mother, they'd do it. If Father Glory said go rape your sister, they'd do it. Worse, if the son of a bitch told them all to commit suicide, they'd do the number on themselves and wouldn't bat an eye."

"Weird, Tee, you're exaggerating," she would respond.

"Maybe so. It's just my gut talking."

Although the Glories never allowed any drugs in there, parents would come in and say their kids had been drugged. And he'd tell them that he tried on at least three occasions to find drugs in the camp. Real potential busts. Unless you'd classify sugar as a drug. One thing they had was bales and bales of sugar. Mostly, they ate some form of vegetable and fruit that they grew themselves. When parents told him there was something fishy in the diet, he would try to make a bad joke. "Nothing fishy in that diet." No protein he could see. Nobody would laugh.

Yet no matter how much he had seen, he'd never gotten used to it. He was always amazed how they'd get the kids to sign over everything they had, bank accounts, cars, clothes, jewelry. If they had trust funds, the Glories would find a way to get that, too. Hadn't he really tried at the beginning, interviewing the kids? They sounded like machines, all programmed with the same script.

"Are you here of your own free will?"

"Yes."

"Do you realize that you have signed away all your possessions?"

"Yes."

"Why did you do that?"

"For Father Glory. For salvation in the spirit world."

It was hopeless. From then on, they weren't people anymore, not real people. And if he stepped out of line, just a tad over the line of law, he'd also get barraged by lawyers from the American Civil Liberties Union. So he tried to keep the so-called rescuers out. Sometimes, if they were determined enough, they got in. Didn't matter. The Glories knew had to handle them. They called him only if things got rough. Not usually these days. They had it down cold.

"That's their right," lawyers would tell him.

"But they don't think for themselves," he'd protest.

"You can't prove that."

Rights and First Amendment, they'd tell him. That covered it all, and he wondered if the men who wrote the Constitution ever figured they'd be faced with something like this. Even when he showed them literature where Father Glory said "I am your mind," the ACLU boys told him about rights and the First Amendment.

He'd paid a pretty price, too, for all this aggravation. Just ask Gladys. Many a night, he would wake, sweating and screaming, and she'd have to soothe him like a damned baby to chase away the lingering memory of that fucking nightmare, the one in which all those eyes kept watching him, all those blank dead eyes. Hell, he was only the sheriff, not God.

"Have you called their lawyer for permission?" the sheriff asked the Harrigan fellow, knowing the answer in advance. Delaying tactics—a favorite ploy of the Glories.

When a distraught relative would call their office in Seattle, they'd get politely referred to a lawyer who would tell them he would "check." It was a question of finding out where the person was, he would say. But he'd rarely call back. And if he did there was enough advance notice for them to be prepared.

If the relatives persisted in going beyond just a visit and got their own lawyer, made too much noise, the Glories would hide the person somewhere else, in another camp, or send them to other parts of the country or the world. The threat of making them disappear was usually enough to call off the dogs.

Sometimes, though, when they felt totally safe about the person in the camp, they might allow a brief meeting, especially if it was a spouse or a sibling. More than one sibling had been captured by the Glories during a rescue attempt. Parents, because they were not part of the peer group and because of their age, weren't nearly as vulnerable.

"Yes," Barney answered. "I called their office. Brown and Kyler. Very old line. Respected. I spoke to Bradley Holmes, a senior partner. He made my teeth itch with his respectability."

The sheriff knew what was coming next. Even the lawyer's snooty name, Bradley Holmes, was intimidating. He could sympathize with Barney's sense of powerlessness. Holmes was the embodiment of the establishment. Through Holmes, the Glories had bought legal respectability. He was a whore in pinstripes. He'd dealt with plenty of those.

"What did he say?" the sheriff asked.

"He said he'd check with my wife," Barney said, shaking his head.

"It's a perfectly legitimate answer. It's her decision." The sheriff nearly choked on the word "decision."

"Oh yes," Barney sneered. "I asked him how long it would take. He said he couldn't tell me. All very calm and measured." When the sheriff deliberately showed no reaction, he continued. "I said I had come out at great expense to see my wife, that she had left a small child at home that she was obviously being held against her will and I would be damned if he'd have me standing around cooling my heels until they had checked. What the hell did 'check' mean?"

"It meant that you could see her when it was appropriate."

"Appropriate?"

"When she wanted to see you." He was trying to be diplomatic. "Look, I'm just the sheriff."

"What you're telling me, then," Barney said, "is that either I see them on their terms or I don't see them at all."

"More or less."

"This is not what I came to you to hear. I came to you for help."

"Sorry. All I can help you with is advice. Just cool it. She's committed. It's over," he said.

"It's like you're protecting them," Barney said, his face tightening.

"I'm not protecting them. I'm enforcing the law."

"Goddamned law. They break up my family and you tell me about the goddamned law."

"Barney," the woman beside him cautioned.

Her rebuke caught him in time and he backed off. The sheriff was used to it.

"It's okay," he whispered.

The sheriff wished it would come to an end.

"Have they got armed guards at this camp?" Barney asked. It was the inevitable question, and the sheriff was prepared for it.

"They don't need them"

"You mean if someone comes in there, guns blazing, they just don't defend themselves?"

"They call me. I defend them. That's my job, to defend citizens of this county against potential criminals."

"How noble."

"Yes, it is."

"I don't like it." Barney pressed. The sheriff knew exactly where his reasoning was leading. Poor bastard. The smell of desperation oozed out of him, spilling into the room.

"They've had incidents," the sheriff said cautiously. At this point, it was always tricky.

"People try to get them out?"

"Some."

"Does it ever work?"

"Not usually."

"Sometimes?"

"Not in recent years."

Barney was silent for a long time. The sheriff was remembering the accidental drownings.

"Have they registered arms with your office?"

"No. We've looked for them." When was this fellow going to catch his drift? "The fact is, Mr. Harrigan, they really don't need them."

What he did not tell them was that they had maintained a kind of hot line between the camp and his office. Usually, though, the Glories were fully able to take care of any wild-eyed relatives that had bluffed their way into the camp.

"We don't really need your help," Jeremiah had bragged. "But when we do you'll be summoned."

They had their own devious ways to get rid of trespassers. Sometimes they said they had no record of the person inquired about. On very rare occasions, they arranged a brief talk with the kid, just enough time for the relatives to get the idea. They were remarkably effective.

Occasionally, some relatives would try to pull a snatch with a deprogrammer waiting somewhere. They had a helluva nose for that. When they sensed that was about to happen, they usually called him on the hot line and he and his men would rush out to the camp. A couple of times, they had missed and some kid had been spirited away, but that hardly happened in the last few years. Usually, when a snatch was tried, it was after the kid had graduated into fund-raising and was plucked off some street corner, but that was always out of his jurisdiction.

His method now when dealing with people loaded for bear was patient, gentle persuasion, maybe scare them a bit, stop them from trying something stupid. Sometimes he would hint at the truth of the process. That always hurt the most. The fact was that the odds were against them, heavily against them. Yet there was one thing he prided himself about. He would never foreclose on their hopes to win back their loved one. Just as long as they didn't try it in his county.

"Are you saying that any attempt to reverse the decision would be futile?" the woman asked. She seemed a good balance for the man—alone, he might have done something he'd regret. He nodded his answer. Decision, he thought? Hell, there was no decision involved. He didn't want to get into that one.

"Its not easy for them to reverse their alliance," was the way he put it. The woman seemed to buy it. The man never would.

They were beginning to eat into his time, try his patience. Besides, his stomach was grumbling. It was nearly lunchtime.

"Look, Mr. Harrigan," the sheriff said, standing up. Behind him was a big map of the county. "Whatever is going through your mind, forget it." He decided to short-circuit any ideas the man might have. He pointed to the map but not to any specific spot. "Their camp is in a little valley surrounded by low hills. It's unmarked. There's a long, winding road. You can't sneak in. There's only this one road. They see you coming. Get my drift? Even if you do find it, they might tell you that she's not there. Sometimes they do. Sometimes they don't. Sometimes they let you meet the person just to see if you mean trouble. Why torture yourself? If you look like trouble they might transfer her out of there. How long has she been in?"

"Nearly three weeks."

"Not likely," he mused aloud, instantly sorry he had said it. "They usually hold them here for six weeks. Then they send them out over the country to fund-raise."

"So," Barney said, his lips contorting into a trembling smile. "You used the word 'hold.'"

"Only a figure of speech, Mr. Harrigan," the sheriff said.

"It implies that she's been captured."

"Don't look for implications; I try not to make judgments. I'm a law officer. I don't sit on the bench."

"But you said ..."

"Please, Barney. There's no point," Naomi interrupted.

"But he knows in his heart it's true. They're holding her under duress."

The sheriff sat down again, tapping his fingers impatiently on the desk.

"I didn't say that."

"But how the hell can they do it so fast?" Barney said.

He'd been through that one, too. There were all kinds of explanations, some scientific that he didn't understand. From his experience, brainwashing was a pretty good description of what they did. They washed the brain all right, washed out all the logic, washed out all the negatives, washed out any power to criticize, to make individual judgments. The fact was that it worked and there was no law against it.

"Tell you the truth, Harrigan," the sheriff shrugged. "I don't know."

"But it's ... it's coercion ... they have no right."

"Rights again?" the sheriff sighed.

"They can't be allowed to get away with it. No way. No fucking way."

The man was on the edge of panic. The sheriff turned to Naomi.

"Talk some sense into him, lady."

His stomach was exploding with pain and emptiness. He needed something to fill it up. He'd have to end it, end it now.

"The fact is, Mr. Harrigan, it's damned near hopeless. I'm not saying that they won't let you see her. They might. They've been through every conceivable kind of ploy. It just won't do any good. What they got in there is a committed woman. She has jettisoned her old life. Accept it. There is nothing you can do." He wished he might have said it another way. Out of pique or arrogance or sheer pain, he had stupidly challenged the man, opened up a possibility for potential trouble. Go home, he cried in his heart. Above all, don't put your trouble on my doorstep. I'm just a man with a job.

What hurt him the most was the knowledge that in Barney's shoes he'd do the same. Go try it then, you poor dumb bastard. Thankfully, Barney stood up, holding out his hand. Now that was odd, the sheriff thought, they usually just sat there until he declared the interview over. The sheriff took Barney's hand. It felt cold and wet, like the hand of a drowning man, reaching out for a lifesaver.

"Thanks for nothing, sheriff," Barney said. "Thanks, America." Naomi turned to face him, nodded sympathetically, shrugged as if in understanding, then followed the man out of his office.

"Leave it alone, son," the sheriff said as they departed.

When they had gone, the sheriff reached down into the bottom drawer of his desk and pulled out a bottle of bourbon. Opening it, he poured it into his cold coffee in the mug on his desk. Taking a deep swallow, he felt it burn as it washed down his gullet. These damned interviews were always setting off those damned recurring images. Tonight he would probably dream again about the eyes.

6

She knew Barney would not leave it alone.

He had, despite all the sheriff's warning, headed directly toward the camp. He had gotten directions through other sources, but he had visited the sheriff, as he put it, on the off chance he might be of some help. The sheriff had confirmed his own powerlessness, although she had sensed that he had some understanding of Barney's pain.

"You heard the man Barney. It's trouble."

"That's why I'm here. Trouble."

"Why must you do this?" Naomi said.

"You know why, Nay," Barney muttered, his determination unwavering. "I've got to see for myself."

"But you haven't got permission."

"Fuck permission. You heard the sheriff. He said those bastards know how to handle us. I need to see her. See for myself."

He turned toward her and patted her thigh.

"I'll be careful. You'll see. Just be cool. I need to see her is all." He pointed to his forced smile. "Like this. Show them this."

She shrugged consent. No point in arguing. She had gone along.

No one had stopped them until they reached what appeared to be a parking lot. There were a few vans and cars parked there. If they had not received specific instructions on how to get there, they might have missed it. In fact, there was nothing to indicate that this was a Glory indoctrination camp. There were no signs. And, as the sheriff had told them, there was a long, winding road, a bridge to cross over a fast running river. Not far, she could see a neat row of barracks-like structures and other cabins. It did remind her of a summer camp.

As they moved into the parking lot, a single man emerged from nowhere and waved. He was dressed in khakis and a lightweight jacket. Around his neck he wore a whistle and an amulet on a gold chain. On closer observation, they saw that the amulet was transparent and seemed to be filled with some liquid. Some religious symbol, she assumed. The man moved in the path of the crawling car and smiled broadly. Barney pulled the car to a stop, opened the door and got out. Naomi stayed inside the car, observing them through the open window.

"I'm Jeremiah," the man said, a smile fixed on his face, putting out his hand in greeting. He was about 35, his curly hair flecked with gray, his expression benign, although behind the cheekbones, she imagined she could see a hard-edged observant look. Put him in a business suit and he might have been taken for an IBM executive.

"I'm Barney Harrigan," Barney said, his voice deliberately ingratiating, salesmanlike, his tone unthreatening, his smile fixed.

"Yes, I know. We've been expecting you."

"Really?"

"Sheriff Moore said you might be stopping by." He nodded and continued to smile pleasantly. "You are trespassing, but it's all right. I'm sure if you waited for a day or so Mr. Holmes would have given you permission."

She could see a nerve palpitating in Barney's jaw. He was, she knew, holding himself together by sheer will.

"So I can see Charlotte?" Barney asked.

"Of course."

He turned and waved, and three people emerged from one of the buildings and headed toward them. As they came closer, she could see two women and one man. She estimated them as being in their early to middle twenties. Since she had no idea what Charlotte looked like, she could only guess that one of them, probably the woman in the center, was her.

Barney, looking increasingly agitated, watched as they came toward him. Naomi could feel his tension. Jeremiah nodded as they came forward. Barney's smile disappeared as they approached.

Naomi noted that they seemed strange-looking. They were all smiling and their eyes seemed glazed. They reminded her of robots.

"Charlotte," Barney called as they came closer. He tensed, started to move forward to greet the group. Then he stopped, waiting. Naomi confirmed that the woman in the center was Charlotte. Her hair was shorn in a mannish cut, reminding Naomi of pictures she had seen of prisoners in a concentration camp. She wore slacks and a frayed sweater.

Charlotte nodded, acknowledging the greeting. She continued to smile, but showed little emotion.

"Nice to see you, Barney," she said with obvious indifference. Naomi could see Barney's disappointment.

"And nice to see you, Charlotte," Barney said. He seemed totally confused by her reaction. What had he expected?

"So here she is," Jeremiah said. "Alive and well. Aren't you, Rachel?"

"Rachel?" Barney shook his head in disbelief.

"The old names don't apply anymore," Jeremiah said blandly. "They have a new life. Isn't that true, Rachel?"

"Oh yes, a new life with Father Glory," Charlotte said. Naomi thought she could detect a sudden glow of ecstasy at the mention of Father Glory.

She simply stood before him, silent, smiling, treating him like a stranger. It must have been galling for Barney. He turned to the woman next to her.

"You did this, Susan, you bitch," he murmured. There was a distinct resemblance between the two women. Obviously, she was Charlotte's sister.

"Rachel is very happy here," the sister said. "Aren't you, Rachel?"

"Very happy," Charlotte repeated without emotion.

"Very happy," the young man said, nodding.

"I'd like you to come home with me," Barney said. Naomi could see signs of rage beginning. His face had flushed and the veins in his neck stood out. "Kevin needs you."

"Kevin will be fine," the sister said. "He has his daddy."

"Yes," Charlotte said. "He has his daddy."

"He needs his mommy," Barney said, tensing further. She could sense the beginning of an eruption.

"There now," Jeremiah said blandly. "You've seen her. Doesn't she look wonderful? She's quite happy. Perhaps you should go now."

"You won't come home?" Barney asked, swallowing hard.

"She is home," Jeremiah said. "Aren't you, Rachel?"

"I am home," Charlotte said.

"But Kevin ..." Barney began.

"Well now, Mr. Harrigan. You've seen your wife. No problem was there. Now it's time you left. The others are having lunch." He turned to the three robotic young people. "You can go to lunch now."

Obediently, the three young people turned and began to head back. "You can't, Charlotte. What about Kevin?" he cried. But the three people did not look back.

"Charlotte!" Barney shouted. "Charlotte!" His voice was shrill. The camp remained quiet. Nothing seemed to stir as the three people walked nonchalantly away, paying little attention to Barney now. When they were out of earshot, he turned to Jeremiah.

"How could you do this to people?" Barney said. He shifted his weight from one foot to the other and his breath came in gasps. He could barely speak.

"It was so nice your stopping by, Mr. Harrigan," Jeremiah said.

"Fuck you," Barney screamed, grabbing Jeremiah's jacket.

"Don't, Barney," Naomi shouted.

"Listen to her," Jeremiah said. "People are watching. The sheriff has been notified. No trouble, please. You are trespassing. You've seen your wife. She's very happy. She's a Glory now and nothing you can do will change that. Accept it, Mr. Harrigan. She has found peace and security. If you loved her you would be happy for her."

Barney continued to hold the man. After a few moments he let go and pointed his index finger at the man's chest.

"You'll be sorry. I swear it. You'll be sorry. I want my wife back. I'll kill you all if I have to. You give her back. You hear. Fair warning."

"I would advise you," Jeremiah said, still smiling, shaking his head as if confronting a spoiled child. "These threats are actionable. It's okay, though. I'll overlook them. I won't report you.

Now, if you don't mind, I have work to do." He looked at his watch. "May I suggest you leave now." He put out his hand.

Barney looked at it and spat on it.

"You lousy fuck," he began.

"Barney, please, don't," Naomi cried.

Barney nodded, his head bobbing furiously. He turned and got back into the car.

"You haven't seen the end of this, you fuck," he shouted. "I'll get you. I'll kill every last one of you. You've murdered her mind, you lousy fucks. You murdered my wife."

"It was so nice meeting you, Mr. Harrigan."

Jeremiah turned and began walking back toward where Charlotte and her two companions had gone.

"You fuck," Barney shouted, starting up the car.

For a brief moment, Naomi thought he might be heading the car in Jeremiah's direction. He turned sharply.

"I'll get 'em. If it's the last thing I do, I'll get 'em."

"Calm down, Barney. Please. Don't make it any worse than it is."

She did not speak again until the car had turned off onto the main highway back to Seattle.

"You should never have threatened to kill them," she said.

"I meant it."

"It sounded like you meant it."

"I hope they got the message."

"I think he did. They might send her away."

He shrugged and they both grew silent.

Despite all the forewarnings, reality had exceeded their expectations. What she wanted most was to still her thoughts, which, in any event, were incoherent. She needed to put everything on idle, to reassemble herself. She was only moderately successful. Beside her, he said nothing, although occasionally his lips would move. She did not intrude on his inner dialogue.

The only logic she could find in why she was here was her own stupidity. This was not her affair. She needed to find the will to go home. This man beside her was not the Barney Harrigan of her comfortable private memories, of her longings and fantasies. Worse, he was looking for his wife. She was far, far out of radar range.

7

They had checked into adjoining rooms at a Holiday Inn just outside of Seattle. After what they had been through, neither of them, she knew, could bear to be alone. They each opened the door between their rooms.

"I'll order hamburgers from room service," he said, forcing her return to the familiar, the prosaic.

"That sounds fine." The thought of food was revolting.

In the bathroom of her room, she took a shower, alternating between hot and cold, deliberately testing her tolerance, as if to validate her physical presence. When she had rubbed herself dry, she pulled her hair back and put on a dressing gown and returned to his room. She felt not the slightest hint of old times, old cravings.

In his room, Barney was sitting at the desk, writing in his notebook. A rolling table had been set. Their hamburgers looked waxy and unappetizing. He had poured a tall drink from a scotch bottle, which stood beside him on the table. When he looked up finally, his demeanor was not as she had expected. He seemed, inexplicably, undefeated.

"Drink?"

"Why not?" she shrugged.

He got up, poured her a scotch, added soda and ice and sat down again at the table, picking up his hamburger, taking big bites. She tried to do the same but could barely swallow. She washed it down with her drink.

"Know thine enemy," he said when he had finished his hamburger. In the camp, he had been reduced to a pleading supplicant. His recovery seemed remarkable.

"Did you see it?" he asked.

"See what?"

"She's not completely there."

"So it seemed."

He ignored her lukewarm response. She remembered Barney's earlier surge of hope. Self-delusion, she thought now. Charlotte was obviously deep in the grip of a religious conversion, whatever else it seemed. However it had happened, however it had appeared, wasn't it still her right? She was, of course, arguing with herself. Accept it, both the sheriff and Jeremiah had urged. Would she? She wasn't quite sure.

Besides, his hope irritated her, as well as the knowledge of her own doubt. She took another sip of her drink. After awhile she noted that he was staring at her. It made her uncomfortable.

"Remember our moment?"

God no, she thought. Was he trying to seduce her, find solace in sex? She had not the slightest inclination. Keep the memory going, she told herself. Keep talking.

She searched her memory. Had there really been a moment? Perhaps. She'd grant him that. She smiled and tapped the table, not knowing what else to do. The fact was she envied Charlotte her bliss. No pressure. No doubts.

"You remember those moments," he said. "Charlotte and I had our moment, too."

Oddly, she felt both disappointed and relieved.

"And I'm going to get her out. Stay tuned."

He was gripped by an obsession of blind hope, she saw, as he ravaged the hamburger in a frenzy, his Adam's apple jumping and bobbing in the ridges of his neck.

"It's there," he said. "I know she's in there somewhere and I've got to shake her loose, get her out. Have you ever seen anything like it in your life?"

"Not really," she admitted flatly.

"Them and their fucking First Amendment." A chunk of hamburger caught in his throat and he had to cough it up and reswallow.

"I don't know the Heimlich maneuver," she said, feeling the alcohol begin to loosen her. Better to banter away her fear, she told herself. Watching him, she felt misplaced.

"They brainwashed her. If I could just get her away from there. That's step one. Inside that camp, she's dead in the water. They won't let her think."

She shivered, drawing her dressing gown around her. It seemed too flimsy a shield and she took another deep swallow of her drink.

"Can you believe how she's changed?" he asked suddenly.

"I didn't know her before."

She had tossed it to him, like a barbed arrow, recalling her raw jealousy. Barney had never come after her like that. The comparison seemed garbled in her mind, unworthy of discussion. She had sought independence, not another alliance. She wanted freedom, not imprisonment. The phrases rang in her mind, like patriotic slogans. When she had longed for him in the cold pit of her bed or in another man's arms, the slogans had sounded like hollow bleats. Again, he began the regurgitation of memory. But it wasn't about her, about them. Accept it, she told herself noting the irony.

"I met her on the beach, picked her up like a beautiful conch. When I talked with her, I heard the echo of myself, all that I wanted. She was so alert, so questioning. Her green eyes danced. She was an avalanche of questions. Why this or that? How come? That was her favorite. How come? It used to exasperate me sometimes. But it never mattered. I liked to be around her. She only had a high school education. She wanted to be a model. Wasn't thin enough. Yet, in my arms, she was as delicate as a flower. Sometimes when I looked at her at night, I used to say to myself, How could such joy happen to me."

He was lost in himself, not knowing how much he hurt her. Nor did she want him to know. So he had found this naive kid on the beach and he had sold her on himself, she thought with bitterness. It was actually what she had wished for him during those first days apart. She had wanted him to find someone just like Charlotte. Time passed as his voice floated in the air between them. She listened perfunctorily.

"I'll get her back," he said again. And again.

He got up, picked up the notebook from the table and sat down again. "It's all in here. Bearing witness. No detail has gone unwritten. Then it goes in there." He pointed to his computer on the desk. "Everyone must know what I'm going through, what others have gone through. Everyone. The world is going to know what these people do. Maybe then they'll understand. Change the laws. Do something. They can't be allowed to get away with it."

"I'd say you have your work cut out for you." She heard her tongue slur the words.

"You think I don't know that." He thumbed through the pages in the notebook. "We just didn't make the sale on the first pass." His face suddenly brightened. "But we got in, didn't we? That damned sheriff didn't think we could do that, and we did it." He slapped his thighs. "We did that. Now we know what we're up against."

His use of the first person plural galled her.

"I've got a couple of bombs to throw." He got up and balled his fist in his palm. "Now that I know what I'm up against. They got one helluva scam going. That Jeremiah. The evil bastard. I'll unload that bastard's wagons."

He was getting up a full head of indignation.

"That fucking sheriff. I'd like to kick him in the cojones, teach him a little bit about America."

His image was becoming distorted. Or was she getting drunk too quickly? Her head was spinning. Still, she let him pour her another drink, hoping for oblivion. Interrupting him, she stood up, her fingers balancing herself against the table, which rolled slightly as she wavered. He caught her just in time, holding her.

"I'd better get you to bed," he said, gripping her waist. She leaned against him, letting him lead her. In the fog of her drunkenness, she felt her dressing gown open, a chill on her exposed nipples. Come be with me, she screamed at him silently. Let's fuck her memory away. He lifted her into bed without hesitation and pulled the covers to her neck. The light fixture above her swam in the molten air.

"I'm sorry," she heard him say. She wasn't sure. It might have been her own words. She was sorry. Sorry for everything. Mostly for herself.

8

They sat in the reception room of the offices of Brown and Kyler, sedately decorated in oils depicting colonial scenes on polished cherrywood-paneled walls. The furniture was early American, too delicate to be comfortable but obviously authentic. On a glossy table, neatly sorted, were Architectural Digest, Antique Monthly, Town and Country and various horse magazines.

"Set pieces," she thought, screaming out Ivy League, DAR, old money, deep American roots, WASP. A beautiful blonde woman, immaculately groomed and coiffed with a simple Junior League wave, answered the phone with a cool disdain. She sat behind a gleaming antique desk. She wore a wire headset and ignored them with an air of carefully rehearsed intimidation. This was Brown and Kyler, old-line, patrician. Naomi felt diminished.

They had come through heavy double doors, replete with colonial knockers. Lettered on it discreetly were the names of an army of partners. The elevator had whisked them to the 39th floor, about which she had made a lame joke about 39 steps, wondering aloud if Hitchcock would pass them in the corridors, if only to break the spell of gloom and despair that hovered over them. It didn't have the desired effect.

Barney was in no mood for jokes. The horror of the waking nightmare going on in his mind was sucking up all his energy, all his focus. He was obsessed. Still, she had not found the courage or the will to leave. On top of everything, she had a slight hangover.

Sitting now in the lawyer's reception room, she continued to cover her embarrassment by thumbing through an Architectural

Digest, hardly paying any attention to the lush pictures and contrived settings.

"I got drunk," she had told him at breakfast. She had three cups of coffee and felt her stomach burn.

In the car, she had asked, Where are we going? She was drifting now, an irrelevant and reluctant observer. Above all she wanted to go home. Yet she yielded to the masochistic pull of it, sailing along like a rudderless ship.

"You'll see," he had told her. She hadn't expected the visit to the lawyer's office. So far Barney had communicated with him by phone.

"Mr. Holmes will see you now," the woman at the desk said cheerfully.

"I'll wait," she said.

"No. I need you with me."

"So I'm a witness, am I?" Was that his purpose from the beginning?

"That, too." Too? She wondered what he meant.

They followed the woman's directions down a long carpeted corridor. Bradley Holmes was waiting for them in a large office. A window wall offered a magnificent view of the Golden Gate Bridge that spanned the pristine bay. It was a clear, cloudless day. She could see all the way to Oakland. Soothed by the sight, she sat down primly on a Chippendale chair. The lawyer had stepped in front of his polished desk to greet them with an eager handshake, warm and friendly. Barney, spruce and slick, in a neat three-piece suit, a smile pasted on his face, slid into a chair as Holmes went behind his desk, leaning back on a high gleaming brown leather chair.

His office was a mass of wood and leather. On his walls were three diplomas. Stanford, LLB; Harvard, LLD. Another announcing admittance to the Supreme Court. Bookshelves under glass held leather-bound classics. In a nook were duck decoys. On the walls were photographs. Holmes with Ronald Reagan, suitably inscribed. Holmes as a young man in crew cut holding a lacrosse racquet. Holmes and a pert, scrubbed woman, he in full resplendent uniform of naval lieutenant, she in a wedding dress. Pictures of children, neat, graceful, handsome. Two pretty girls and a lovely-looking boy. On his desk was a picture of a baby in an old-fashioned pose, pinkly naked on a pillow. He wore a charcoal gray suit, a red striped tie, a pinstriped shirt on a field of blue, perfectly matching his eyes.

His life was, she decided, like the reception room, like his name—patrician, comfortable, old money, old family, impeccable. Barney, on the other hand, like an actor in a drawing-room comedy, shanty black Irish, swathed in an Ivy League costume, his pain carefully tucked under his vest, exchanged pleasantries. She, the neurotic Jewess, here to bear witness, looked on, ten times removed, a bit player.

Through the window, she could see the life of the city. Up there on the 39th floor they heard nothing of this turmoil below. A tall clock swung its pendulum in a corner. She listened as both of them dodged around the main point, waiting for the other shoe to drop. He had not explained to her why he had come, and she did not ask.

"You really should have waited for permission," Holmes said, his voice stentorian, dripping with authority. "And you did threaten them, which was a big mistake. You can't go around threatening people, Mr. Harrigan. We could take action, you know." She had seen his eyes drift to his time book open on his neat desk.

"Maybe I was over the top," Barney admitted pleasantly.

"You can say that again. We may, indeed, decide to take action."

"I was angry and upset."

"You might have been better informed on what to expect."

"Probably. It came as a shock, seeing Charlotte," Barney said with an air of exaggerated calm.

"Yes," Holmes agreed. "It always does. It is quite understandable. You see, Mr. Harrigan, your wife has had a profound religious conversion. It's not my religion or yours. We can only understand it in context."

"Yes. I see that now."

"She is an adult woman. She has made her own choice. Believe me, I know how you feel. I would feel the same way if my wife or any of my children had taken that road." His eyes moved to his family pictures. "But in the end, I would respect their decision. Indeed. I would have no other choice." His voice was soothing, in keeping with his persona and his surroundings. "No legal choice."

"She wasn't very communicative," Barney said. He paused and Naomi felt his peripheral glance toward her. "There are lots of issues here. We have a child." Barney cleared his throat. She could tell that some plan was emerging. He hadn't discussed it with her.

"Yes. I understand."

She wondered where he was heading, alert to nuances, her mind suddenly cleared. He had said he had more bombs to throw.

"They have nothing to fear from me," Barney said unctuously.

"Perhaps not from you, Mr. Harrigan. But you surely can understand their paranoia. There is an army of unscrupulous people out there. Deprogrammers. Bent on destroying this experience. They kidnap the convert, subject him or her to beastly experiences, cut away the spiritual root. It violates not only our moral sense but the First Amendment to the Constitution, which protects every American's religious liberties."

"I understand perfectly."

"Do you?"

She could sense the hard suspicion behind the imperious facade.

"Certainly, in terms of the legalities and its consequences."

"You don't think she was brainwashed, then?"

Holmes had leaned back on his chair, making a church steeple with his fingers, a fat cat playing with a tortured mouse. There is no contest, she wanted to cry out at Barney, watching him squirm behind the contrived facade.

"I don't know what that means," Barney said. He was surprisingly up to the mark, not missing a beat.

"There is no legal definition. A religious conversion is a religious conversion."

"I suppose."

"You saw no physical coercion at the camp. No attempt to keep her there by force."

"No," he said, appearing thoughtful and attentive. "Nothing like that." He paused. "But I had to see for myself. Anyone would do the same when their life blows up in their face, not knowing the cause." He looked pointedly at the Holmes family pictures. "Anyone would do the same."

"So you've seen it. I would have arranged the visit with less of a trauma on yourself."

"I know that now. You're not exactly given a road map on how to react." Watching him, Naomi saw a nerve palpitate in his cheek. He must have felt it and lifted his hand to hide it, shamming an itch.

"There is no such thing as brainwashing," Holmes said. "There is even some doubt about its being possible even when it is present, although there has been much written about it in connection with the Chinese communists who, when Mao was alive, attempted to put a stop to any aberrant behavior by what they deemed was reeducation. In the Korean War, books were written to explain what had happened to our prisoners. All of these so-called prison converts eventually returned to the States. This does seem to indicate that so-called brainwashing is not really credible."

She was surprised at her own reaction to his words, which transcended her defenses and natural distaste. They seemed perfectly reasonable, articulating what was, despite what she had seen, her point of view. He was obviously pressing the point home.

"I have seen nothing, nothing in law, nothing in psychiatry, or anything that passes as science to offer a different view. In other words, I do not believe that brainwashing occurs."

"I haven't studied the matter with that much thoroughness, Mr. Holmes," Barney said, picking up the lawyer's cadence. She could see why he was such a good salesman, as he struggled to parry Holmes' suspicion.

"Believe me, Mr. Harrigan, I have studied all aspects of the matter, researched many cases, tried some myself." He looked toward Naomi, perhaps for approbation. "We are a country of laws, not men."

The pedantic platitude severely tried her patience.

"The Glories are a bona fide religion, with approval of tax exemption by the Internal Revenue Service. They have a perfect right to exist, to proselytize, to conduct their spiritual business. You may argue with their recruitment methods, their practices, even their ideology. However distasteful, however reprehensible to your moral standard or point of view, however they affect your life, they have an unalterable legal, ethical and moral right to exist. That must be central to your understanding of the matter." He turned toward the window, seemingly bored with his explanation, which, she realized, he must have repeated many times. Barney, too, must have heard or read it himself many times over in the last few days. Then why was he here?

"I have not come to argue the point, counselor. What good would that do? I haven't the luxury of choice. I'm here about Kevin."

Kevin, she thought. Kevin? A cold chill shot through her.

"Our child," Barney said.

Holmes bolted upright in the chair as if something had just hit him obliquely.

"I ...," Barney began, then faltered. "... I want her to have him. It must be obvious to you that I'm not supportive of her new religious belief. More power to her. If I wasn't enough, if her family wasn't enough, so be it. Her choice is her choice."

The blood had drained from Holmes' face, washing the color from his sailboat tan. Barney pressed on. Naomi felt squirmy, fidgeting. Not Kevin, she pleaded silently.

"I'm a salesman. I sell computers. I travel a lot. I can't be a proper father."

"They put the children in camps," Holmes began. "Like communes. I can see it if the child is a product of two members or the church ..."

"I'm going to divorce her as well. Give her a chance for Father Glory to pick a new legal spouse. I understand that he does that little service." There was no mistaking the sarcasm. Holmes reared back in his chair, considering the point.

"It's perfectly legal, as long as there is consent by both parties," Holmes said, his equilibrium recovered. He steadied himself and reconstructed the church steeple.

"So I'd like to start proceedings to divorce my wife and give her custody of the child. Actually, I would like to turn the child over to her immediately."

"Are you sure?" Holmes asked.

"Barney ..." Naomi began, disoriented. Barney quieted her with a flicker of his eyelids and a sharp look of rebuke.

"Immediately. He's in Fort Lauderdale with his grandparents. I want her to have him immediately. She's his mother."

"And you're his father," Holmes said, casting a surreptitious eye on his own family pictures. "It's quite ..." A cloud seemed to fall across his face.

"Irregular?" Barney said, slowly. "Or simply wrong? Is that what you mean?"

"I mean," Holmes said, "that you should think it over."

"I have. I want her to have the child immediately."

"I don't think you know what you're doing. You're under considerable stress." His voice broke, drifted, searching for its timbre. "It's a totally regimented life. At least give the boy his right to choose ..." Holmes was obviously uncomfortable. Beads of perspiration had sprouted on his forehead.

"You don't think he'll have a good life with the Glories? You don't think it's good to be robotized, controlled at every level? Told when to think or shit?" He pointed to Holmes' family pictures. "You mean you wouldn't recommend it for your own children?"

"Leave my children out of this." Holmes was losing control, and still Barney pressed on.

"You'd like that, wouldn't you? Mr. Superior Intelligence. Mr. Superior Morality. Okay if the Glories wreck other people's lives. As long as it doesn't touch yours. How the hell do you sleep at night?"

"I demand ..."

"You're as much a part of their apparatus as my wife. What do they pay?" He looked around the office. "Pretty good, I'd say. Good enough for your fancy antiques, your fancy office, your fancy schools for your kids, fancy dresses for your wife. Let's talk about rights ..." He was wound up, pounding away with indignation. She watched Holmes attempt to mount his defense, but his facade had been breached.

"They have a right to counsel. Everyone has a right to counsel."

"More rights shit. Rights? You can shove them up your ass. What you and I are talking about is money. Money. Pure and simple." He stood up. Taking a thick envelope out of his inside pocket, he threw it on the desk.

"On hundred grand. A down payment."

Holmes looked dumbly at the envelope.

"Here's what I want. I want you to tell your clients that I've agreed to give her the boy. Shit, I would never give him to those bastards. Tell them that all I want is for her to pick up the child outside of the camp. If possible outside the county. Get my drift? If you do that there are two possibilities. She sees her son, it jolts her to walk by herself. Doubtful, right? Second option goes into effect. We snatch her. Attempt a deprogramming. If we deprogram her and get her back, you get five times what's in that envelope. I mean business, Holmes. If they don't bite on either of these options, then you find a way to buy her out. I'll raise a million if I have to and you can take what you want. I don't care how it's done."

Holmes sat back in his big red chair, unable to react.

"I . . . I don't know what to say."

"Say okay. Say I'll try. Say you'll do it."

"You're demented," Holmes said.

"Determined would be more accurate. I'll make more trouble than you ever dreamed about."

Holmes shook his head.

"I can't."

"Yes you can," Barney said between clamped teeth. "Yes you can."

Without another word, he grabbed Naomi's hand and helped lift her out of her chair.

"Lets get the fuck out of here."

They moved swiftly out of the office, through the corridors, into the reception room where they slowed down to a walk. He offered a benign smile to the girl at the desk, who smiled back primly. Then he pressed the button of the express elevator.

"Please, please, please," he whispered.

She started to speak. She was totally confused by his tactic. It made no sense. Had he lost his moorings?

"Not now, Nay. Not now."

He looked above the elevator door watching the red digital lights flicker. Behind them, a bell sounded persistently, pleasantly trilling, like in a department store. The elevator came. The door opened.

". . . why yes, Mr. Holmes, they're . . ." The girl's voice disappeared.

The door closed. Barney leaned against an elevator panel and closed his eyes.

"Are you all right?"

"Yes. Fine."

He opened his eyes and they both watched the digital numbers move swiftly as the elevator hurtled downward. It did not stop at the lobby level. As it reached the level below, he poised himself at the entrance, holding her hand.

"What is it?"

She held his hand, following his lead, running toward an exit sign. They came to a door, which he swung open. They were in a courtyard, between two huge trash bins. She followed him up steps, into the street, where he kept on running. The street descended sharply downhill, and she had to strain her leg muscles to keep from falling. Her chest ached. A sharp pain speared into her side. Madness, she thought. He's gone crazy.

Faces red, sweating, gasping for breath, they kept moving through Union Park, into some side streets.

"I can't," she protested between gasps.

"All right."

He looked behind him. Pedestrians moved laconically, self-absorbed. Cars passed in the ordinary flow of traffic. Holding her arm, he guided her into a coffee shop. They took a booth in the back. She felt the sharp pain in her side subside as she watched him. Patting his perspiring face with a handkerchief, he opened his collar and the little gold pin that held it together fell on the plastic table.

A waitress came up to them.

"That hot outside?" she said with a shrug. He managed to give her his order.

"Scrambled eggs. Two coffees."

"Toast?"

"Yes. Yes."

She could see that all he wanted was to get rid of her. Finally, they cooled down.

"I don't understand," Naomi said.

"I know."

Saying nothing more, they waited as the waitress, looking at them archly, brought two coffees, which she placed on the table in front of them. It had all happened so fast, like a projector revved up, offering senseless images.

"You were wonderful," he said finally, patting her hand. She wanted to draw it away, but she held it there. The touch of his flesh now seemed alien and she was genuinely alarmed.

"Was there really a hundred thousand dollars in there?"

"Yes. And a note on the envelope. And I marked all the bills." His handkerchief was soaked. Taking off his jacket, she could see his shirt was wringing wet, stuck to his body. The curl had gone out of his hair and her dress clung moistly to her back.

"Did you see the bastard? That moralistic hypocrite." He was in the throes of a deep inner excitement, the explanation of which eluded her. She realized that his mind had been spinning endlessly for days, churning with plans, options and alternatives.

She was only beginning to glimpse the extent of his scheming now, the singleness of purpose that drove him forward, like a computer guided missile. He seemed very much in control.

"Yes, I saw that," she agreed. "But what I didn't see was what your intentions are. I'm confused."

"I'm working on a number of tracks at once. I want them to see I mean business, that I would go to any lengths to bring Charlotte out, pay any price. I want them to know that I mean trouble."

"That message came out loud and clear."

"He may even bite himself, the greedy fuck. Find a way to get her out of the camp. Tell them that I brought her son, that I am giving him up. If that doesn't work, there's the other alternative. Buy her out. Ball's in his court. I don't care how it happens, only that I'm working every angle I can think of, no matter how far-fetched. This is a way, and I'll fight it any way I can. You saw her. You saw the challenge. "

Her confusion was not completely dispelled by his explanation.

"It is a challenge," she conceded.

"Takes fire to fight fire," he said, looking at his watch.

It occurred to her that he was observing time for a reason. As if to hide her scrutiny, she lifted her coffee cup, but continued to watch him over the rim.

"I have a ..." She was about to say "right," editing it quickly. "It would be nice to know these plans in advance. After all, I am you chief witness."

"I know," he said lowering his voice, watching the door. "I'll try to be more candid in advance." He paused. "There was a note in with the hundred."

"Note?"

"You might as well know. It's yet another track."

"You've lost me."

"I want him to be at risk as well. See where I'm willing to go. I wrote on the envelope: This is the payment I promised you and I signed my name, and gave him the number of the motel. That and the marked bills has got to scare the living shit out of him. You saw his office, all that facade of respectability, the old-line firm. That's what the Glories bought. And what they bought has to be above reproach, Caesar's wife. Above all, he wouldn't want to expose himself to the slightest hint of corruption. He might go for one of the first two alternatives."

"He didn't take it. You left it on his desk."

"His word against ours."

"Ours?"

She felt a sour backwash in her throat, the upsurge of indignation.

"But it's a lie," she said, feeling foolish.

"Just one more ploy," he corrected.

"You are devious, I'll give you that."

"That's what I want him to see. I want him to convince them that I'm more trouble than Charlotte is worth."

"And you think they'll respond to that?"

"I hope so." He paused and glared at her. "After what you saw at that camp with your own eyes, Nay, anything goes."

"But this …" she began, putting down her coffee cup. He was attacking the heart of her, her vaunted moral position, the sacrosanct center of her. "The means doesn't justify the ends." It was literally the bedrock of her political philosophy, the fundamental cog in her value system.

"You want me to roll over and die. Do nothing. Accept my fate. And Charlotte's. Surrender? Those bastards have attacked me. They've broken up my family. Do you think they fight fair?"

"I didn't say that," she countered, confused now. "This is no time for a rational discussion." For the moment, she decided, she would take refuge in that. Was she running away? Like before. The image of her dead baby hovered before her mind, like an apparition.

"Why did you come then?" he asked, striking into the soft center of her guilt. "You knew it wouldn't be a joyride."

"I came because …" but she could not go on. How could she possibly explain her motives, her guilt. I must leave, her reason told her. Instead, she put down her coffee cup. The waitress came back and slid the scrambled eggs in front of each of them. Looking at eggs, she felt the beginnings of nausea.

Rising unsteadily, she went into the ladies' room. It was filthy, smelling of urine, the bowl of the toilet rust-stained. Doubling over, she vomited. It took a while to clean herself up. I must get out of here, she vowed. Run. He was using her, part of some bizarre plan known only to him. She wanted to hurt him, to tell him about the fetus, the baby. Would it hurt, really hurt? Yes, she decided, she must clear the air between them, reveal her true motives, foreclose on her acting against the grain, against her principles, principles that were a fundamental part of her life.

When she came back to the table, two men had joined Barney. Again, he had outfoxed her, had made plans involving her without her consent. Hiding her anger, she slid in beside him.

"This is Pat O'Hara." Immediately, she sensed the Irish kinship. O'Hara was their age. He hid his eyes behind dark mirrored sunglasses, and his craggy bony face was partially obscured by a scraggly rust-colored beard. What in the world was he hiding? A skinny chest was covered by a faded denim shirt.

"And Roy Smith." He was a chunky black man with a rim of steel-wool beard around thick lips. His skin shined like ebony and his large, amused brown eyes mocked the world in a sea of white. To greet her, he raised two fingers in a macho gesture of acknowledgment. Sitting across from them, she noted in the way they reacted to each other that they were a twosome, on the same emotional wavelength. Comrades. Mr. Brains and Mr. Brawn, she silently snickered.

"Naomi Forman," Barney added. "She's my friend. It's okay."

O'Hara assessed her, his mouth set in a tight line of noncommitment.

"If you say so," O'Hara said. He spoke softly, perhaps deliberately so, but there was a conspiratorial air about him. Apparently they had been in the middle of a discussion. She noted, too, that Roy had eaten her scrambled eggs and was just scooping up the dregs with a piece of toast.

"I don't say you can't figure out a way," O'Hara said, dismissing her, although she felt his reserved judgment. "Just get her out of the camp. The sooner the better. The longer they keep her, the tougher it is."

"That's the game plan. Get her out. You got to work," Barney said.

O'Hara nodded.

"I need the body."

"That's the point of the exercise."

"In three or four weeks or so," O'Hara explained, "they'll put her on the street selling whatever, or into one of their businesses. They could even send her out of the country. You won't know where she is. They're clever bastards. You're already becoming something of a nuisance. If they think you're going to be a trouble-maker, they might shift her around."

"You think maybe I've blown it?" Barney asked.

"Who the fuck knows," O'Hara said. "You're not the only one rattling their cage."

"We'll just have to act as fast as we can," Barney said.

"All I'm saying is that they can't be underestimated," O'Hara pointed out.

The waitress came, took away the dishes and refilled their coffee cups.

"None for me," Naomi said, swallowing away a new wave of nausea.

"Will it work?" Barney asked. "The deprogramming?"

"I can't guarantee that," O'Hara said. "Most of the time. Depends."

"On what?"

"How they've twisted her head. She's terrorized, scared shit-less. Her mind has gone to sleep. It's a sin for them to think."

So he's a deprogrammer, Naomi thought, resentment rising. Again, he had not consulted her. He had said he was operating on many tracks. This seemed like one too many. As if responding to her thought, Barney said, "He's a deprogrammer. Used to be at the camp."

"At the camp?"

"Jeremiah's honcho," the black man interjected. "Zachariah's what they called him."

"Takes one to know one," O'Hara said, making a lame attempt at humor. When no one laughed, he shrugged. "I'm not proud of it. But I've got credentials."

"Mrs. Prococino mentioned him," Barney said. "Remember?"

She hadn't. Nor did Naomi like either of them.

"Roy here saved me," O'Hara explained. "It's a long story."

Roy nodded. She didn't want to know.

"You're planning to kidnap her," Naomi said, looking at Barney, who nodded.

"No choice about that," Barney replied.

"None at all."

"You saw her."

"It's wrong. Against the law," Naomi muttered, her indignation rising.

"Hey. Which side is she on?" O'Hara said.

"Ours. Don't worry." Barney patted her arm. She withdrew it.

O'Hara turned his mirrored glasses toward her, then took them off, showing nervous darting hazel eyes lost in a network of red veins. He fixed them on her and she turned away.

"The first law is the law of nature. That came before the law of the land. No one has the right to take away a person's free will. When they do that, they take away your mind, and when they take away your mind, they take away your being." She was sure he had given this lecture many times, although it sounded like something fresh and new. A "but" charged into her mind, until a new wave of nausea held her silent.

"You won't hurt her?" Barney asked.

"That's their scam," O'Hara said. "She has been hurt. In the worst possible way. My job is to open up her mind, snap her out of it. I know the way into it. I was once there myself. I know how it's done."

He seemed a most unlikely prospect, costumed with macho contrivances. He had put on his mirrored glasses again, retreating.

"They took away seven of my best years. I'll never forgive them for that."

"Seven years," Naomi echoed flatly.

"Hard to believe?"

"You don't look the type that would join," she pressed, finding her strength again.

"I didn't join," O'Hara said patiently. "That's mistake numero uno. You don't join. You are captured. That's a problem in itself. Blaming the victim."

"Please, Nay," Barney said. "I've checked him out. He's saved nearly a hundred people from not only the Glories but other cults as well."

"It's his business," she shot back. "He's a ghoul profiting from your pain. How much are you paying him?"

"Twenty-five grand, lady. And all expenses. For me and my people."

"Your people?" she cried. "So you've got an army of thugs."

"Just me," the black man interjected. "I'm his people. I'm his thug."

"I think you've got a doubter here, pal," O'Hara said. "Maybe I should split."

"No ... please."

"Suppose it doesn't work?" she asked, with mock innocence.

"Then the shit hits the fan. She goes back into oblivion and they charge us all with every bullshit thing they can throw at us. It's happened to me. I've got suits pending in four states. That's what happens to the money, lady. Lawyers. It turns out I do it for love."

"Love. What do you know about love?"

"More than anybody," O'Hara mused. "That goddamned word. How these cults have putrefied it, insulted it. Those poor, sad victims. I've come to hate the word."

"Sad," Naomi said, with sarcasm. "Very sad."

"Worse than that," O'Hara took a deep breath into his thin chest. "The entire process is devious and malicious. Out-and-out mind control. A ruthless mind-rape hiding under the mask of religious freedom."

"You said you were in it once. It means you believed it." Naomi said, hot for argument. She had no faith in these men.

"Please, Nay," Barney said.

"It's okay," O'Hara said, lifting his hand like a traffic cop. "I understand where she's come from, Harrigan. She has to be educated." He turned to Naomi. "I don't mean that as an insult. You've seen the lady in question. How does she look to you?"

"How she looks is not the issue. She's there by choice."

"We'll have to disabuse you of that little nugget. For her there is no choice. Her mind is in cold storage. She has absolutely no control over her present actions, no free will. Remember Jonestown,

Waco, that cult in Japan, France, Africa? Do I have to mention the World Trade Center? It freezes my tongue just to think about that one. Those people were programmed. All Jones, Koresh, Bin Laden and the others had to do was pull the switch. They had these people totally brainwashed. And the poor bastards believed those jackasses who run the show were the messengers of Jesus or Allah or whatever deity comes to mind, and some that don't. Hell, they really believed these guys had a pipeline to some divine source. We've all seen the results. Those poor saps did their bidding into oblivion. Just step over the line, folks. Paradise awaits. And the Bin Laden idiots. They really believe they were going to find 72 virgins with dark eyes. That's supposed to be paradise? Come on now. That's no reward, that's a headache, 72 cackling virgins all looking at that hard thing. Good God, what's that monster? You going to put that ugly thing in me? Picture it. What dumb shit."

His sick humor and posturing grated on Naomi. He was stringing together incidents and creating half-baked theories to prove his thesis. She was not convinced. People do stupid things. Yes, there was evil in the world. These people were indeed evil, but that did not justify his wild theories.

"Okay," O'Hara said, as if he were embarked on a new beginning. "Your wife in there. How did she strike you?"

"Like some other person. Not my Charlotte," Barney answered.

O'Hara glanced at Naomi.

"I never knew her before," Naomi said hesitantly, softening her belligerent stance. "To me, she seemed well ... exhausted."

"At this stage they usually are. My job is get them back to where they were before they were brainwashed ... at least, start them back. Jog their minds to work. They believe at this point that it's a sin to think other thoughts than what they're told to think. I know it's a confusing concept. We don't know that much about the human brain. One theory is that by manipulating information and exhausting both the body and the brain, you actually change the chemical balance. Hell, there are lots of other theories. The fact is that it works. And people like Father Glory are willing to use it for their own greedy ends. I know him. He's just a ruthless son of a bitch who uses these kids to line his pockets. They get nothing. They're just slaves. He gets everything. You should see how he lives in his mansion, with his yachts and limos and private jet. Hell, those poor kids would kill for him. Now there's a cliché. Do we need any more evidence? There's nothing, nothing on this earth more precious than freedom. Nothing."

He seemed to retreat into reflection.

"How can you argue with that, Nay?"

"I'm not arguing," she said stiffly, although her mind was groping for ways to counter him. Suddenly she had one.

"Okay," she began. "I'll grant you that maybe you do have a kernel of truth when you talk of how the Glories and other cults manipulate people who fall into their net. I can understand the idea of temporary changes. Control diet, sleep, information, exhaust people, maybe you have a point, but how does it explain those suicide bombers who worked for Bin Laden? You're talking about process. Were their diet and sleep controlled? We've heard a lot about sugar. Did these Arab suicide bombers pig out on Twinkies? Or was it pizza that put them over the top? Seems that there was a bit of a difference in the so-called process."

She had lashed out, flailing indiscriminately, but determined to make her point. O'Hara nodded.

"As I said, I understand where you are coming from. The fact is that that Bin Laden's followers were brainwashed practically from birth. They were halfway into his cult to begin with. The concept of paradise is drummed into them from the get-go by their so-called religious leaders, and they validate it five times a day. They are indoctrinated by their teachers and their schoolbooks from the moment they are aware and can read. These books are filled with hatred and calls for violence, self-sacrifice and, yes, self-immolation if necessary if it's for the cause. The indoctrination preaches against so-called infidels, meaning everyone who doesn't believe what they believe. Obedience to the divine, as interpreted by their leaders, is taught as a duty. Soon they are dry timber, ready to ignite if they fall into the cult's recruiting net and are further brainwashed by Bin Laden or any self-appointed guru with charisma, focus and determination. In a short time they can snap into suicide and go out a kill themselves if ordered to do so for whatever reason the boss feels is justified. Just fiddle with the message, shift the calibration just enough to get them fully committed.

Takes effort, patience, time, skill, focus, organization. There you have it. Suicide bombers locked into the cult mindset, brainwashed ... no different from the Glories. None. Father Glory says die, go for it, and they will, just like Bin Laden's boys."

He stopped abruptly for a long moment and continued to hesitate as if pondering whether to inject another idea. She had observed the maneuver and was puzzled by it. Then it passed and O'Hara continued. "Problem is you can't deprogram them so easily. I do one-on-one. Think about doing them one-on-one. There are thousands, maybe millions of them. There is a solution, of course. Kill the leaders and the followers are disoriented, jumping around like chickens with lopped-off heads. But then, that gig is not on my resume. I don't do mass deprogramming. Not qualified. Just call me the professor of cult and leave it at that."

She had listened patiently, trying to understand.

"Contents noted," she said. She'd have to think about this. She had heard these ideas before but she had never been moved to accept them. They were, after all, contrary to her mindset and convictions. "There is still the moral issue to consider."

"Jesus," O'Hara said. "I've heard that morality bullshit before. He turned to Barney. The real question is, can you trust her?"

She felt their eyes bore into her. Yes. He was right. That was the ultimate question. They had given her an out. She tried to rise, but her body stayed rooted to the seat. The moment passed.

"Yes. We can trust her," Barney said exchanging glances with her. She felt her own will sucked out of her.

"Okay then. Here's the skinny. You get your wife physically out of that camp. I'll get her mentally out. I can't give you any guarantees, but I'll try my damnedest."

"So it doesn't always work?" Naomi said, still determined to carp.

"Not always. As I said, that's when we get into trouble. Depends on the person."

"You've got to do it with Charlotte," Barney said, his desperation showing through his resolve.

"I'll try my damnedest." O'Hara looked at Naomi. "For starters, we've got to get her out of that damned county. The sheriff is too scared to oppose them. They've got him stalemated. He sees himself as being stuck between a rock and a hard place. Also, I'm sure they've already got wind of something going down. They're good at that."

"How can they know that?"

"Who the hell knows?" He turned toward Naomi. "Hope you're right about her."

"I'm right." Barney said without hesitation.

She wondered about his certainty. She wasn't certain about her own loyalty.

"Just get her out of the camp. They could get itchy and do something stupid."

"Like what?" Barney asked, confused.

"Don't even think about it," O'Hara said. "These people are ruthless. They'll do anything to protect themselves." He stood up. "I'll be reachable at my mobile number any hour of the day or night." O'Hara scribbled his number on a piece of napkin and gave it to him. Barney put it in his shirt pocket.

Naomi watched as O'Hara's gaunt figure emerged from behind the table. The black man stood up, a slab of black granite.

"Trouble is," O'Hara said, "I get tired explaining it. The fact is it's there. Shit happens."

Without turning again, the two men moved toward the door and into the street.

"Under what rock did you find him?" Naomi asked when they were out of sight. "He's one cocky, surly bastard."

"If he saves Charlotte, I don't care what he is. He's been there. Who else would take this on? It's nasty work. Besides ..." He turned to look at her, not just at her, but trying to see inside of her, begging, imploring. Probing her were the eyes of a trapped animal. "What choice have I?"

He had a point, she decided. What was hers? She felt like a moth dancing around a flame, mesmerized.

9

"Who would have thought, back in those days, it would come to this?" The words had come out of nowhere, a sniper's bullet, whining into her mind. She had leaned her head back on the headrest of their rented car. He had left the other one at the parking lot that served Holmes' office building and called the rental agency to pick it up. "Just a precaution. It's like undercover work," he mumbled. It baffled her, like most things that were happening. His mind was like a river carving out its own course through a jungle, devious, relentless, surging here, trickling there, skirting obstacles, but always with one objective in mind, finding the open sea, freedom. It was just one of a hundred images that occurred to her.

"I'm glad you're with me, Nay," Barney said.

Had she figured in his grand design from the beginning? Or was he improvising? The irony was that predictability was one of her reasons for rejecting him.

"I'm going to get her, Nay," he said fiercely.

"If anyone can, you will." Her response sounded gratuitous. He was a far cry from the memory of him that she had carried around with her for so many years. Or had her way of perceiving things changed?

"I always wondered ..." she began haltingly, "... why you never came after me, Barney," Like this, she would have added. But she choked it off. The comparison was odious.

The car moved steadily. He was suspiciously calm. She saw no tremble in his lip, no palpitation in his jaw, no flicker of his eyelid.

"It seemed a fait accompli," he said, after a while. "You didn't want the constrictions of commitment." His words seemed pedantic, contrived, although his reasoning was clear. "Your life was elsewhere, independent of me. I was also embarrassed. I did a ridiculous thing."

"Not ridiculous, Barney," she admitted cautiously. "I feared your commitment was too ... too overwhelming. I felt pushed."

"I figured you just didn't love me enough. When you love someone, nothing matters. You don't make decisions of the heart with your head."

"I wanted my independence. On my terms."

"I know. That told me you didn't love me enough."

"But I did."

"Then you wouldn't have left. No matter what."

"We were different. Our lives were in different places. We had different values. Different aspirations."

"I found that out."

Now she was being the fool, and it embarrassed her.

She waited for more, but it did not come. So he did remember, but it was all part of his yesterdays. Irrelevant. Leaning back, she closed her eyes again. There's a lot to be said for exorcising thought, she told herself, remembering O'Hara's words: It's a sin for them to think. At that moment, she envied Charlotte her perceived sense of bliss.

He maneuvered the car into a parking space in the motel lot, then hurried into the lobby. When she caught up with him, he was waving a pink telephone message.

"Pay dirt," he said.

She looked at the message.

"Between four and six," he said, looking at his watch, as he hurried to his room. Following him, she went through his room into her own. In the bathroom, she undressed and stepped into the shower. Time to clear away the grime. She turned on the taps full blast. The spray bombarded her and she bent down to let it hit her head. Pound some sense into me, she begged.

Standing in front of the mirror, naked, rubbing herself dry, she removed the steam on the glass with the flat of her hand. When she saw her face clearly, she made her decision. It wasn't her show. It was time to pack.

Personal desires aside, she told herself, deliberately cryptic, as if she were hiding her real motive from herself. It was not pleasant confronting that reality. She had, indeed, harbored illicit hopes. He was lost to her irrevocably. All her longings were pure fantasy, sexual wishful thinking. All that desire and fantasy had disappeared. It was over.

Maybe there was some guilt in it, but the real reason was, well, unworthy. Like reading the obituaries looking for widowers. Besides, there were more compelling moral reasons. What she had seen at the camp was through his eyes, not her own. She agreed with Holmes. A religious experience was mysterious and personal, however it came about. Charlotte had both a legal and moral right to be where she was. O'Hara was obnoxious, his reasoning faulty. He was caught in an obsession of revenge. None of it had anything to do with her emotionally. Intellectually she was revolted. They were bending rationality, invoking unproven science, inventing methods of repression, cynically playing head games, intruding on Charlotte's private inalienable right. Such thoughts were at the very heart of her political and moral convictions.

The law had been honed out of years of experience, the wheat removed from the chaff. It was Barney and O'Hara intruding on Charlotte's will, however despicable the methods of the Glories. They, too, were indefensible, but that didn't excuse what Barney and O'Hara proposed to do with Charlotte's life.

Cleansed of indecision, she came into the room, dressed in slacks and a blouse, and headed for the phone to make her plane reservations.

"It worked."

His voice jolted her and she put down the phone, breaking the connection.

"Worked?"

"I think so." He held his notebook in his hand. "He was blood-red mad. Calling from a phone booth. It took him a while to settle down."

"He's getting you Charlotte?"

"It's not as simple as that." He looked at his watch. "I'm going to Lauderdale to pick up Kevin."

"Kevin? Have you gone crazy? Are you going to give them your child?"

"Don't be ridiculous. Do you think I would do that?"

No, she thought. No matter what, he wouldn't do that. He began to pace the room, putting his fingers through his hair.

"It's Byzantine, I know. He needs his out, too. They'll think they're getting Kevin. It's so incredible, they'll believe it. He agreed. The bastard agreed. He liked it. Can you imagine? The hypocrisy of those people. They'll also think they'll be getting rid of me and, at the same time, have a future recruit for their fucking army. I made one condition, which is the real scam. That I hand Kevin over directly to Charlotte. Outside the camp. A shopping center. They'll bring her in one of their cars. We beat it back and forth for a while. Like a prisoner of war exchange. It has to be credible to them."

"I've lost you."

"He's setting it up for us to snatch her."

"And the money?"

"Hell, he bought the deal. I don't care about the money. It might break me. I'm a salesman Nay. Money is a replenishable resource. Besides, all the bills I gave him so far are marked. Evidence that money passed." He waved his notebook. "I've got all the serial numbers in here."

"He must know that."

"Maybe so. I told you, he's a shrewd bastard. Also, corrupt as hell."

"Everybody's corrupt in this deal."

He ignored her remark. His mind was not concentrating on her subtleties.

"I've discussed it all with O'Hara."

"He approves?"

"If it gets Charlotte out of the camp and out of the county. That's the objective."

"But she'll be protected. You think O'Hara and his goon can just up and get her? Do you think the Glories are that stupid?"

"Holmes says there are no guarantees."

She noted that his optimism had faded.

"Showing her Kevin might change the game plan, make her walk on her own."

"Maybe," Naomi agreed.

"Hell, he's got his own risks to take. Not that we haven't got some problems. The Glories won't go out of Sheriff Clausen's county. That's an absolute condition. It gives them a sense of security."

"And O'Hara's taking the risk?"

"Yes."

"For more money?"

Barney nodded.

"You're going to put your child through this?"

"It's his mother."

She watched him pace. Stopping, he faced her.

His words echoed in her mind.

"I'm hoping that Kevin's presence might shorten the time it takes to deprogram her, gnaw at Charlotte's sense of guilt, affirm the tie between mother and child. Hell, there has got to be something in that. How can a mother give up her own child?"

She averted her eyes, directing her hand toward the phone. It would not obey her.

"Please, Nay. If this doesn't work, I don't know what I'll do. In the meantime, stick with me. I need you here. Call it moral support."

"You can use that word?" she said. She felt cut in two, stalemated within herself. Against his passion and obsession, she felt powerless.

"You're using me," she muttered lamely.

"I'm using everybody, Nay. I know that."

He looked at his watch again.

"I've got to go. With the time difference, I can make it back by two tomorrow. Can I count on you, Nay?"

When she didn't answer, he moved back to his room and she stretched out on the bed, watching the ceiling. Don't think, she begged herself. He came back into her room, carrying a shoulder bag and his notebook.

"You can drive me or I can take the car," he said gently. When she didn't answer, he said, "I can't tell you how much I owe you."

She grunted a goodbye and, in the distance, vaguely heard the rented car cough, sputter and drive away. Alone in the motel room, her sense of disorientation heightened. As if to fix her identity and willpower, she called the office, forgetting the time differential. The endless ringing informed her and she called her boss, who was out for the evening. Then she called her mother.

"I'm in Washington, Mother," she said, after hearing the high-pitched cackle of the familiar voice. As always, she could sense her attitude, poised between suspicion and sarcasm.

"Say hello to the President."

"Not that Washington, the state."

"So far?"

"I just called to see how you are."

Her mother lived in this perpetual state, waiting for the ring that would be the clarion of disaster.

"You're all right? No troubles?"

From years of experience, she knew the rhythm of a placating response. Long ago, she had rejected confidences. The generation gap had become a chasm.

"I had a spare moment."

"A conference or a man?" Her mother larded her disapprovals with wiseacre accusations. Mostly, the spears fell on a strong shield, but sometimes they hit the mark. Naomi searched for the reasons she had called.

"There was something I wanted to ask." Even to herself, she sounded wispy and tentative. Then an idea emerged.

"As long as everything is fine, you can ask. As long as there are no arguments." It was merely banter. They had little in common. Her mother's widowhood was a closed world of games and charity work, predictable opinions, a ghettoized mentality. She lived embedded in her roots.

"Were we ever religious?" she asked.

"Religious? You were bat mitzvahed. Your father went to shul when he was alive. I light yozeit candles. Of course, we were religious. We're still religious. We're Jewish."

"I mean really religious. I mean about God."

"Naomi? Is there something you're not telling me?"

"It's important, Mother. Think for a moment. I want a serious answer. Were we religious? When I was growing up, did we believe in God?"

"Where is the question? We're Jewish. Read the Bible."

She was doing badly. The problem was that she was not sure what she was asking. Then her mother said, "Naomi, no matter what, you'll always be Jewish. No matter how many scutches you go with, although I don't hold my breath. No matter if you marry one. No matter if you convert to the goyim. God knows who is Jewish and who is not. No matter how topsy-turvy the world gets."

She felt how fiercely the sense of belonging lived in her mother.

"You are what you are, girlie."

"And no one can take that away, make you different?" She felt foolish, asking a child's question. Worse, she was asking it of someone inert and narrow-minded.

"Different? Who can make you different?" Her mother paused. "You called me from California to ask these questions?"

"I think that if I believed in God ..." Naomi faltered.

"Not believe in God?" her mother responded indignantly. "That's a sin. That's only words. Of course you do. I told you. You're Jewish. That's the problem with all you young people. You're all confused."

"You can say that again."

It was one of her mother's umbrella generalizations.

In her circle there were absolute truths. Belonging, Naomi thought suddenly. Was that what she wanted to ask? Everybody was thirsty to belong, to be part of something bigger than one's self.

"But I did not have a choice in that," Naomi protested. "I was simply born into it. I'm Jewish because you and Dad were Jewish." Her words sounded simplistic and naïve, and it frightened her.

"From Washington, the state, you're calling? Are you smoking that potsy?"

"Pot." She paused. "No, mother. I'm not stoned."

"I love you, my darling. I don't understand you. But I love you."

Tears welled in her eyes.

"And I love you, Mother," she said. Why, she wondered. Sometimes she would dismiss it as merely sentimental, a mysterious biological imperative. I love her because she's mine, she thought. It had nothing at all to do with logic. Then why had she killed her baby? Their baby? No one could ever be truly independent. Independent of what?

When she hung up, despite the confused conversation, she felt better. Applying her makeup carefully, she went to the lobby, bought a newspaper, read it over a drink in the bar. Injustice was everywhere. It was like a wasting virus, spread over the carcass of the world. Nests of them were everywhere. Another metaphor imposed itself. The vines of morality were being choked off by the weeds of cruelty, fanaticism, indifference, greed. It was good to feel something about all this, she thought.

In the coffee shop, she ate part of a club sandwich, then came back to her room and put on the television set. Every channel had something banal and boring, just one other indicator of the world's declining values. One had to resist that, as well. Restore standards. Give thinking decent people hope. Inspiration. Her spirit soared. She had put principle before self. She had faced the problems of the world head on. When aloneness descended on her, she could take refuge in the thought that she had given her life meaning by involving herself in the life of mankind, in the bigger picture.

She had left Barney because his world was too narrow, too earthbound. What he called home and hearth meant stagnation, control, boredom. In her world, there was room to grow. His world was a hothouse, stultifying, pedestrian, dedicated to the pursuit of money, things. She felt pride again in the decision that she had taken years ago, a young girl with a purpose. It had taken courage and guts to do what she had done.

She felt strong again. In control. No, she concluded. She had no right to participate in the travesty that Barney was concocting. It was immoral, against her grain. However obnoxious the Glories were, Charlotte had every right to her life, as she chose to live it. Other factors had brought her this far. Other vulnerabilities. Above all, she must stand by her principles.

For a long time, she looked at the telephone. Then she called Sheriff Moore.

10

An objective frame of mind was an act of will, Sheriff T. Clausen Moore thought, as he sped towards the motel. At that moment, he had many reasons to be subjective. The call had interrupted his weekly poker game in the middle of a winning streak.

"She just won't talk to anyone but you, Sheriff," Perry, his most trusted deputy, who was on night duty, had told him. The sheriff had written down the number but had not called back immediately. Nevertheless, it disturbed his concentration and he began to lose heavily. His recollection of her was surprisingly clear although she had said little. "Urgent," Perry had told him the woman said, causing unneeded speculation at a time when business matters were supposed to run on idle. He was, after all, entitled to a little relaxation.

In the end, of course, duty prevailed. It always did. He wished others would have his sense of responsibility. Naturally, Gladys thought he was too rigid on that point. He attributed his zeal to the fact that he was dirt poor as a child. Hard early times had conditioned him to responsibility, and it deeply disturbed him that he could not convey this ethic to everyone. The way to success was diligence. He had kicked the asses of all three of his boys to get them to understand.

When he had called her back finally, 300 dollars lighter, his sense of diligence had frayed very thin.

"I will not talk about this on the telephone, sheriff,"

"I can assure you it's not tapped," he told her testily.

"It's not only that," she said. "It is too important to be trivialized by a mere telephone call."

That sounded haughty. He hated conditions of any kind, especially when dealing with anything that had to do with the Glories. He had enough of it from them.

"I promise you won't be wasting your time," Naomi said with just the slightest slur of derision. Before leaving, he had had another beer.

"What is it, Tee?" one of his friends asked.

"Glories."

"Shit."

When he arrived at the motel parking lot, he had not yet reached a plateau of objectivity. Naomi was waiting in the shadows at the edge of the lot as they had agreed.

"I thought you had gone home," he said.

"I should have," Naomi said as he turned off the headlights. She came into the car and sat beside him. "I should never have come."

"Oh, shit. I drove two hours to hear this."

There was a long silence and he wondered if she could detect the smell of beer. He had run out of mints. Turning to face her, he waited as the oval of her face became clearer. He could not see her eyes, lost in black shadow pockets, but he could sniff the odor of betrayal. It was all too familiar.

"I'm not sure about this," Naomi began tentatively, pausing, groping in the silence. They always began this way. He waited, absorbing her nervousness. From years of experience, he had learned the value of silence. It was not yet the moment for reassurance.

"Can I be hypothetical?"

"It's your dime," he said, sighing. He was beginning to feel tired.

"All right then. If you interdicted ... stopped a crime before it began, does it become an official arrest?"

"What kind of a crime?"

"Let's say any kind."

"Can't you be more specific?"

"No."

"Then we have nothing to talk about."

"I'm doing this very badly," Naomi said. "What I'm trying to say ...".

"You don't want him hurt. You don't want him to be in any trouble." He smiled, although he knew she did not see it. "Do you seriously believe that what you're about to tell me is unique?"

No sense beating around the bush. It was too late for games.

"He's going to try and kidnap her," she blurted. "He's got this idea that if she sees her child, she will go quietly. If not, they're going to kidnap her. I want you to stop it and I don't ..." He joined her in finishing the sentence.

"... want him hurt."

"Exactly."

The fact was that the sheriff didn't want him hurt either.

"And you don't want him to know that it was you who blew the whistle?"

"It's not that I'm cowardly," she snapped. "Or thinking of myself."

"Has he got a deprogrammer?"

"Yes."

"Who?"

"A man by the name of O'Hara."

"That one. He's tough. I knew him when he was on their side. Nothing like a reformed addict. Actually, they say he knows his onions."

"Then you're in favor of the vile practice?"

He paused. He'd have to be more cautious, he rebuked himself. He was too tired.

"How the hell are they going to do it?"

"The deal is to get her out of the county, out of your jurisdiction."

So that's it, he thought. He speculated that money was changing hands. He'd leave that one alone. If that was the case, he didn't want to know. They probably think he's also on the take. There was some logic in that, he knew. Votes could be characterized as a legal bribe.

"Figures," he muttered.

"It's too complicated to explain. There are wheels within wheels. You said you have close contact with them. Just warn them and tell them to keep the woman in the camp. Its that simple."

"Nothing is that simple."

"I think what Harrigan and O'Hara want to do is repugnant."

"Even if it works?"

"Yes. Even if it works. It's wrong."

He had to test her now, to know where she was coming from.

"You want his wife to stay with them?" he said. "Is that your agenda?"

"I resent that inference," she snapped, fuming.

"Just doing my job."

"Good. My motives have nothing to do with anything but principle." There was a slight tremor in her voice. He was alert now, his mind fully awake, his sense of objectivity steady and strong. He had heard that before. Principle! Whatever the motive for her betrayal, it was immaterial. He represented the forces of law and order. It was enough to tamp down the glob of disgust growing in his gut. It didn't matter one whit that he would do the same if it were his wife, his kid.

"All I can say is thanks for the tip. You have done your duty as a good citizen."

Did she detect a dollop of sarcasm?

"I betrayed them," she mused aloud.

"You can't have your cake and eat it too."

"Sheriff," Naomi said. "Are you a man of feeling, a man of compassion?"

He hadn't expected that. There was the hint of judgment about it, which rattled him.

"Considering what I do," he said slowly, "yes." In his heart, he knew he had long ago buried compassion and hardened himself to pity. Real feeling was not in the province of his business life. He was a professional. "I am not paid to feel." Perhaps it was the darkness, the woman's invocation of private principles, true or not, that made him feel inferior to her moral standard. This woman, he knew, was a sucker for that, a bleeding heart that really bled.

"What that woman, Mrs. Harrigan, thinks and feels is her business, her life," Naomi said.

"You don't believe she was coerced? Brainwashed?" It could be some kind of trick, he told himself, a new ploy. He'd have to be on the lookout for that.

"Everybody who believes in something strongly is brainwashed. She gave herself to them. That's her right."

"Are you trying to convince me or yourself?"

"I'm convinced. That's why I want her left alone."

"And her husband not hurt?"

"Yes."

He considered her offer carefully. T. Clausen Moore lived by his word. It had been the slogan of his last campaign, and he had come to believe that it really might be close to the truth. He had never lied to Gladys, had always kept his word to the boys. Maybe he wasn't perfect, but he was not dishonest. "A man of his word." Sometimes he wished he had the stomach for corruption. He'd have been a lot richer.

Stalling, he pressed the automatic button that brought the window down, letting in the cool air. Like her, he too, had constructed a facade of principle around himself. Sometimes it seemed imposed on him.

Since he was a boy growing up in West Virginia, he had personified a certain kind of rough leadership, whose main value was fairness. It was a mysterious quality, he acknowledged to himself. "What does Tee think? Let Tee decide. If Tee does it, I will." Not the stuff of officers and gentlemen. More like a sergeant or foreman. Knowing the limits of this mysterious talent had kept his aspirations sensible. One thing about Tee, people said, he's a fair man.

The Glories had tested his veracity. From the moment they appeared in the county, they had imposed on his fairness, stretching it to its outer limits. He was a family man, a Christian churchgoer, a faithful husband, a strict father, a reasonably good man. In his heart, he held no truck for the Glories. In fact, he detested their sinister practices, their abuse of real religion, their way of proselytizing young people. But just as long as they stayed within the law, he had to be fair. And he was. Maybe even a little fairer now that they controlled a bloc of votes. That consideration was being fair to himself and his family.

"Let's suppose ..." It annoyed him to be hypothetical, but if he was going to make this deal, he'd better damn sight get some assurances in return. "... we abort this one. What are the guarantees that they won't try again? The Glories hate trouble."

"They'll keep trying, sheriff. We both know that. Barney ... Harrigan ... is very determined. I'm also very worried about his son."

"And your conscience?"

"Sheriff," Naomi said firmly. "I have to live with this. It may be principled, but it won't do much for my conscience. I'm betraying their trust. Fact is I'm very worried about Barney and his son."

"Suppose you just tell him that you told me all about it and that's that?"

"I've thought about that. You can't imagine how big a step this is for me." She seemed to want to say more, but she held her silence.

"All right," he said, after mulling it over. "But I can't guarantee that they, the Glories, won't take some action."

"I'm betting that they won't," Naomi said.

"Me too."

"So we have a deal?" she asked.

He hated the word and its implication.

"I'll deal only on Harrigan. I'm afraid I'll have to be rougher on O'Hara. He got past me a couple of times. Besides, Jeremiah will press the point."

"I don't care about O'Hara," Naomi snapped.

"Good."

"As long as Harrigan is safe. And his son." She hesitated, showing her concern.

"Leave that to me," the sheriff said, waiting for a response. When none came, he asked: "Now tell me what the plan is."

Naomi's voice came at him haltingly at first, then in a torrent. She had undoubtedly rehearsed it first in her mind.

11

The body of Charlotte Harrigan lay beside the rushing waters of the deep creek. Barney Harrigan, body stiff, head bowed, stood beside it, staring down at the open-eyed, inert face illuminated in a puddle of yellow light thrown from a flashlight carried by one of the sheriff's men. Naomi had turned away. Her face was buried in her hands as her body shook with quiet sobs.

"I'm sorry," the sheriff said. He hadn't bargained for this. Outside of the circle of light, he made out the phantom figures of Jeremiah and Holmes, the lawyer. Deeper in the shadows there were two other barely defined figures.

In the distance, the barracks-like buildings of the camp were dark and calm. Obviously, great pains had been taken not to disturb the slumbering inmates. Inside of himself, the sheriff felt the acid pain eating at his resolve.

He wished that Barney had made it easier by collapsing in grief. He could understand the mime of grief. It had a predictable momentum and could simplify the immediacy of interrogation. When the news of the woman's demise had been reported, his job was to bring Barney the news. It was awful. He had the little boy with him now. Thankfully Gladys had taken him and was caring for the boy at home. Poor little guy. He hadn't a clue about what was happening.

"Sorry, are you?" Barney said, lifting tearless eyes. "They killed her mind. They might as well have killed her body."

Debating a response, he held back. No point in exacerbating the situation. Behind him on the bridge, an ambulance was parked.

Technicians waited with a stretcher. The young doctor who had officially ascertained the death stood a few steps behind them, fingering his stethoscope. Three of the sheriff's deputies stood around observing the scene.

Kneeling, the sheriff studied the woman's face. The eyes were open, as glazed and empty as they were in life. The old nightmare of the eyes flashed across his mind, forcing him to turn away. He was conscious of the mute audience watching his performance and coughed to mask the movement, an involuntary spasm of revulsion. Waves of nausea seized him and he feared rising. He wished he had the authority to close the dead woman's eyelids, divert the accusation of the dead eyes.

The woman's moist hair was matted, the skin drawn back taut against the cheekbones. Her lips were parted, as if she had gone panicked and screaming into the void. The legs were drawn out straight, the arms pressed against her sides, her dress pulled tight over her knees. So they had wrapped her for special delivery, he thought. All neatly packaged. No longer of use.

"Death by drowning," the young doctor said, moving forward.

"Murdered," Barney corrected, his voice carrying. Peripherally, the sheriff saw the lawyer move toward them.

"No evidence of that, Harrigan," the sheriff said, standing up, feeling a tingling weakness in his knees. He felt a retch inside his gut and it took him a moment to steady himself.

"You've all got blood on your hands," Barney hissed. He was keeping himself under tight control. "Don't tell me 'sorry.' I will not hear 'sorry.'"

"It was a genuine accident." The calm voice of the lawyer intruded.

"You," Barney said, pointing a finger at Holmes. Oddly, he didn't go beyond that one word. The sheriff sensed that something was going on in his mind, some plan that he was cooking up.

"Too bad, Harrigan," Holmes said. "A meeting had been arranged. This is simply a cruel coincidence. An accident."

"Fuck you," Barney sneered.

"I'm sorry, Harrigan. That's all I can say."

He came closer, whispering now.

"I'd advise you to forget this. Accept the facts. They have credible witnesses. Make more of it, they can keep you in court forever. Think of your son."

"Credible witnesses? What bullshit." Barney looked at his wife's body. "That's part of my life down there on the ground," He stood over her for a long time, as if in a trance. His mind seemed to have drifted away, probing some dark corner of himself. Holmes retreated.

The sheriff turned and sought out Jeremiah, well hidden under a mask of impassivity. The sheriff could detect neither remorse nor anxiety. Under the calm, he sensed an air of annoyance. He searched himself again for the lever of professional objectivity.

"How did it happen?" he asked.

"She slipped, fell into the river. We tried to save her. It was too late. I called you immediately." Jeremiah shrugged, the words, floating out of his mouth on a puff of vapor. He moved further into the shadows drawing the sheriff with him. Near the creek, two of his officers were inspecting the area now, their flashlight beams searching among the crags and rocks that sloped down to the rushing waters.

"You can't just say accident," the sheriff snapped. "We're in a fucking bind here."

"Just do your job, sheriff," Jeremiah said simply. "And I'll do mine." The sheriff felt the implication of control but let it pass.

"I'm gonna do it," he said with what he knew was boyish bravado. He looked up the rise toward the sleeping camp. Poor bastards, he thought. Now this!

"She couldn't sleep," Jeremiah said, his words clipped and precise. "The incident with her husband and what was to come disturbed her calm and she wanted to take a walk."

Had she been told what he had conveyed? He doubted it. In fact, he doubted the explanation given by Jeremiah.

"Since when do you allow a stroll at night?"

Jeremiah glared at the sheriff, ignoring the question. The sheriff felt his pores open and the sweat slide down his back. I am still the sheriff here, he told himself, beating off a convulsion of anger.

"Everyone is free here to do as they wish here," Jeremiah said through a tight smile. How many times had he heard that? It was pointless to persist along that line.

"I'm going to make it easy, sheriff," Jeremiah said sneeringly. The sheriff balled his fists impotently.

"See how dark it is? New moon. They went for a walk. Amos and Rachel's sister, Mary. She apparently went too close to the edge and slipped. Simple as that."

"Didn't they try to save her?"

"Of course. But they couldn't get to her fast enough. The river, as you can see, runs fast. It is dangerous. Note we have posted signs after the last incident five years ago." Shit, did he have to bring that up, the sheriff thought. The memory still disturbed him, but that too had had witnesses. Glories. "She drifted down a ways," Jeremiah continued. "They reached her finally, then fished her out of the water and called me. I tried mouth-to-mouth and had you called immediately. Obviously, it was too late."

The words had flowed in a measured cadence, matter-of-fact, like the Pledge of Allegiance. He detected, too, the total absence of comment. Jeremiah had offered no editorials. The dead were useless to him.

"Have you told your leader?" the sheriff asked, remembering the protocol. "The head of the church."

"Of course," Jeremiah replied, pausing for the next question, like a boxer bracing for the next jab. In terms of alertness and agility, the man had him dead to rights, thought the sheriff. He felt leaden, his mind plodding and inert. Hold yourself together, he begged himself. He wished he could go home now and talk it out with Gladys.

"I hope we can put a cap on the publicity, sheriff," Jeremiah said suddenly, showing where his major interest lay.

"You know I can't control that."

"Try."

It came at him disturbingly like a command. There was no attempt at subtlety or obfuscation. "Hush it up" was the way it translated in his mind.

"I've got that other thing brewing back in my office." His own attitude filled him with self-disgust. "I've still got O'Hara in custody."

"I think we can dispose of that. The church already has. Release him. We'll get him sooner or later."

"And this Harrigan? What about him?"

"He has no reason to stay."

"I'm afraid you haven't heard the last of him."

"Remains to be seen."

His eyes drifted to where Holmes stood watching him from a distance. Barney had not moved from that spot over his wife's body as if he had rooted there.

"Better get the body away," he called. The technicians sprang to life, placing the dead woman on the stretcher. Barney followed it somberly to the ambulance, Naomi beside him. He heard the slam of the ambulance door and the creak of the bridge's wooden planks as the vehicle drove off.

"You said they were with her," the sheriff said to Jeremiah, motioning with his head at the two sentrylike apparitions that stood nearby.

"I told you that," Jeremiah said with a flash of annoyance.

"Just routine," he said, moving forward, hearing Jeremiah's footsteps following.

"What's your name?" the sheriff asked, confronting the young man who was, incredibly, smiling.

"Amos."

"I mean your real name."

"That is my real name."

"We'll provide it," Jeremiah interrupted. "For your records."

"What happened?"

The young man's eyes sought Jeremiah's, who must have nodded, setting off the tape recorder in the boy's mind. It would be futile, the sheriff knew. He half-listened as the young man delivered his speech like a litany, his lips fixed incongruously in a smile.

"She couldn't sleep. She said she wanted to take a walk so me and her sister, Mary, went with her. It was very dark, but we followed close by. She walked along the river. Then suddenly she went too close, then slipped and fell into the water. She started to drift away but he got her finally and we both pulled her out. Then we ran up and got Jeremiah. He came immediately and tried to revive her."

"I told you," Jeremiah said. The sheriff shrugged and turned to the girl, Charlotte's sister. There had been a distinct family resemblance. Studying her face, he could not see the slightest sign of remorse.

"It doesn't bother you?" he asked. Her eyes moved toward Jeremiah.

"Is that relevant?" Jeremiah asked.

"It is to me," the sheriff said.

"He wants to know how you feel about Charlotte's death, Mary."

The woman hesitated, then her smile inexplicably, broadened, her glazed eyes opening like saucers.

"Rachel has been summoned to the spirit world. She is happy on the other side. Father Glory is seeing to that."

"I thought it was an accident," the sheriff said sarcastically. He felt Jeremiah's flash of contempt.

"That was his method. His will. God wanted her."

"Yes," Mary said. "God wanted her."

"Poor child," the sheriff murmured.

"I know it's hard for you to understand," Jeremiah said with forced sweetness. It was another sermon he had heard many times before.

"Tell him what happened, Mary," Jeremiah pressed. Mary began immediately in a rush of words that barely floated into the sheriff's consciousness. They were almost word for word Amos' account. While she spoke, she smiled, which was very disconcerting.

"So you see," Jeremiah said, "a simple accident. We have two credible witnesses. Nothing left but to wrap it up." For the first time, the sheriff noted Jeremiah's tension. The son of a bitch is nervous, he thought, restoring a shred of self-respect. His cohorts in the church hierarchy must be pissed off. They didn't need this. Nobody needed it, least of all the sheriff.

"The Heavenly Father would like this matter disposed of as quickly as possible." It was a blatant admission, and the sheriff pressed his advantage.

"Does he?" His sarcasm was deliberately blunt. Father Glory's involvement could be a double-edged sword. Dispose of it quickly or else. It was a ringing threat to both himself and Jeremiah. In that totalitarian world, Father Glory pulled all the strings.

"It was an accident," Jeremiah said, lowering his voice. "A simple accident."

"You're totally satisfied about that?" the sheriff asked.

"Totally."

"Could it have been suicide?"

Jeremiah gasped, not expecting the jab.

"Why suicide?" he asked. "She was happy. She'd been reborn. She found faith." His voice rose. "She found Father Glory."

"No need to get defensive. I am, after all, the sheriff in this jurisdiction."

Jeremiah paused, obviously gathering his wits.

"Even if it was suicide, where's the crime?"

"Crime? Whoever said anything about that?"

"Your implication was quite clear." He paused. "You seem to have forgotten our earlier conversation."

"I'm afraid I haven't."

"I've made it easy for you, sheriff. It was an accident," Jeremiah said, his confidence restored.

He tried to find Jeremiah's eyes, but they turned away. In the absence of any evidence to the contrary, he'd have to go with it. Like the others. He detested the idea. This one smelled to high heaven, especially in the light of what the Forman woman had told him. It was too coincidental, too pat. It was murder, he decided in his gut. He had informed Jeremiah about what was planned, had even taken O'Hara into custody. The fact was that he was an accomplice. He told the Forman woman to keep her silence for the time being. There was no point in pushing the envelope. He looked toward the dancing beams of light still searching along the shore of the stream.

"So long as we understand each other, sheriff," Jeremiah said, sucking in his breath.

He'd have to think this out, he told himself, more as a sop to his esteem. Used to be an idyllic place, he thought sadly, sweet air, low fertile hills, nice people, a good place to raise a family, the American dream. How did they ever let this black wind of evil blow through here? He turned away, depressed and empty.

Naomi stood on the bridge, elbows along the handrail, looking downward, her complexion ashen. He walked toward her.

"A can of worms," he said, searching for an approach that would convey his feelings and mollify her. "I feel awful about this," he said directly. "They say it's an accident, they have witnesses ..."

"Do you think that's the truth?" the woman asked.

"Maybe. Maybe not. It wasn't your fault," the sheriff said. "You did the right thing. So did I. Forget it. This had nothing to do with what you told me."

"If I hadn't betrayed them would this have happened?"

"They knew."

"Holmes?"

"I'd bet the barn on it. No one can be trusted around here."

"Goes for me, too, I guess," she whimpered. "I betrayed them."

Her self-accusation softened him.

"I wouldn't be that hard on yourself. I told you. It wasn't your fault."

"I'll have to tell them."

"I wouldn't. Not now."

A scream rent the air. Barney had grabbed Holmes and they were scuffling. The sheriff's men had him quickly in hand, separating them. Two of them held Barney, who futilely resisted his containment, snarling like an animal.

Holmes brushed back his hair and patted his clothes, trying to restore himself to a semblance of his former dignity.

"We made him a substantial settlement," he said. "It offended him."

"Blood money. The dirty bastards. They kill her and want to pay me off."

"It was very generous. There is still the boy to think of. It's perfectly legal and honorable. A practical consideration that shows the compassion inherent in the principles of the Glorification Church." His pomposity was galling.

"Bullshit," Barney snarled, calming. He pointed a finger at Holmes. "We still have our own debt to settle."

"It's been settled," Holmes said, showing no sign of nervousness. "A donation to the church. In your late wife's name."

Barney's tongue seemed to freeze in his throat. His body arched, then collapsed in the men's arms as if all his bones and muscles had turned to jelly. The men dragged him to the sheriff's car and propped him beside Naomi, who sat impassively beside him. They drove back to his office in silence.

Back at his headquarters, the sheriff found that O'Hara and the black man were asleep in one of the holding cells. He'd deal with them later.

"There's a motel on my way home," he said. "We'll talk in the morning."

He looked at his watch. It was nearly two. He could think of nothing to say to them, no real word of honest comfort. In the brightness of the morning sun, Harrigan would have to face the deep chasm of his lost life, the Forman woman would have to deal with her oppressive guilt, and he'd have to figure out how to keep his own balance.

What he had done was merely warn them, abort the snatch. A simple phone call.

"We know," Jeremiah had told him.

"How?"

"We have our sources. We have no intention of being part of this."

So Holmes, the loyal retainer, had played his own game. Holmes was a whore.

His mind was too fatigued to confront that now. What he needed was Gladys, his rock of reassurance.

He registered them in separate rooms and left them at the motel, relieved of their oppressive silent accusations. Deep in his fatigued mind, he sensed some mysterious ordination, as if events had been manipulated by a force determined to bedevil him.

Yet even when he crawled into the warm high bed that he and Gladys had always shared during their married life, he could not fully offer his body to the security of sleep. He knew what he feared most of all.

"You okay, Tee?" Gladys stirred beside him.

"Hell no," he murmured, reaching out to feel a warm haunch where her nightgown had rolled up. It occurred to him that he was the only one of all the others who had crawled safely back to a warm, familiar nest. He felt heavy, leaden, betrayed by something he could not quite understand.

More than twenty years ago, they had come away from the dead coal towns of West Virginia. Their escape had been miraculous. For redneck hillbillies they had built a good life here at the country's edge, safe and snug. Got us our dignity back. In poverty and hopelessness, there was no dignity, only despair, reflected in the burned-out Appalachian hills.

Now it had charged back, and he could smell the oppressive dust of failure again, a dust as evil as the one from which they had fled. It, too, seemed to have come out of the ground, putrefying everything, creating its own empty-eyed army, like the one he used to see crawling along the old mountain roads.

Sheriff T. Clausen Moore, he mocked to himself. Once the title had been as royal as king. Now the crown's glitter had paled. It had turned out to be papier-mâché!

"Could lose my badge," he whispered to Gladys. Most of all she feared the economics. Often she had said, "No more white bread and lard spread. I'd choke on that, Tee."

"I'm afraid, Gladys," he said. "If I let go now, we could be in trouble. The boys got their dreams." One of them, Teddy, the oldest, wanted to be a doctor. The others were also coming up with expensive dreams.

"Wouldn't sell my soul for myself," he muttered. Usually, the thought could absolve him from all blame.

"God provides," Gladys said. The hell he does, the sheriff thought. It had taken him years and distance to expel the old fire and brimstone of the itinerant preachers who promised salvation for a bowl of soup, performing incantations that would never leave his memory, however hard he had tried to drown them with ridicule.

"Yeah. And if God ain't good, we're all in trouble," he said, knowing in his heart that Father Glory's sad, dead-eyed kids could not possibly get grace from a loving Lord, if there was one.

"The Harrigan boy all right?" he asked.

"Wants his mom. He woke up and I held him while he cried himself to sleep. Perry said she drowned."

Perry was his deputy.

"An accident," he heard himself say.

She turned toward him and started to knead his muscles. Her touch always soothed him. She was a big woman, amply endowed, encased in tight flesh, a warm, soft presence.

"You'll always be my littlest boy," she told him often. They had known each other since they were kids. Even then, there were no sharp edges to her. A simple country girl, that's me. He had never known another woman, nor had he ever felt the desire to explore.

"Leave all the bad out there, Tee." Her universe was him and the boys, and he had never let her down. The world outside was ugly, full of predators, killers, thieves, liars. You didn't bring the mud of despair into Gladys' house. Other women had special needs, hidden desires, secret dissatisfactions. Not Gladys. Other men, he had observed, yearned for something different. Not him. When her presence billowed around him, he was snug in a safe harbor.

"What's right for us may not be right, Gladys."

Kneeling over the dead girl, he remembered that he wished he had closed the lids, hidden her dead stare. The Forman woman had blamed herself and he had acquiesced, hid his own guilt.

"Wanna good one, Tee?" Gladys said. "Clear your mind."

He felt her caresses begin, her tongue sweet and velvet.

"Feel good?"

Anybody took his Gladys away, he'd go through the fires of hell. He imagined his loss. And Harrigan's.

"I can't keep my mind on it, Gladys."

Gently, he edged her away. There was no way to clear his mind ever again. He had swept the leavings of his rage into some secret vault within himself. There didn't seem to be room for any more of it. He had always known that what they did out there in the camp was against some higher law, some irrevocable law of nature. Some day men would catch on and then a new law would find its way into the books.

It will pass, he had told himself. But it wasn't passing. One day, they'll have us all. He felt himself slipping into the pit of sleep. Then suddenly in the pit, he was wallowing in the gelatinous mass of squidlike eyes, rolling around him, smothering him unblinking, oily with a stench so overwhelmingly foul that it jolted him awake again.

"That was no accident," he gasped.

"You all right, Tee?"

He reached for the telephone, pressing the pre-coded number for his office.

"Wake O'Hara," he told the man on duty. "I'm coming over."

12

Naomi lay on her belly on a high knoll from which they had a commanding view of the road, which snaked from the main highway. Roy, beside her, surveyed the landscape, training the telescopic sight of his rifle on the road, butt against his cheek, the flat of his large black thumb caressing the metal of the sight.

"Lousy sun," he said.

They were on a level with its rising face, the big bright blinding globe of sun rising over the hills, shooting fresh spears of light over the valley. Roy, shielding his eyes with his palm, squinted ahead.

"We'll get a clear view when they move lower."

She sensed his enjoyment of the tension. She could tell he liked guns. Boys like guns, she observed to herself, another strategy to squelch analysis, reverse the traditional path of her thought patterns. If they're so big on mind control, then I'll control mine, she told herself firmly, shivering in the morning chill. The sun was brightening, but not yet warming.

Naomi's dossier would read "kidnapper," and she wondered if she, too, would be at a loss to explain it. "You'd have to live it," she told her imaginary inquisitor.

She had lived it all right, taken the long journey from reason to action through guilt, remorse and contrition, participating deliberately in her own private revolution of self.

"Your choice," O'Hara had told her.

"No choice," she had answered pugnaciously. "Not after last night."

For most of what remained of it, she had lain naked in her motel room, afraid to douse the light. Someone, a thing, a force, was peeling away everything that protected her, layer by layer. It had eaten away her skin, her bones, and now was tearing at her vital parts, her innards. What was it they were looking for? She accepted the pain of it. Welcoming it, in fact. What she needed most of all was punishment. Contrition would hardly do the trick. Even guilt had lost its sting.

The force, the thing, whatever it was, had detonated her value system, sprung all the circuits. Being in charge of herself was the irreducible bedrock of all her aspirations, her body, her mind, her being. A human being had the right ... no ... the mission to direct his or her own destiny. So look where it had led her. The rebuke was gratuitous. It could never erase the reality of her dead baby, mask its inchoate screams, now joined with Charlotte's, whose life she had also aborted. She wanted to be hanged by the neck until dead, to go screaming into the mindless void.

She had heard his soft knock and had opened the door, without asking who was there, hoping it was the executioner. Instead it was O'Hara, leaning against the jamb in his mirrored glasses in which she could see two images of her nakedness, just one more way to shame herself. He shuffled in and she got back on her bed, pulling the blanket to her neck.

"I thought you were in custody."

"I was, indeed. Me and Roy. We are released under our own recognizance."

"The sheriff must trust you then."

"More than you think."

Slumping in a chair beside the bed, he removed his glasses, as if it were a signal to reveal himself. She did not speculate how he got there. Perhaps he was an apparition.

"I know what guilt is," he said with surprising gentleness. "I've been picking yours up all night."

"How could you possibly know?" she asked, then nodded. Of course, the sheriff had told him. It occurred to her suddenly that they were now allied with the sheriff in some way.

"I've got hundreds of dead souls on my conscience."

"What about dead bodies?" She felt a sudden tremor of hysteria.

"My contract was to kill minds."

"This won't go away," she said.

"It never does." He paused and sat down again. "But you might work it through. Make moves. Checkmate it. Like me."

"You?"

"I told you. I've ruined more lives …" He shook his head and emitted a low, giggling trill. "I was the best they had. Father Glory's golden boy. I made Jeremiah look like an amateur. I was Zachariah, the prophet of evil. My hands will never be clean. Never."

"But how is it possible?" she said, studying his face.

"You mean how did I get involved in the first place?"

"Isn't that always the key question?"

He averted his eyes and sucked in a deep breath.

"You really want to know?"

"Yes. I do."

"It's not as dramatic as you might think. Actually, the way people fall into this trap is … more or less … the same story. Repetitive. Boring."

"Tell me, since I'm in this. Don't ask me why or how," she said. "But I am sort of entitled."

He did not smile. Shrugging, he turned away, paced for a few moments as if assembling his thoughts, then began to talk.

"I had just broken up with my girl. My parents had died. I had lost my job. I was lonely, on edge. I felt lousy, rootless. I got to Seattle, roamed around. Did drugs. Got busted. Then these two lovely ladies approached me. Man, they told me I was the greatest thing on wheels. I needed that. I felt like shit. Next thing you know, they were working on my guilt. Your life is a turd. Now do something worthwhile. They told me they had this project that helped mankind—fed the poor, healed the sick. Come hear about it, they urged, throwing this trip on me, this love-bombing, this burst of sweet, soothing affection. At the time, that's what I needed most of all. Before I knew it, I was out at that camp. Then pow. I was in it up to my ass."

"Just like that?"

"Just like that."

"I'd say you were weak-minded."

"Yes. You would say that. The thing is they caught me at just the right moment. Everybody has just the right moment. Especially if they're wandering alone. Alone!" He shook his head. "I used to do it myself. I could pick a good prospect out of a crowd, could smell them out. It gets easy. You look for the open ones, the searchers."

He shook his head, then started to pace again.

"Hell," he said turning toward her suddenly. "Aren't we all searching for the same damned thing?"

"Are we?"

She noted to herself that his pose of certainty had disintegrated. Like her, the mask of his convictions had hidden his humanity. Yes, she knew, we are all searchers. But for what? She felt a sudden clarity of insight. To escape from loneliness, that was the comfort of living. To be one with the rest of mankind. To be touched by others, recognized, appreciated, loved. The awful pain of life was to emerge into the world out of the womb, alone. All our lives we must search for the cure for that pain. She felt a great rush of emotion as she contemplated these thoughts.

"How did you get out?" she asked.

"Roy. I saved his life once. Actually, he was mugging me and I decked him. The cops wanted to bring him in. He was a three-time loser and this would have put him away for life. I said it was just a misunderstanding, that he was a buddy of mine. He owed me this favor. One day, he caught me on the street. Knocked me cold. Then he had me deprogrammed. Simple as that. Big black bastard. Just returned the favor. Now we're in it together. Sucked in. Like a whirlpool. That's my life now. Saving others."

"Who don't want to be saved."

"But they do. In their hearts, they're screaming to be let out."

"Zachariah," she repeated.

"Yeah. Zachariah. He's the one, according to them, that made it with Mary, Jesus' father. How about them apples? Don't ask me to explain it all. It's like they ripped out all the pages of the Bible, put it in a shredder, then pieced it back together their own way. They got this book, The Book of Glory. It's printed just like the Bible we know. Oh, they do have it down. Religion, this bird, this so-called Father Glory, has discovered that it is the most secure scam of all, believe it or not. Hell, it's under the protection of the U.S. of A."

"You think he, Father Glory, believes in what he's preaching?"

"Yeah, I think he believes it or has come to believe it. Sometimes people who realize their ambitions or dreams begin to believe that some higher force has guided them to the pinnacle. Who knows? But he has built an organization under the guise of religion and he's figured out a way to get people to believe it implicitly and keep on believing it. His goal is to keep them from not believing, which means he has to prevent them from getting out into the real world again and fit them into some new one, a world in which they, he, the big bastard, holds all the strings."

"But why?"

"Megalomania. Power. That's where it's at. Control. Son of a bitch wants to run the world. Hell, it's not a new fantasy. People make up schemes like that all the time. Religion's the way. Promise 'em salvation in the other world. That's pretty heady stuff. Do as I say and you'll make it to some eternal nirvana. If not, I'll see that you rot in hell or some place where you'll be in pain for an eternity. Scares the shit out of people. Make 'em believe that and they'll rape their mothers, castrate their fathers and serve up their little kids for dinner."

"You sure make it sound creepy, O'Hara."

"It is creepy."

She wished she could argue against his supposition. But she knew that there was historical and contemporary evidence so compelling that it was futile to oppose it.

"Like I told you. If I really wanted to I could do it to you. Just lend me your head and give me your time."

"Never."

"Never say never. I'm not saying that some didn't get away. But not you. Hell, you're raw meat. A do-gooder. That makes you halfway there. The do-gooders were always the easy ones to turn."

Despite her doubts, she let his comment pass. Nor did she wish to put it to the test.

"Is it as simple to get them out of it?" she asked.

"Harder out than in. They've been programmed by experts. I've got to crash through the barriers that have been put in place. It takes some doing." He paused. "The fact is that all of us have been programmed by others to believe what we believe. Even you. You've been programmed to believe that people can't be ogrammed to do things that are against the grain, against standards of morality and behavior that are, in your mind, compassionate and good. Believe me, your mind is not as open and free as you think it is. Might be some of the things you think are right are bullshit."

"Maybe. That's why I'd like to keep an open mind about everything."

"Doesn't seem too open to me."

"I'm willing to be convinced."

"Okay. Then come with us, Naomi," he whispered. "Let me show you."

"Show me what?"

"We're going to split open Charlotte's sister. And Amos."

"Split open?" The image frightened her. Worse, it suggested terrible acts of violence.

"Deprogram," he said. "An ugly word, I know. I prefer to call what they do deprogramming. What I do is try to bring them back into the real world. That's what we're going to do to Charlotte's sister ... Mary, they called her. Her real name, you must know, is Susan. And Amos."

"How are you going to get them to consent to this?"

"We're not going to ask their consent, Naomi. We're going to take them."

"Kidnap them?"

"Just as we intended to do with Charlotte."

She was stunned by his assertion.

"After what we've just been through?"

He observed her for a long moment.

"Do you believe that Charlotte died by accident?"

It was a question she did not want to confront and her hesitation told him what was self-evident. She wasn't sure.

"Are you suggesting...."

"I'm not suggesting anything," he snapped. "All I'm saying is that the testimony of Charlotte's sister and Amos is suspect and that we're entitled to the absolute truth."

"But they may have told us the truth."

"Accidents don't happen like that. Not there. Nobody gets up in the middle of the night for such a simple act as a walk. Nobody.

In that place? And no witness ever tells the same story in exactly the same way. It's a patently obvious cover-up. You don't know these people. I do …" His words trailed off. "Been there, done that."

"Murder …" Her voice shut down.

" 'Nuff said."

"So you really think that Charlotte …" Again her voice shut down.

"That's the point. We want the witnesses to tell the truth. We won't be able to get at that until their minds have been released, until they've been deprogrammed."

"Have you considered the risks, O'Hara?"

"Completely."

"If things go wrong …"

"I've got 48 hours."

She was startled by his assertion.

"I don't understand."

"Sheriff Moore. He's in on it. He set it up."

"And you trust him?"

"It's not uncommon," O'Hara shrugged. "I often get help in the strangest places. Yes, I trust him. We were once adversaries and I think we know each other. I believe he's fed up with hiding his own instincts. He doesn't believe them. In their hearts, most people know what bad is. He's bet his career on my nose and he's given me 48 hours." He shook his head. "It's a gamble. It's too short a time. But it has been done before."

She caught his undercurrent of uncertainty, which confused her, making him more human than she had imagined.

"Sometimes I can't break through. No matter how hard I try."

How had things gone this far? This was beyond mere emotional risk. Despite the sheriff's alleged consent O'Hara had invited her to participate in an illegal act, an act with dire consequences.

"How can you trust me? I've already betrayed you once."

She hadn't meant to reveal that. He showed no shock at her revelation.

"The sheriff?"

He nodded.

"He told me not to talk about it. Not yet."

"Doesn't matter now. Your instinct's wrong, but it probably didn't matter. They apparently knew. My guess is that they didn't want the hassle."

"Are you saying that they drowned her because they didn't want the hassle? Good God. Does Barney know?"

"He blames himself. Not you."

"And you? Who do you blame, O'Hara?"

"Them. Always them."

"But what I did," she began, then hesitated. O'Hara interrupted her.

"Don't be so hard on yourself, Naomi. Believe me, I know the power of guilt. The trick is to channel it in a positive direction. I'm offering you that chance."

"I'm not sure I'm up to it," she sighed, feeling enervated.

"Your call."

"But the risks," she managed to protest. "For you. If things go wrong, they could put you away and throw away the key."

"What's one more risk?" he said, snickering.

"And Barney?"

"After what they did to his wife, Barney is gung-ho."

"Will it bother him to have me along?"

"Will it bother you—that's the question."

"But why do you need me?"

"Good question, Naomi. We need to convince people like you that it is possible to brainwash human beings into mental slavery and force them to do unspeakable acts."

"What do you mean? People like me."

"People who think that every human being is essentially good," he said slowly. "The self-righteous ones. People like you, the bright ones who believe in the sanctity of human will, who believe in freedom and morality, the idealists. Without you, we all lose and the bad guys get away with murder."

"Isn't that a bit strong?" She felt her old argumentative self reassert itself.

"Not strong enough. What you need is a demonstration."

"Maybe so," she sighed. They exchanged glances. He started toward the door, then turned.

"Tomorrow at eight. In front of the motel. If you're there, you're there. We won't wait."

13

Beside her, she felt Roy tense, noting that the butt of the rifle pressed an indentation deeper into his dark cheek. His eye squinted into the telescopic sight, quivering the dark nest of wrinkles beside his temples. Below them, coming down the long winding camp road that sloped toward the highway, she saw the two cars, moving like toys on a plastic track, the sheriff's car pacing far ahead as a camp van followed.

O'Hara had explained the strategy so as not to frighten her with the implication of killing and violence. There was a point in the winding road where it snaked in a deep loop following the river's bend, hiding it from the sheriff's pace car, which, speeding up, reached the four-lane highway and pressed forward at full throttle.

According to the prearranged scenario, the sheriff's intention would be clearly stated. He had come to the camp merely to complete the investigation of the site in full light. The objective was to get the investigation over quickly. To complete the paperwork. He would assure them that all he would need was the statements of Mary and Amos to be given at his office.

Naomi had little doubt that the sheriff's disarming hillbilly innocence would lull them into a sense of security. The lure of a quick and happy ending would be a powerful attraction to Jeremiah and Holmes. And, sure enough, there they were: Jeremiah, Holmes, Mary and Amos, moving slowly down the snaking road in the camp van, smugly oblivious to this small force ranged against them.

Crouching behind scrub brush about a hundred yards above the road, O'Hara and Barney were waiting, ski-masked, armed, fiercely formidable for the surprise assault worked out by O'Hara with combatlike precision. She doubted that their disguise would be truly effective. It was more for drama than dissimulation.

Beside her, two quick shots popped in her ear, leaving an echo. The bullets shot out the van's tires and the vehicle shivered to a halt. Rising, she followed Roy to O'Hara's van. He slid into the driver's seat and she jumped into the rear. Inside, it was fitted out with shackles welded into the metal floor, and two bunks of canvas stretched over metal piping. On one of the bunks were two obscene-looking rubber masks. Through a grill behind the driver's seat, she could observe the road ahead. Light also spilled into the dank rear cabin through a tiny grill in the van's back door.

She had never experienced this sense of covert danger. The excitement, despite her fear, was strangely thrilling; the aura of criminality charged her with titillating energy. It was another dimension of action she had never glimpsed before. She felt herself wavering between exultation and revulsion.

The van ground to a halt at the edge of a stand of trees not far from the stalled camp van.

Roy's tap on the inside panel was her signal to open the double panel doors in the rear, which she did with shaking fingers. A spill of bright sunlight poured into the van's interior. Above the cooling motor's ping, she heard the driver's door click open and soon saw Roy's glistening face peek inside. He carried a submachine gun. "Just in case," he said, crouching in the van's cabin, noting her eyes riveted on the weapon.

She managed to keep alert through her fear, listening. She heard heavy footfalls, then a jumble of voices, a brief woman's high-pitched scream, then silence. Scuffling feet and grunts came closer. Looking out, she saw Barney and O'Hara, in ski masks, dragging Amos and Mary, who seemed deliberately stiff-legged and weighted as if they had been taught some countertactic. O'Hara had a submachine gun slung over his shoulder.

Barney and O'Hara had the two victims gripped under their arms, as they tugged the inert bodies forward. Roy, in a ski mask now, ran to meet them, the gun at the ready. He reached immediately for the amulets that they wore around their neck and, taking a knife from his belt, cut the chain that held them.

Then he helped O'Hara and Barney heft the bodies into the rear of the van, quickly locking their ankles and wrists into the shackles. Roy's dark fingers slipped the masks over the heads of the two prisoners as the doors slammed shut. Barney climbed into front of the van, tearing off his ski mask, as it shot forward with O'Hara at the wheel. It bounced over rough terrain until it moved out on to a smoother surface.

Naomi noted that he was still holding the chains with the amulets.

"What's inside? Holy water?" she pointed to the amulets with her chin.

"Inside this?" He raised them and held them up. The amulet was in the shape of Father Glory's facial likeness.

She nodded.

"Nothin' much. Just cyanide. Enough to kill you in seconds."

"You're not serious." Roy was a joker.

He smiled and broke one open.

"Smell," he said holding the broken amulet under her nose.

"I'm not sure," she said, sniffing.

"Burnt almond. No holy water."

"But why?"

"It's a cult thing. Gateway to paradise. Part of the bullshit."

The assertion stunned her into silence as she watched him break open the other amulet and pour the contents on the floor of the van.

"Good for a quick bye-bye," he said with a laugh. She didn't join him.

She watched the two victims struggle against the shackles, masked heads bobbing, like hideous monsters out of a child's imagination.

"Won't do you any good," Roy barked, moving his hands to hold their heads still, pressing them together as if they were basketballs. The strong pressure quieted the heads like some miracle of healing.

"Is that necessary?" Naomi asked hoarsely. She felt compassion well up again. She hadn't expected this particular aspect of violence.

Roy turned to her and nodded, shrugging. She had been told what to expect but had not been prepared for the reality. Fighting terror with terror, O'Hara had said. She imagined the horror that Amos and Mary must be feeling trapped in the darkness.

Her eyes drifted toward Barney, who squatted on the floor against the closed doors, turning occasionally to watch the road through the grillwork, his hair matted with perspiration, his face distorted with tension. His persona seemed to have metamorphosed. Like the Glories, she noted, with irony. He was not the Barney she had known. Hate hung on him like a pall.

Turning away, she looked at the two shackled prisoners in their grotesque masks. These were human beings, and she was an active party in their suffering, perhaps the cause of it. Still, she held her rebellion inside. Keep an open mind, O'Hara had urged. The gift of his vulnerability had won her—if not her heart, her mind, which she permitted herself to open to what to her were new ideas.

"It will not be pretty," he had warned her. She clung to the memory of his emphatic voice. "Remember Charlotte," he had added.

She leaned against the front panel, her body absorbing the shocks of the washboard road over which the van proceeded. Looking through the grill behind the driver's seat, she saw a pine forest closing in on them. The motor strained as the van climbed upward. The bumps grew worse. Roy's arms held the two bodies upright, to prevent injury.

"Jes' hold on, folks. Won't be long," he said cheerfully. After a time, the van stopped. Barney swung the door open while Roy unlocked the shackles. When the young man started to flail his arms, Roy held them, twisting one behind his back.

"Won't do you no good to make it hard," Roy said. O'Hara came around to the rear to help them out. They did not struggle. O'Hara led the boy over the unfamiliar ground, Barney followed, carrying a submachine gun slung over his shoulder. Naomi wondered if he was prepared to use it.

"Help her," O'Hara ordered. Standing, Naomi banged her head on the van's ceiling, but the blow revived her reflexes. Jumping to the ground, she held the woman's arm, as Barney, holding the other arm, brought her up the path to a weathered log cabin.

Inside, it was surprisingly comfortable. A large mottled animal skin rug covered a planked floor. The furniture was worn but serviceable. The room was dominated by a stone fireplace with wood already set for a fire. On one side was a kitchen with a chipped porcelain sink, a stove and refrigerator. Open shelves were well stocked with cans and cartons of food. Barney and Roy unslung their guns and placed them in a closet, closing it by snapping a combination lock around two rungs. Apparently the cabin had been well prepared. It was not far from the camp but well hidden and, ironically, still in Sheriff Moore's county.

The main room led off to another three rooms. The entrance to each of these rooms was barred by thick planks, which had to be pushed aside through thick metal braces. Roy and Barney led Amos to one of them, while she followed O'Hara and Mary into the other one. In the harsh light thrown by a single bulb, they entered a windowless room. The windows had been sealed from the inside with thick wooden planking. A worn double mattress devoid of sheets lay on the floor. Adjoining was a room that contained a sink and a toilet. The door had been removed.

Naomi's eyes searched for signs of escape. None were apparent. The room was quite obviously boxed in, a well-protected cell. To break out of it looked impossible.

"This is awful," she muttered.

"I know."

O'Hara turned to Mary, then peeled off the hideous mask.

Mary gazed back at him with hatred, her face and hair plastered with perspiration. Removing an ugly leather gag, he quickly ducked a wad of phlegm that shot out from between her lips. Naomi expected her to scream. Instead, she hissed: "Father Glory will see you in hell." The effort to speak so suddenly started a paroxysm of coughing, and specks of saliva dribbled over her mouth.

"You are in hell, baby," O'Hara muttered, offering a cruel smile.

"Susan, you dirty little lying bitch," Barney shouted from behind her.

She hadn't seen him enter. The words burst out of him, fists balled. He lifted both his arms as if to strike her.

"Don't," O'Hara screamed grabbing him. Barney lowered his arms. "Stay with Roy."

Barney looked at Mary for a long moment, his face contorted with hatred. He muttered a curse and let himself out of the room.

"Resist the devil and he will flee from you," Mary shouted defiantly, repeating it as a mantra. "Resist the devil and he will flee from you. Resist the devil and he will flee from you."

Her eyes seemed to roll back upon herself, as if her mind was retreating to a place of safety. She began to clap her hands and raise her voice until it screeched like that of an injured animal.

Mary's rant was relentless, the words tumbling out her endlessly. It was obvious that she was inducing herself into a trance state. Her throat muscles strained as the words spewed out of her.

"Let's leave her now," O'Hara said.

"Like this?"

"I told you," O'Hara said. "My way."

"But it's cruel."

"It always hurts to get born," he said.

They left the room and O'Hara replaced the planks, although it did not shut out the sounds of Mary's screaming. Sniffing, Naomi smelled the aroma of frying bacon.

"Tahm for eats," Roy said, from the kitchen.

"He used to be a chef," O'Hara said, collapsing in one of the chairs, stretching his scuffed boots in front of him.

"The boy's more docile," O'Hara said. "She'll be a hard case."

"It's the bitch that we need to break," Barney muttered, his face frozen into a grimace of hatred. He was a stranger now, lost in a swamp of revenge.

"You've got to hold on, fella," O'Hara said with almost pedagogic patience. "What you see in there"—he motioned with his head toward the girl's room—"is no one you ever knew before." He looked up suddenly. "What was she like before?"

"Susan. Who can remember? Doesn't matter," Barney said. "She took my Charlotte."

"And God knows how many others."

"I don't care about the others."

Roy came forward, balancing four plates of food.

"Coffee's comin'," he said cheerfully.

He put the plates on the table and pulled utensils wrapped in napkins from his hip pockets. Then he went back to the kitchen and brought out a pot of coffee and ceramic mugs.

O'Hara got up and went to the table. Roy sat down beside him and immediately stuffed his mouth with eggs and toast. Some yolk dripped onto his chin.

"Better eat," O'Hara said. Barney shrugged and got up. Before he could negotiate a mouthful he put it down and banged the flat of his fist on the table, shaking the dishes, tumbling a piece of toast from its pile. O'Hara looked at him and shrugged, then turned to Naomi.

"I'm not hungry," she said. "Give her mine."

O'Hara and Roy ignored her and continued to eat with a relish that offended her. She turned away in disgust.

"We eat. They don't," Roy said. "Eggs is no good cold."

"They don't?"

"Not now," O'Hara said.

"They're human beings."

O'Hara continued to eat and Roy soaked up the eggs with bits of toast, as if deliberately flaunting greed.

"You better," O'Hara said with a full mouth. "Both of you. You've both got work to do." He pushed the plate in front of Barney, emphasizing the command. With effort, Barney picked up a strip of bacon and put it in his mouth, washing it down with steaming coffee. Behind the door, Mary's litany continued, but the decibel level was steadily dropping.

"The canary's getting tired," Roy said, picking the now-dried egg from his lip.

"How can you deny them food?" Naomi said, her previous resolutions to herself faltering in this atmosphere of cruel indifference. O'Hara turned to her and shook his head.

"I said it won't be easy."

"But to starve them ..."

He pushed his empty plate away. "We have to weaken them," he said. "Tire them out. That's the way it began. That's the only way it can be reversed. Like an army softening up the enemy before the attack." He paused and stood up, walking toward her. Although he wasn't a big man, his presence loomed up at her. Grasping her shoulders, he forced her to look at him. "We're gonna feed them. Just enough. But we're not gonna let them sleep." He tapped his forehead. "The problem is in here. We're fighting terror with terror." He watched her for a moment, then his voice became gentle. "I know how it looks."

"How it is," she corrected. "You can't do this to people."

"Better than dead," Barney blurted.

"It's the only way," Roy said, rising on big, muscled haunches. He slowly pushed aside the planks that held Amos' door and went in. O'Hara quickly replaced the planks.

"What's he going to do in there?"

"Just sit. Keep him from sleeping." He shook his head. "Look, Naomi, we've got to get them to put down their guard. To exhaust them. Same methods used by the Glories. Trust me. I've done it for both sides many times."

"Trust you?" Naomi sneered. "How can I? This offends me."

"I said it would."

"But you've put them in a prison."

"Physical. Not mental. Which is worse?"

"Never mind," she stammered, groping for a thought that might salvage herself. Two wrongs don't make a right, she told herself. It seemed futile, childish. Charlotte's dead face floated back at her, taunting, defeating her rage.

She couldn't eat but she did have a cup of coffee. Barney, moody with mourning and bitterness, sat at another end of the table, writing in his notebook. She couldn't blame him. Not really. Nor could she summon pity for him.

She became aware of O'Hara offering instructions in a flat, authoritative tone, a monologue that outlined the housekeeping conditions of their stay. There was one extra bedroom, with twin beds. They would take two hours' sleep and two hours' duty, which meant sitting with the "subjects." So they had become less than human in their identification as well. Roy would keep sandwiches and coffee handy around the clock, including providing the "subjects" with oatmeal mush three times a day. There was a shower out back, O'Hara pointed out with an attempt at humor, "if you begin to smell skunk on your body." No one laughed.

In the brief silence that followed, they could still hear Mary's voice. It had become diminished to a harsh, brittle whisper.

"When that stops," O'Hara said to Naomi, "you go in there and sit with her. Make sure she doesn't get any sleep. You, Harrigan. Be sure to get those planks back." He looked at his watch. "I'm gonna get me some sack time. I'll be going around the clock." Stretching, he lumbered across the room to the bedroom, stopping before he opened the door.

"When Roy goes out," he said to Barney, "you go in."

"What should I do?"

"Doesn't matter. Just don't let him sleep. Think of them both as a roast cooking. I'll be coming in and basting them from time to time."

"Let her stew for awhile, then go in. Watch her. Let her scream."

He went into the bedroom, leaving Barney and Naomi alone together.

For a long time, she did not turn to face him, although she found herself listening to his breathing, imagining she could hear his heartbeat. Its thumping rhythm had a vaguely familiar sound and she remembered often how she had listened to it, her ear against his chest, a counterpoint to the music in her heart. She cursed the memory, down to the tiny brain cell that spawned it.

"It was my fault, Nay, not yours," he said. It rang hollow in her mind.

"I was the weakest link," she replied, feeling a tight, hard glob form in her chest. "I didn't hold." In searching for her own absolution, she had discovered that image and it seemed apt. It was neither the time nor the place to explain her convictions. They had already caused enough anguish.

"No one is to blame but them," he murmured. His gaze felt hot on her cheek. Still she did not face him. Don't release me, she howled within herself. Not now. Thankfully, he did not wait for a response. "All I want is the truth of what happened to Charlotte. Those two know. Jeremiah ordered it. It's a no-brainer. We need their testimony. I owe Charlotte that."

Odd, she thought in a burst of clarity, how the mind comes up with motives. He had found an excuse for his revenge.

"And then?"

"Then?" Without seeing his expression, she was certain he looked at her pointedly, perhaps with bitterness.

"We'll have grounds for a murder conviction. It's a start. We have to expose them, dismantle them. Bastards. The truth is ... I'd rather kill them."

She shuddered. But she knew he was being honest. That part of him had not changed. Vengeance was powerful, escalating, feeding on itself. She had seen it too often in her work. Fire with fire, the spokesman of authority always said, responding to protests. The beleaguered always replied in kind, forever escalating violence, until death became as commonplace as weeds. It insulted man's capacity for forgiveness.

She felt a spiraling self-righteousness, the old feeling of moral outrage. For her, it had always been the only reality. Now she could only cling to it like a drowning victim grasping for flotsam, helpless in the white water.

"How do you fight evil?" she whispered, as if her mind had generated the words without her will.

"Like this," he said. She turned to face him.

"You can't fight evil with evil." What was she protesting? she wondered. She was in it with them. In the silence that followed, she recalled the woman in the barren room.

"I'm going in."

Getting up, she put her ear to the door. Mary had quieted. Removing the planks, she grasped the doorknob.

"Lock it after me," she said. Barney rose immediately as she opened the door and entered the room.

Mary was squatting on the mattress, her head resting against the wall. Harsh light from the single bulb washed out her pale face, fleshed and pimpled from a bad diet. Her hair was still matted, her forehead shiny with perspiration, her eyes vague, her lips pressed tight together, slightly puffed.

Naomi leaned against the wall, then let her body slide to a sitting position as she watched the woman, unsure of whether or not she was aware of Naomi's presence. Time passed. Naomi wondered if she had succeeded in inducing a trancelike state. Mary didn't move. Even her fingers lay immovable as icicles, palms up, on her thighs. Her eyes were open, their gaze fixed.

Naomi decided there was no need for talk, although she was not sure whether or not Mary was in a waking state. Suddenly, the woman coughed. A rasping sound wracked her chest, forcing her body to react. Her eyes drifted toward Naomi. The vagueness softened, although the look was now forlorn, helpless. Pity rose in her.

"Would you like a drink?" Naomi asked.

The vagueness faded now as Mary's body stiffened. She sat upright in the bed, nodding, offering a thin wan smile. Naomi rose and went into the bathroom. The chipped sink was stained brown, with only a single faucet. Opening the tap, she dipped her fingers into a slow trickle of cold water.

"No glass," she said.

"Never mind," Mary croaked. Her ranting had wasted her voice. Naomi paced the room, feeling the woman's gaze fixed on her, like some searing beam of light.

"Resist the devil and he will flee from you," Mary said, oddly calm.

"I'm not the devil," Naomi shot back, surprised at her reaction.

"What then?" Mary asked pleasantly.

"Just a woman. Like you," Naomi said softly, sliding back into a sitting position against the wall.

"Father Glory will protect me," Mary said hoarsely. "I have nothing to fear. Satan never wins. Father Glory wins, always."

"He didn't win with your sister," Naomi said.

"She is in the spirit world."

"You should have left her alone," Naomi said, forcing a rebuking tone.

"We saved her. She was in the grasp of Satan."

"She was perfectly happy with Barney."

"Never. She was only happy with Father Glory."

"She had a husband, a child, a place."

"He lied to you." A veil seemed to lift from the girl's eyes. "He was Satan. He was cruel to her."

"And the child?"

"Satan's child."

Naomi shivered.

"All they want is the truth. About the way Charlotte died."

"I told them that. It was an accident."

"They don't think so."

"I swear on my life."

"On Father Glory's life?"

Mary hesitated and smiled benignly, moving closer, to the edge of the mattress.

"Yes," she said. "On Father Glory's life."

Mary held out her hand, reached over and touched Naomi's knee. Naomi let it rest there, looking deeply into the woman's eyes. They seemed bottomless, serene, despite the condition of her face.

"Don't you believe in the concept of love? Love is the most important emotion in the universe. Without love, there is nothing. Love transcends all. Jesus was the personification of love. God's love child. He did not succeed because his mother defiled love with Zachariah. Only Father Glory can save mankind now from the hell that awaits us all."

Her words poured out, honeyed, smooth and gentle.

"These men do Satan's work. They have no right to defile me. No right to do this. You'll see. They'll …" she hesitated. "They'll force me. That's the way they do it. You'll see."

"All they want is the truth," Naomi said lamely.

"Do you think I lied?"

It was the one reality that she had refused to face.

"They don't believe you."

"Do you?"

She hesitated, digging her teeth into her lower lip. Mary got off the bed, crawled across the floor and toward her, without taking her gaze from Naomi, clasped both her hands in hers.

"You must save me from them," she whispered. "We are women. We understand."

"Father Glory is a man," Naomi said, unresisting, feeling the strength of the woman's grip.

"Father Glory is God's true child," she said with overpowering certainty. "Look around you." Inadvertently, Naomi tore her eyes away from Mary's gaze and searched the room, then returned her gaze. "Out there is only defilement. Loss of purpose. Chaos. Destruction. Someone must save us. We are suffering because we have turned away from God. Only Father Glory can save our souls. He is the true Messiah."

"How?" The word seemed a compulsion, wrung out of the mud of her disbelief. Father Glory was a fraud, her mind told her.

"By love. Love." Mary pressed, unclasping her fingers, holding Naomi's shoulders, bringing her face close to hers, until the eyes unfocused.

"Help me," she whispered. "Resist the devil."

"But how?"

Mary paused, her eyes boring into Naomi's.

"Sneak away from here. Tell my brothers and sisters. Tell Jeremiah. They will come and get us. Please. They have no right to do this to another human being."

The words were like a match to the dry tinder of her soul. She felt the conflagration rise. Suppose they had told the truth, Naomi reasoned.

"I'm human," Mary said. "Like you."

Yes. She felt the pull of the woman's humanity, the plea from her depths.

"I told them what they planned to do to your sister," Naomi said slowly, as if the words had been pulled out of her.

"Of course you did," Mary said without a pause. "Because you knew it was evil, Satan's work."

"But if I hadn't ..." She felt a sudden constriction of her tongue, as if it had been glued to the roof of her mouth.

"God told you what you must do. To save her."

"But she died."

"With Father Glory in her heart and soul. It was your gift to her."

"My gift?"

Naomi felt her thoughts tumble, cascading down the ruts in her mind, washing away her guilt. She savored the sense of release. Of freedom.

"Save me," Mary said. "Save us from Satan. Both of us."

Mary held her now in a warm embrace. Naomi felt her soft breasts against her own, the sweet goodness of her. The woman continued to hold her. She lost track of time. Then suddenly, she heard the planks begin to be removed outside the door. In a flash, Mary was back on the bed in the same position in which Naomi had found her.

O'Hara stood in the doorway, his eyes squinting into the brightness. He carried a leather-bound Bible and a briefcase.

"Get some sleep," he ordered, watching Mary, ignoring her. Naomi rose limply. She felt drained, beyond fatigue, yet still tasting the strange high of exhilaration. With a glance at Mary, whose eyes faced the planks where the window had been, she moved toward the door, blocked by the pervasive figure of O'Hara.

"Time for the cavalry," he said, making room for her to pass.

14

"Services for Charlotte Harrigan," a tiny headline in the local paper read, followed by a single paragraph: "Services were held today for Charlotte Harrigan, 25, at the Glorification Church. Mrs. Harrigan, a native of New York City, had been a recent convert to the Church. She died over the weekend of accidental drowning."

Shaking his head in disgust and frustration, Sheriff Moore balled the page in his fists and flipped it into the trash can where it lay, appropriately, amid the Styrofoam cups and ashtray leavings. He had not expected, nor had he wished for more accurate coverage. They had cremated her. Everybody in the county played the game and there was no question in his mind that the Glories were set to buy up the local paper from the Kildare family, who had owned it for three generations. They take over, one step at a time.

Soon they would own the whole county, just as they owned him. No sense wallowing in remorse. It was too late for that now. The Glories had tarnished them all, and those they could not control they bought. It chilled him to think of it. County by county, town by town, they could take over the whole fucking country. He'd seen it happen here, the outraged citizenry fighting the Glories and their high-priced carpetbagging lawyers making them dot the i's and cross the t's. The best he could hope for was a checkmate. Nothing more. And if O'Hara, Zachariah, let him down, he was finished.

As the day progressed, so did his second thoughts. He was a fool to stick his neck out. Too big a risk. And that O'Hara had a rap sheet as long as his arm, mostly after he had started deprogramming for a living.

He remembered him as Zachariah, the ferret eyes, shifty and clear. It was hard to tell if he was part of the scam or a believer. Who knew? Now he was bedded down with the bastard, risking a career, hating himself for his sudden surge of do-gooder baloney. Forty-eight hours, he'd given them. Not much time, he knew. O'Hara had pleaded for more, but he feared that more time would be dangerous. The Glories weren't dumb. They might catch on to who was behind it. He looked at his watch. Nearly a quarter gone.

"They're here, sheriff," Perry, his deputy, said, bursting in on his bleak thoughts.

"All right."

He tidied up his desk, stepped on the trash can to smash the paper further into the rubbish, then straightened his tie and assumed a position of authority, hands clasped on his desk, chin jutting out, the very model of assertive virtue. He had ducked them all day, communicating briefly on the phone, assuring them that he was on the job of pursuit.

Jeremiah and Holmes came in and took seats opposite the sheriff. Holmes crossed his legs self-importantly, always the patrician, with his charcoal gray pants pressed razor sharp, his shoes shined, his long socks creaseless. Jeremiah in his khakis looked, as always, officious and superior. They waited until Perry had left. He had brought them steaming mugs of coffee, which he had perched on cork coasters on the edge of the sheriff's desk.

Behind the sheriff, more for show than action, was a county map with an overlay and marks in red and green, indicating potential hideaways. He had scrupulously left out where he knew Amos and Mary were being held. By the way Jeremiah and Holmes looked at him, he had no doubt that his veracity was in question.

"It was a clumsy attempt," Jeremiah said. "I could smell O'Hara through the ski mask. Playing his games. As if we didn't know." Raising his eyes he looked at the sheriff.

"Smell's not evidence," the sheriff said weakly.

"I was there; you weren't," Jeremiah snapped.

"You should have been there," Holmes echoed.

They were like a comedy team, each playing to the other's timing, as they had done on many other occasions and confrontations. "You were there to protect us," Holmes said, embellishing the point.

The sheriff had expected the accusation, thankful that it had come up so soon. He needed to get it out of the way, clear the air.

"You were in front," Holmes said. "Suddenly speeding away at almost the exact moment when the tires of our car were shot out."

"There was no need to keep you in view," the sheriff said. "You were going in the same direction. You knew the way. You were coming in for paperwork. I wasn't taking you in." He gathered his resources, pulling together his energy for the blast of indignation that he had planned. Was it the right moment?

"And then to suggest it might not be them," Jeremiah snarled. "Just whose side are you on?"

Now, he thought.

"The law." He spat out the words, feeling the flickering flame of righteous anger charge out of his mouth and nose as if he were a dragon. When the point was made, he deliberately calmed.

"I'm not saying it wasn't them." He lowered his voice. "Hell, even you said release O'Hara. I did. And I'll admit he and the others are logical suspects."

Futile smoke-blowing, he knew, curling into unlikely crevices. He was deliberately dropping red herrings. How they hated not to control people and situations. Taking comfort in that, he pressed on.

"Anyway, all the roads out of the county are covered. No sign of that van."

"And the Forman woman? And Harrigan?"

"Checked out of the motel I put them in."

"Yes. We know," Holmes said. Had the sheriff expected them to roll over dead? It annoyed him to know that they were taking countermeasures, doing their own detective work.

"Maybe they've gone back east," the sheriff said. "He made arrangements to ship his wife's body back to New York."

"Yes. We know that, too."

The sheriff was no longer able to disguise his irritation.

"Busy little beavers," he sneered.

"He's around here and you know it," Jeremiah snapped. It was a carefully calculated surprise attack, complete with pointed finger. His frustration was fully revealed now. Play it easy, the sheriff begged himself, feeling the sour backwash begin in his throat. To gain time, he picked up his coffee mug and sipped the tepid liquid. He had not laced it with booze. He needed every ounce of alertness.

"I could also put out an all points to other jurisdictions," he said with a slow West Virginia drawl. It was time for slow talk now, hillbilly blarney. Out here, it had always been a worthy and effective shield. For vote getting, he had carefully masked it, avoiding the caricature, like keeping his belly flat with hard exercise.

Holmes uncrossed his legs and Jeremiah's head pivoted as his eyes searched the nooks and crannies of his office.

"You know that won't do," Holmes said.

Resisting the use of a pointed finger, Jeremiah said with lowered voice: "No big-city publicity."

So they were scared, too, the sheriff decided, swallowing away the sourness. He knew they hadn't yet checked with higher authority. The thought triggered an inner chuckle. An image emerged of Father Glory himself golfing with toadying disciples on the private course on his North Carolina estate. He wondered how deeply the machinery of this religious scam could be shaken by his plan. Deprogram and get those two deadheads to confess. A long shot, he admitted, but worth the effort. For the first time in years, he felt again the power of his office, the sweet authority of the badge.

"I'll find them. Don't worry," he said, with what he hoped would be indisputable conviction. Not once, he noted, had they mentioned the real issue.

"You'd better," Jeremiah said.

"Why so concerned?" he asked innocently. "They're not parents. You could sue their ass. No jury would be sympathetic."

Holmes and Jeremiah exchanged glances, suggesting the sheriff's dubious credibility. He knew that they could sue only if the deprogramming failed.

"We have nothing to hide," Jeremiah said, dismissing the unvoiced issue. Holmes made a steeple with his fingers, a ruse of contemplation, nodding as a signal for Jeremiah to continue. "They can be made to lie."

The sheriff snickered. So they were already drawing up a defense. Yet, even if the deprogramming opened up a different explanation for Charlotte's drowning, it didn't mean prosecution. He might cook up a perjury case. Or it could be murder. What he wanted, more than anything, was truth. Truth! The idea of it fired him up. A man had his dignity to protect.

Even a successful deprogramming did not assure a permanent breakthrough. Without sympathetic backup, like parents, spouses, siblings or friends who cared, Amos and Mary could drift back, unable to cope with the reality of mental rebirth. He hadn't quite thought that one through. What, if anything, would be done with Amos and Mary once they had reemerged and told the truth? The excitement of his original idea, complete with the reprise of heroic music in his brain, was fading quickly.

"Just find them as fast as possible," Jeremiah continued. "Before ..." He paused, letting the threat hang in the air. The fanged possibility bit deeper this time, along with another nagging foreboding that drifted in the back of the sheriff's mind. Something said or left out. An ominous silence. He searched for it in the chaos of his thoughts.

"We want no trouble out of this," Holmes said from behind his steeple.

"I told you, I'll find them." The sheriff hesitated, wetting dry lips with his tongue's tip. He'd have to go get them in 36 hours. More time and there was no holding back the Glories and their various snoops. The cold grip of fear squeezed his heart, forcing it to pound like a bass drum.

"You realize that they want to make something out of the accident," Holmes said, referring, at last, to the main issue, avoiding the word "drowning."

The articulation of the obvious confused the sheriff. Perhaps they wished to deliberately show him their legal hand, as if they were prepared to shoot down any deviation from the original explanation. He ignored that aspect. No sense getting ahead of events.

"Sometimes," he said, to deflect the path the conversation was taking, "you should let some of these people go if there's going to be trouble." Instantly, he knew it was a mistake. A flush rose along the sides of Jeremiah's neck.

"How many times do I have to say it?" He looked at Holmes who folded his steeple and shook his head.

"They are not under any duress," the lawyer said.

"No lectures," the sheriff shot back, surprised at his vehemence. "Not now." It was not only the irritation of their pressure that moved his anger, it was their perpetual denial of their brainwashing scam.

"With that attitude, how can he be objective?" Jeremiah asked, throwing the line to Holmes.

"I don't know," Holmes said.

"Maybe we should read him the Constitution. In particular, the First Amendment."

"He doesn't want lectures."

The sheriff waited for the little byplay to simmer down. They were toying with him now, playing intimidation games. He did not react, wanting them to think they were roasting him.

"We won't settle for anything short of returning our people to us," Jeremiah said sharply. He stood up. "Intact."

"I'm no miracle maker," the sheriff protested.

"Then become one," Jeremiah said, his dammed-up anger showing signs of spilling over. Holding himself back made him rigid, and he had the look of cold marble. He had them scared, the sheriff thought. There was, he supposed, a little victory in that. And he had successfully resisted their intimidation ... for the moment.

Again the elusive idea floated in his mind. What had they avoided saying?

"I can't guarantee nothin'."

"Neither can we," Jeremiah said, with an ominous emphasis on the "we."

Like a dark floating cloud pregnant with storm, he watched them recede from his office. He dipped his hand into a bottom drawer and drew out a half-full bottle of Jack Daniels, pouring a stiff drink into his now cool coffee, swallowing it in large gulps. Swiveling back, he turned to face the window, observing the lawyer and Jeremiah stride purposefully to their car in the dusky fading light. Partners in evil. The killer and his mouthpiece. The odd image disturbed him and he turned away.

Maybe he'd better call the whole thing off. Still, what nagged at him could not be netted by his conscious mind. Concentrating, he flushed through the tunnels of memory, confronting only blackness.

15

O'Hara, pale and ghostly in the dappled moonlight, leaned against a tree, looking like some twisted aberrant outcropping. Near a fringe of evergreens at the perimeter of the cabin, the sheriff parked his car on a hard dirt rectangle cluttered with rusting debris of another era. There were lots of neglected cabins in this part of the country, used more frequently back in the '60s, when living off the land and drifting was fashionable among the hippies and flower children.

Seeing O'Hara waiting, the sheriff moved toward him. At close range, O'Hara's eyes seemed hidden in dark shadows.

"Anything?"

"The man will blow out first," O'Hara said. "Maybe tonight."

"And the woman?"

"A hard case," O'Hara shrugged. "She's in it real tight. I need more time."

"They're leaning on me."

"If we break them and it's all lies, they'll stop leaning," O'Hara said, his words harsh and hurried.

"And if they aren't lies?"

"Heavenly deception, remember? They're programmed to lie."

"Hope you're right, O'Hara. It's my ass if you're not."

The sheriff was sorry he had revealed the cutting edge of his panic. In the dark, under the pale, mysterious moon, he felt his courage waning.

"I'd bet my life on it," O'Hara said.

"That's a big bet. How can you be so sure?"

"Hell, not long ago, you were more sure than me."

In the pause that followed, he felt O'Hara's inspection and the discomfort of his own vulnerability. Fear had undermined his certainty.

"If you want, I can stop now," O'Hara said. "It's a freebie anyway. I can pull out."

The sheriff avoided a response, shifting his weight. He was in it now and at least four people knew it, four strangers. He had never before given his trust to strangers. Any one of them could turn him in for collusion, a formidable aspect of corruption. He had abetted a kidnapping. Exposed, he could not possibly avoid the consequences.

"It's important. The truth is always important," O'Hara said, as if to bolster him. Above all, he knew O'Hara was right.

"It could have been just a suicide," the sheriff said.

"Just?"

"I didn't mean it like that."

"Or murder."

The sheriff sighed. He had turned over all the possibilities in his mind. Secretly, he hoped it was murder. He could do something with murder.

"And if you crack them? What about after?"

O'Hara scratched his wispy beard in contemplation, another sign that this thing between them had not been thought out as carefully as the sheriff would have liked.

"What about protective custody?" O'Hara suggested.

"Maybe," he agreed. It was always a possibility, but he'd have to convince some judge it was absolutely necessary. All he wanted was a weapon against them, something to use if necessary, something to protect his sense of self. In a pinch, his integrity. "But if I can't?"

"There are rehabilitation places. The problem is that if the Glories want them, they'll go get them. They know the places. Depends on the stakes."

"They'll have to testify. They can't be hidden forever."

"After they come back to reality, they may not want to be involved at all. They may want to forget the whole thing. Live with it."

There was another possibility that had gone unconsidered.

"The point is that they'll be free to act on their own conscience. But their freedom will be fragile. They'll be mad as hell about what happened to them. Some run from the horror. Others try to get even."

"Like you?"

"They pissed away ten years of my life. One lost decade deserves another." He laughed, a short, self-mocking, joyless trill. The sheriff shivered. The idea still spooked him. He had heard the explanations a thousand times. Still, his mind did not fully grasp it, and he felt ashamed for his cowardly willingness to surrender to their power. It was that shame that goaded him now. Their practices needed to be exposed. Maybe then the laws could be revised. Whatever happened inside the human brain, the idea of mind control was wrong, a crime against people. There needed to be a law.

"I said 48 hours," the sheriff said. "I'll keep my word."

"I never questioned that."

It soothed him to know that his word still counted.

"And the others? Harrigan and the woman?"

He heard O'Hara suck in his breath; a hint of doubt passed between them.

"He's still madder than hell. And she's not totally convinced," O'Hara said, after a pause. The sheriff did not like the hesitation.

"She wasn't before," the sheriff said. "I worry about your trusting her." A cloud floated by the face of the moon. O'Hara's features vanished.

"I don't. But once people confront the reality they understand." It was O'Hara who had wanted the Forman woman to accompany them. "Call it a challenge. Her kind is the real enemy, the compassionate liberal-minded do-gooder. Without converting them, we lose." The sheriff was not convinced, but he had consented. He hated the type. Too naive. Evil had a way of winning against their kind.

The sheriff's panic began again. Perhaps it was the sudden blackness. A wind rose, shaking the pine needles, creaking branches. A chill swept through his body.

"What was that?" he whispered. They were silent for a few moments, listening to the unfamiliar sounds of the forest. He had imagined footsteps, sensed human movement.

"Hear anything?" the sheriff asked, calmed by the buzz of a jet in the distance.

"Just the sound of paranoia," O'Hara said, deliberately lightening the mood. The sheriff felt the weight of O'Hara's hand on his shoulders. He recoiled.

"You are jumpy."

"I'm on the line, O'Hara."

"We all are." The weight of his hand increased. "It'll help to believe that you're on the right side, that you're making a statement for mankind." He seemed mocking, sarcastic, faintly ridiculous.

"You sound like a preacher."

"Maybe I am. I proselytize for a free mind these days."

The sheriff felt the weight of the man's hand lift. He was jumpy for good reason. He had a great deal to lose. He looked at his watch and read the radial dial.

"Twenty-four hours more. That's all I can give you."

"I know I'll have the man by then."

"That's not enough."

The cloud passed and suddenly he found himself peering into O'Hara's suddenly revealed agate eyes, reflecting the moon's light, recalling the old nightmare.

"If you can't break her by then, set her and the boy loose, and fade away. Take Harrigan, Forman and the black man and get the fuck out of my county. I'll see that Harrigan's kid gets back safely. Gladys has really bonded with the boy. She'll take good care of him until Harrigan can take him again."

He was picturing a map in his mind. "After you all clear out, I'll send my men here." He paused, going over private consequences, knowing it would be better for them to do this now, to release the two Glories and disappear. But he checkmated the thought, then remembered the nagging pull of silence, the omission.

"You had better be gone before they get here."

"That won't satisfy them ..."

O'Hara said more, but his words swirled away, like fog clearing. He remembered suddenly what had been unsaid.

Harrigan's child! Holmes knew that Harrigan had gone back to get him.

An ominous idea lingered briefly, then floated away. Paranoia, he decided. There were limits. Weren't there?

16

Naomi heard Roy's heavy tread creaking on the old floorboards, then the clatter of a pot on the stove. Roy was preparing their captives' meal, a mass of gruel, oatmeal. Barney was in with Amos. They had worked on him all day and he was clearly exhausted.

In the time she was with Amos, between their onslaughts, he seemed like a bird with broken wings, disoriented, exhausted, shouting incoherently as if in a hallucination, repeating bits and pieces of biblical phrases. He had banged impotently against the walls, had pissed in his pants, lying in them, refusing to take them off.

There was no question that Amos was shedding layers of resistance. It was as if they had mounted some private holocaust on one man and were leading him into the showers of poison gas. Never once had he looked at her. Perhaps it was his sense of shame or confusion as his mind tried to burrow deeper into a hole, all exits closing around him. Not like the woman.

When finally she was relieved by Roy, she went back into the main room and lay on the couch, listening and waiting. Barney was in with Mary, keeping her awake, savoring his role in the mental torture of his former sister-in-law.

Naomi had tried to talk with him, but the distance between them had widened. Besides, he had his notebook, his confidante. The more he wrote, the more he seemed to slip away, lost in a brooding silence. He frightened her now, and she wondered if he could be trusted alone with Charlotte's sister.

Then it was O'Hara's turn again. He motioned for Naomi to join him in Mary's room. Witnessing again. They seemed determined to make her a believer in their methods. She followed reluctantly. When she observed the process, it made her angry. She was revolted by it. She came into the room, sitting on the floor, her back to a wall. O'Hara sat on a stool in front of the mattress. Mary sat cross-legged, staring into space. O'Hara's strategy was, at first, simply to ignore her, looking away.

Suddenly he attacked and Naomi was instantly alert. She dared not voice any objections as she watched his relentlessly cruel verbal onslaught, questioning, probing, offering nonstop answers to his own questions, arguing a kind of theology of the absurd. It went on for two hours, but O'Hara could not seem to penetrate Mary's defenses. Then he stopped abruptly and they left the room. Naomi was appalled but said nothing. In fact, she was proud of Mary for resisting.

"He's cooking," Roy said when he had come out of Amos' room for the third time that day. "He'll break soon," he muttered, standing over her, holding the steaming gruel on a tray. "He's exhausted and disoriented," he added, showing no emotion.

Later, she had O'Hara had gone back into the room where they held Mary. Again, she observed the tactic, continuing to root for the woman.

The procedure seemed to follow a pattern of relentless rebuttal with O'Hara trying to force a response. Come on: Engage me, he seemed to be shouting. The woman remained stubbornly uninvolved. "I need more time," O'Hara had cried. "More time." Watching him at his obscene work was devastating. But she hung in, determined to keep her promise to Mary, to find her a way out.

The procedure began with a condemnation of Father Glory's lifestyle, his mansion, his private yachts, his reputed wealth. O'Hara showed pictures, read from books which outlined his worldwide business operations, his interlocking corporations, his newspapers, his political fronts—all outlined in words and documents that seemed authentic. He read passages from the Bible, ridiculed their theology, punched holes in what he said was their misstatements of biblical lore.

And yet, as shocking as the information was, as damning to the Glory Church, its tenets and practices, its dissimulations and disguises, Naomi still had trouble convincing herself that what was happening here was necessary or good. Everyone had rights, even to be fooled. Didn't everyone in a free society have the right to believe in any deity, living, dead or imagined? Wasn't what they were doing here as wrong as what the Glories did, or what other cults engaged in? This was America. Her heart cried out for the two young people undergoing this terrible, deliberate cruelty. She wondered how long she could prevent herself from taking drastic action.

But she held her silence. Perhaps it was her innate sense of fairness, the do-gooder instincts that O'Hara had railed against. So far she had borne witness but had not been convinced. Again they left Mary's room and O'Hara went in with Amos.

When he finally came out of Amos' room, he looked exhausted. His eyes seemed to have sunk into deep, dark hollows. The events of their earlier discussion lingered bitterly in her memory. This O'Hara, Zachariah, was nothing more than a manipulator, more a force of negative energy than a person. A living fixation, an obsession.

Nothing that had happened in the last few days could be understood in the light of any of her previous frames of reference. Even Barney was an enigma. His entire persona had done a flip-flop. He was now more than a stranger, if that was possible, an alien being, as if infected by a cosmic disease. Even the most fleeting memory of their good times together left her with wretched disgust. And over this scrim of gloom, the dead face of Charlotte imposed itself, leaving Naomi shattered and confused.

Yet through the maze of horror and soul-searing revelation, the woman in the other room had truly touched her, recalled the purest blue flame of her compassion. "Save me." The words clanged in her mind, a giant bell whose sound continued to reverberate, chattering her teeth with its vibration. "I must," she promised herself.

At dusk, she seemed to have found the moment and the courage to act. Barney had collapsed over his notebook, lost in the deep sleep of exhaustion. O'Hara had returned to Mary's room. She could hear a marathon of pounding words, screams and protests, mostly O'Hara's. Roy was with Amos.

She crept toward the front door, rising when she found the knob. There was no form to her plan, no calculation. Only escape!

She had to warn others about what was happening here. Somehow, she had to get the word out.

But the sheriff was in it, she warned herself. She would have to find her own way to the Glory camp. The idea horrified her, but she pressed on. She had to find the right course. Alternatives fumbled impotently in her mind. Mother! She wanted to call her mother.

"Just listen, Mother. Stop interrupting."

"Just come home, darling. Be safe."

Come home? All the cruelties she encountered in her job, all the stories and photos of atrocity and carnage, all the political horrors recounted in their data banks, were impotent compared to this. Nothing made sense here, except the immediacy of the violation, what she was witnessing here in this place. No other evil could justify this one. She felt the old politics of her life rumble back staunchly in her mind, the values that she had clung to, sacrificed for. They had been challenged by these events, shaken her surety. Now her confidence was returning. Wrong was wrong. The moral imperative was all. Everything else was secondary. The beast inside of us was still the beast.

She turned the knob of the door to the outside. Turned harder. It was locked. The bastards had locked them in. So much for trust.

"What is it?"

The door's rattle had awakened Barney.

"I just wanted air."

She watched him yawn and stretch, wondering if his tired eyes conveyed suspicion.

"It's awful, Barney," she said in a sharp pleading whisper.

"I know," he shrugged.

"This ..." She hesitated. She had wanted to say worse than that, uncertain how he would take it. She was certain now that his eyes glistened with suspicion. Certainly hate was in them as well.

"Like birth, as O'Hara had put it," he said softly. "Not pretty. Full of pain and mess." The image recalled an earlier guilt, making her cringe. He turned away and opening the notebook, picked up the nub of his pencil and began again.

"Did you write that down?"

"Yes." He nodded, patting the pages. "Not a detail must go unrecorded. This is my record of their infamy. Somebody has to bear witness." His eyes filled with tears. "My bible," he stammered. "I'm Job writing his story. They crushed my life."

"But Job believed in God." Her words sounded ridiculous.

"You think so?" he asked. "Then Job was a liar."

Never had they talked about God. Such concepts were foreign turf, the business of others. Yet God had been invoked. Some day, she would have to think about that, the power of the idea.

"Tough nut." It was O'Hara. He had come out of the girl's room, slamming the door, sliding the planks angrily. "Your fucking sister-in-law's a stone wall."

"Better get in there," he said to Naomi. "Don't let her sleep."

"What about food?"

"No food either."

"But ..." She aborted the protest. No. She didn't want him to lose confidence in her loyalty. Not now.

She went into the room, stifling now, the stink of sweat and stubbornness pervasive. Mary lay naked on the sweat-stained mattress, breathing hard, her face turned to the wall.

"You all right?"

Her body appeared twisted and stiff. At the sound of Naomi's voice, Mary turned to her. Through the glaze of her eyes, Naomi could see the stubborn hate.

"You promised." Her tone was accusing, acid-edged. She did not wait for a response. "He raped me. See." She spread her legs, showing her woman's parts. Naomi turned away. "He made me do unspeakable things, sinful acts. I told you he would."

"No. He couldn't."

But the woman seemed convincing, genuinely abused. Was it possible?

"You'll rot in hell with them," Mary said. "Father Glory is watching, testing us." The woman slid upward on the bed, arching her body against the wall.

"I've resisted. Father Glory will be proud." She fastened her eyes on Naomi. "You must help me."

"I'll find a way."

"No, you won't. You're one of them."

"I'm not."

Mary turned her face to the wall.

"He tells me these terrible lies about Father Glory. Unspeakable lies. Father Glory is a man of love and peace, the new Christ. He has come down to earth to help mankind. Resist the devil. Resist the devil." The incantation began again and continued for a long time. The woman's agony poured out of her, accusing, attacking.

"You are no different from them."

"No. I am different. I believe this is wrong."

"Do you?"

"Yes."

"I haven't done anything to them," Mary said hoarsely, after another long recitation. Naomi watched her, her heart full of pity. Who was this woman? Barney had provided no relevant details, identifying her merely as Charlotte's sister. Her suffering was the only reality to be observed. Had she loved and been loved by parents, by friends, by a man? Had she aspirations? Dreams? Ambitions? Did she make plans? Had they been thwarted? What were her disappointments? Her defeats? Why had she wandered into this life? What had she needed? What was missing in her life? Why had she helped bring Charlotte under the spell of Father Glory? What had passed between the two sisters? What had they suffered together? Without knowing the answers to these questions, why did these men persist in torturing her?

"How did you come to this, to Father Glory?" Naomi asked.

"Life had no meaning before," Mary said softly, sweetly, offering a broad warm smile, so out of character with her condition. "I did awful things. I was garbage. I took drugs. I prostituted my body with men and women. I stole. I cheated anyone who gave me the slightest chance. I spent a year in jail for stealing. I worked in an old people's home and would steal their spending money and jewelry. There were no depths to my degradation. Once I fell in love with a man who made me have relations with animals for other men to watch. I had three abortions ..."

Naomi's heartbeat leaped to her throat.

"Three?"

Mary's eyes had locked into hers again.

"I was not a human being any more. I was possessed by evil. I split my parents' marriage by telling my father lies about my mother and my mother lies about my father." She hesitated and her lips trembled. "I told her . . ." Mary's eyes seemed to glow out of their sockets, great spears of light, probing. "That my father was my lover. She committed suicide. I knew she would. I gave her the means. I bought a gun and gave it to her."

"My God."

"I was the epitome of evil. I had no sense of right or wrong. Satan's child. That was me. Like most of us out there in what people say is the real world. What do you think is out there? Greed. Horror. Striving only for pleasure. Hurting other people. There is only hate and misery outside. I have been saved by Father Glory." Suddenly, she stopped talking, waiting for the words to penetrate, her eyes boring into Naomi's. "I had to save my earth sister. She came away because she knew that her life was shameful. She was having affairs with other men. She was not even certain that Kevin was Barney's child. She hated her life, detested all the horrors around her. Her psyche was diseased. You should have heard her. All Barney ever thought about was money, material things. When he was on a business trip, she would prowl the streets, find men, fog her mind with alcohol. I had to save her from that." Naomi quailed before the alleged confession. "Are you so perfect that you dare to judge us that have found spiritual happiness? Are you so perfect that you can judge me?"

In the silence, Naomi knew that an answer was expected.

"No, I'm not."

"Where is your decency? You're just like them. You have no sense of sharing. No real love. Look around you. Everyone is manipulating everyone else for their own personal gratification, pursuing pleasure, money, material things. Open your eyes. What do you see around you? Poverty. Despair. Smugness. Self-righteousness, sensuality, promiscuity. What is out there is the putrefaction of man's true purpose, which is to love one another. Listen. Observe. See the hypocrisy, the venality, the lies. Don't you want to scream out your protest? Make good happen? Root out the devil in man?"

"Yes. Of course I do." Her retort had come without her thinking, blurting out.

"No, you don't," Mary snapped, burrowing in. "You are in it with them. No better than they. You should have left Charlotte to her happiness. It was you that killed her. You and them. That monster out there. Can't you smell the stench of Satan on them? Not only Barney, but that black devil and the man that calls himself O'Hara. Oh, we have heard a lot about him. Satan's messenger."

Tears streamed out of her eyes, cascading down her cheeks.

"They can do what they like with me. My spirit will live in heaven with Father Glory while theirs and yours will rot in perpetual hell. I believe in love and goodness and the power of God to make things right. What do you believe in? What is your life that has led you to this? I am a woman like you, flesh and blood." She pinched her breasts, leaving fresh pink imprints on her flesh, ignoring the pain. "Father Glory saved me. Father Glory is my master."

Naomi felt herself drowning in a pit of remorse. The woman's anguish had gotten through to her. How could she participate in this, this travesty? She felt a volcano of indignation rise inside of her, bursting through the skein of guilt and fear.

"Was Charlotte's death an accident?"

The woman smiled, shook her head.

"After what I've been saying, how can still ask me that?"

"I need to know."

"Yes. It was an accident."

In shame, Naomi hid her gaze from Mary, standing up, pacing the room now, sensing the militancy and indignation rising within her. Her resolve stiffened. I will fight them, she vowed.

The opening of the door recalled her sense of caution.

"Hang on," she whispered to Mary, stretching out her hand to touch her shoulder. The woman blinked her eyes and nodded her understanding.

"Eats," Roy said cheerfully, coming in with a steaming bowl of oatmeal. He looked at the naked woman, who made no attempt to cover herself, defiant, as if her confession to Naomi had given her additional strength.

"Naughty, naughty," Roy said with a leer.

Naomi could not bear it. She walked out of the room, alert now to her own stealth, determined now to free these people. She would find a way. She must find a way. They had no right to torture these people. No right. The main room was deserted. Listening to the door of Amos' room, she knocked softly.

"Yes." It was Barney's voice. "Where is O'Hara?"

"He went out."

"Out?"

She inspected the room. She heard Roy's voice berating Mary. Bastards, she muttered under her breath, crossing to the door, determined to break it down if it prevented her from leaving. Miraculously, the knob turned. For a moment, she held it partly open, listening. The damp night air was heavy with mist, thick with the scent of pine and earth. Her eyes probed the darkness as she slowly, silently, shut the door, breathing deep, in an effort to still the loud pumping of her heart. She must find help, she told herself.

Stepping softly, she stopped to listen, then moved cautiously forward. She felt the hard dirt path under her feet, halted, listened, waiting for her eyes to focus in the sparse light. Nearby, the metal of the van gleamed and she crouched in case O'Hara was there. Then she hid behind a clump of overgrown shrubs.

Listening, the sounds of the night grew louder. She had expected absolute silence, but her ears picked up unfamiliar sounds, the creak of moving tree limbs, the rustle of pine needles, the hum of the wind. A city girl, she had no sure knowledge of this, only memories of childhood outings, city parks. Yet she felt the exhilaration of freedom, the joy of escape, and with it, the purity of her mission. She was finished with manipulation. Her instincts, she was certain now, had been right from the beginning.

17

Somewhere out there, O'Hara lurked. Naomi moved out of the protection of the shrubs. Crouching, she moved forward. Her eyes picked out the narrow path ahead. Behind her she saw the cabin, outlined in the dim light. It looked peaceful, innocent, another example of false images. She shuddered, then moved forward, step upon cautious step, senses magnified, alert to her pores.

A twig snapped under her foot. She paused, waited for a reaction. When none came, she straightened and began to walk again.

The woman had pleaded for help. Outrage quaked inside of Naomi, prodding her swiftness. Soon she could hear the truly familiar city sounds, the whooshing of tires, of cars moving, a jet plane overhead. The road moved downhill and soon she was running, gasping to fill her lungs.

Suddenly the ground beneath her feet disappeared, and she was hurtling through the air. She felt a sharp, painful impact on her shins, then the hardness of the ground as she lay supine under a great weight.

"Damned bitch."

It was O'Hara's hissing voice, the smell of him enveloping her. She struggled on her belly, feeling her arms pinned to the ground, her legs leaden with his weight. The palm of his hand was pressed against her mouth.

"Don't scream. Don't move."

He slowly released his palm, her throat belched out a brief scream, then the palm clamped down again.

"I said don't."

Struggling until she felt her ribs bursting, she quieted, finally surrendering to his superior strength. When she was still for a few moments, he withdrew his palm, waited to be sure her silence was assured, then slowly got off her, lifting her roughly. Her face felt bruised and she spat dirt.

"You're a pretty sight."

"I want to get out of here," she snapped, finding her voice, which sounded shrill and coarse.

"What will satisfy you? Haven't you caused enough damage?"

"Don't send me on that trip. It won't work. Not again."

"So she got to you finally. I thought she might, but I had hoped you'd keep an open mind, resist her."

"Making her suffer like that ... it's inhuman, immoral. I can't bear it. After all she's been through."

"Oh," he said with sarcasm. "So you know what she's been through?"

"Yes. I know."

"She told you."

"Yes."

"And you bought it?"

"Of course I did. Why would she lie?"

He shook his head and spat on the ground.

"You poor, naive, stupid bitch."

"I'm immune to your name-calling."

"That's a good sign. How come you're not immune to her bullshit?"

"I believed her."

"Of course you did. You're just naive and ignorant of their tactics. Heavenly deception, woman. Lie. Lie. Lie. Any lie is permissible if for the cause, if it fits into Father Glory's master plan, his cynical and misguided so-called theology. Wake up, woman. Don't you get it?"

She refused to be intimidated. Finally, he shrugged and grabbed her upper arm.

"I told you it wouldn't be pretty."

"Hah." She shook him loose and laughed. "There's an understatement."

He stubbed a toe into the hard ground.

"Did she say I raped her?"

Naomi hesitated, but did not answer.

"And you believed it?" he asked, his tone gentle.

"She . . . I can't say . . ."

"She told you how she prostituted herself, had relations with her father, caused her mother to commit suicide. Had sex with animals for the gratification of other men. All that garbage. On and on. Right?"

"None of your business," Naomi said belligerently. "It was for my ears only."

"Your ears only. That's a lie. I taught them lies like that. She's been programmed to regurgitate these lies, make them sound like truth."

"I don't believe you."

"Now she wants you to save her, right, rescue her from us, Satan's messengers. And you, being a naive fool, have fallen for it. Here you are. Off to the rescue. Off to call in the Glory cavalry. How dumb can you get. "

She felt a growing hysteria begin inside of her. Her chest ached and she swallowed hard, unable to speak.

"Stop taking these people at face value. You don't take me at face value. Why them?"

"She's suffering," Naomi whimpered, "That's face value enough."

He shook his head in obvious exasperation.

"And you believe her. Good God. I'll bet you even believe her about what happened to her sister."

She hesitated.

"Why should I doubt her?" she said, trying to hold fast to her convictions. Hadn't she observed the woman's suffering with her own eyes?

"And you think all this is wrong, a mean exercise. Inhuman. Immoral."

"Yes. Yes, I do."

"And last night. Our discussion."

She shrugged, then nodded tentatively.

"You were deprogramming me. Making me believe you."

Coming forward, he held her shoulders. His face was no more than an inch or two from hers, lost in vapors. Humiliation gnawed at her. The smell of his sweat-soaked manliness repelled her.

"All right," he said, after a long pause, grabbing her arm, dragging her toward the cabin. "You can do and say what you like, but it will have to wait. I can't let you go. I'd really like to get you out of my sight. But I can't."

He thrust her roughly through the cabin door and she fell against the table, rattling oily dishes. A coffee mug fell to the floor and shattered.

He slid open the planks that held Mary's door. With the heel of his fist, he banged on it, shaking the house. Roy, neck muscles tensed, came out.

"What the hell ..."

He sized up the situation quickly, his eyes roving toward the open door. Quick as a cat, he sprang forward and locked it from the inside. Reading O'Hara's eyes, he slid open the planks that barred Amos' room.

"What is it?" Barney said, poking his head out.

"Is he on the verge?" O'Hara asked. Barney shook his head.

"Go get him, Roy. Ready or not. Sweat him till he breaks. This lady Judas here won't quit." Roy sprang forward and went into Amos' room. O'Hara turned to Barney.

"Keep them both barred." Barney nodded.

Angrily, O'Hara dragged Naomi into the girl's room and threw her roughly to the floor, where she lay inert, watching in horror. Mary was flattened against the wall, rearing, like a trapped animal, her fingers locked like claws.

"What did she tell you?"

With his foot, he prodded Naomi's ribcage.

"Don't," Mary said, scowling.

"What did she tell you?" O'Hara said again.

"You know."

"That I raped her."

"You did," Mary screamed.

"What else?"

"About her life. What she went through."

"Drugs. Prostitution. Right? That her life was garbage. That Father Glory cleansed her. Her incest with her father, her mother's suicide. Her jail terms. All that degradation. Until she found the sweet light of Father Glory." The words spewed out of him. "That she was Satan's child until she was rescued by Father Glory."

Naomi nodded.

"That there was no sense of sharing, no real love. Everyone manipulating everyone else for personal gratification." He shook his head. "Open your eyes. What do you see? Poverty? Despair? Smugness? Self-satisfaction ..."

"Stop it," Naomi said.

"Can't you see it, woman?" He pleaded. "Programmed. I know because I used to put it there. I taught this tactic."

He turned away and moved closer to Mary, still reared against the wall.

"You're not going to the spirit world. The Heavenly Father is angry with you."

"He's not," Mary shouted.

"Look at her. You sent her out to save you. If the Heavenly Father cared, he would have let her pass. He hasn't the power you thought he had."

"He does."

"He lies to you. He always lied to you."

"No."

She shook her head from side to side.

"All he wants is money, more and more money."

"No. No. No. No."

"He makes you lie and cheat and steal. And do worse things."

"He does not."

"The Heavenly Father has cut you loose. He is angry with you. You were not true to him. You failed him. That's why she's here with us. He did not have the power to let her pass."

"It is all lies."

"And your mother didn't commit suicide. You know that, Susan."

"I'm not Susan."

"She died of cancer. And your father was killed in an automobile crash with you at the wheel."

"That's not true."

He took out a clipping from his pocket, and read from it.

"'Stuart killed in automobile crash. Mr. Samuel Stuart of Bedford was killed today when the car in which he was riding hit a telephone pole.'" He looked at Naomi. "From Barney."

"All lies. Lies. You know that's not true."

"There was no crash?"

Naomi felt the woman's eyes, pleading now, focusing on her with savage alertness.

"And the abortions?" Naomi blurted.

"Those. That was my idea," O'Hara said. "I put that frosting on the cake."

"It's true," Mary shouted. "How could you know?"

"The Heavenly Father hates you, Susan. That's why you're here. He wants you banished from him. Father Glory wants you banished."

"Resist the devil. Resist the devil. Resist the devil."

The mantra began again, in a rising crescendo. She stood up on the mattress. Facing the wall, she flattened her body against it, repeating the words.

"How did Charlotte really die, Susan?"

The litany continued.

"Father Glory hates you. Hates you. Hates you."

His eyes bugged out as his voice rose. He ground a fist into his thigh, watched her and shook his head.

"Locked in tight as a drum," he whispered, then shouting: "Dammit, Susan. I'm trying to set you free." He turned toward Naomi. "People like you ..." But he left the sentence unfinished.

"I'd do the same thing. Just like her," Naomi said.

Without comment, he helped her to her feet. He knocked on the door. Barney slid open the planks and they came out into the other room. Then they went into the room where they kept Amos.

Roy looked up from a squatting position near the bed, his face glistening in the raw light. The young man sat stiffly in the center of the mattress, Indian style, thin, gaunt, looking like an Eastern ascetic. He had wrapped his arms around himself as if he were literally holding himself together. His eyes were closed.

"Been like that for a while," Roy said. "I nearly had him. He was really starting to break." He shrugged.

"I'm never going to forget this," Naomi said. "Never."

Ignoring her, O'Hara turned to the young man. Falling to his knees, he put his face close to the boy's ear. Naomi leaned against the far wall. Her knees felt weak and her head spun. Her flesh felt alternately icy and feverish.

"It's all right," O'Hara said gently to the young man. He gripped his shoulder. "Amos."

Amos opened his eyes, cautiously at first, then wider. They were moist, less glazed than she had seen them earlier, showing a feeble flicker of alertness. O'Hara turned away from him and nodded at Roy, putting a finger to his lips.

"Everything is fine now," O'Hara said, turning again to Amos. "We know. Mary told us the truth about the girl."

Amos closed his eyes again and shook his head from side to side, as if trying to escape from himself. O'Hara pressed his attack.

"The Heavenly Father is very pleased with you. You have done your duty."

Tiny sweat drops burst out on Amos' forehead. His head rolled back, his Adam's apple strained against the taut skin of his throat.

"The Heavenly Father is very proud of you. But he is very upset with Mary for what she had told. You've resisted Satan very well, Amos."

The young man writhed, as if another person was struggling inside of him. Naomi was frightened, too mesmerized now to contemplate her indignation. O'Hara glanced toward her, flashing a thin, sardonic smile.

"Mary's sister was gripped by Satan. You and Mary had to do it. She was going to run to them, hurt all your brothers and sisters. Jeremiah told you how important it was. Didn't he?"

Amos nodded.

"Bastard." Barney croaked. Roy gripped him quickly, putting a heavy arm around his neck. Barney strained for a moment, shuddered, then quieted.

"She had to die, didn't she, Amos?"

He nodded.

"And you and Mary had to do it because it was important to the Heavenly Father, wasn't it?"

Amos nodded vigorously.

"But you knew she had gone to the spirit world and you had done a good thing?"

Again he nodded, and O'Hara continued to stroke his shoulder. He had stopped writhing. An odd process of unstiffening began, as if his bones and muscle had suddenly turned to jelly.

The room seemed to Naomi to be floating in space, encased in a bubble. Inside, it was airless. Nothing stirred. She felt helpless and inert, protesting as in a dream. They've made him say that, forced him. She wanted to cry out, but when the scream came, it was not hers. Like the cry of an animal caught in a trap, Amos' shattering scream speared out of the vacuum of his consciousness. Like a flashing knife, it sliced into the room. She felt the sharp sting of some unfamiliar pain.

The young man clung to O'Hara, the lost son to the searching father, his body wracked with sobs. An exorcism. It was the first idea that came to her, although she was uncertain as to what had been exorcised. Barney had collapsed as well into the thick brawny arms of Roy, who held him upright, like a puppet whose strings had been cut, helpless.

"It's all right, Jack,"

"They ripped you off, Jack. I'm sorry."

After a while, the young man calmed. Lifting his head, he showed them a tear-stained face, nose running snot.

"Just breathe deep," O'Hara said. "You're free now. That's the important thing. You're safe now."

Safe, she sneered. Suddenly, the lifeless puppet that was Barney sprang to life, twisting out of Roy's grasp, lunging for Amos. Before he could reach him, Roy stopped him with a hard karate chop to his lower back. Barney, gasping, fell to his knees.

"Not his fault," O'Hara said, standing up.

"Pay dirt," Roy mumbled. "He's out."

He looked at Barney, still in pain, gasping for air.

"Sorry, man. It won't do no good." Reaching out, Roy helped Barney to his feet.

"Can't blame him," O'Hara said.

"Who then?" Barney whispered.

"That's the point. Who?" He looked at Naomi.

"Still not convinced?"

"He'd say anything," she shot back. She turned toward the young man, drained, weak with exhaustion and fright. "Look at him."

Without a word, O'Hara grasped her arm and led her back to Mary's room. Roy and Jack followed behind them. Barney recovered somewhat, stayed in the main room. Surreal, Naomi thought, trying to fix it in her mind, preparing it for recall. Surely, she would have to tell this. She tried to imagine how differently she and Barney would see these events.

18

Mary's head was still turned toward the wall, but the noise of their coming stirred her and she began again. "Resist the devil. Resist the devil."

O'Hara thrust the young man in front of her. He dropped to his knees on the mattress, his eyes staring at the girl, who, in the brief turn, had seen his face. Grabbing Mary by the hair, O'Hara forced her down to her knees, then braced her shoulders with his thighs. In this position, she could only avoid confronting the young man by closing her eyes, which she did.

Roy had come forward, kneeling near the boy, locking his body in a wrestler's embracing hold. Watching the scene, Naomi's thoughts tumbled in confusion. What she was witnessing impinged on her vision of reality. Yet back in some deep recess of her mind, she felt a spark of fascination. It magnetized her, held her in suspenseful anticipation. At the same time, it appalled her.

Barney stood mute leaving against the wall of the room. He said nothing, his eyes narrowing as he watched the scene unfold. She could tell that something was brewing in his mind, something that was sure to result in something awful.

The young man began to melt again, tears rolled down his cheeks. Strained sobs burst out of him.

"Tell her, Jack," O'Hara said, holding the girl's hair as if he were reining a recalcitrant horse, riding her. The girl's head strained against his grip.

The young man was too choked with emotion to speak.

"Stop this," Naomi begged, but it sounded more as a helpless bleat than a firm command. She could not find the will to act.

"You helped drown your own sister. It's straight to hell for you now. Straight to the burning pits. Tell her, Jack. She was there beside you, drowning the life out of her own sister. Before God, you have shamed yourself. Thou shalt not kill. Thou shalt not kill." He repeated the words through clenched teeth.

Jack looked up suddenly, calm and clear-eyed. Roy stroked his shoulder.

"It's okay, man. It wasn't your fault."

"It was her," he said, oddly rational, considering his state. "She told me it was all right. She told me Jeremiah said it was all right."

Mary slowly opened her eyes, directing them at the young man. Her gaze was burning, powerful, as if her entire being was concentrating its heat. Naomi saw the power of it, the force of faith, cosmic and mysterious, reaching out for the young man again. Quickly, Roy's big paw shut out the gaze, taking the full wad of spit that ejaculated out of Mary's mouth.

"Satan," she croaked. Then suddenly, belying her helplessness, she cried out in an ear-splitting screeching yell, "Do not forsake me, Father."

"Stop it," Naomi screamed, as if in counterpoint. "Enough of this."

Still, O'Hara did not release Mary, pulling tightly on her hair, bending her head further back, as incoherent sounds gurgled in her throat.

"You killed her," he hissed. "You know you killed her. You committed the worst sin of all. You killed your own sister, blood of your parents."

Mary clamped her eyes shut, beginning her incantation again. "Resist the devil. Resist the devil."

"Damn," O'Hara said gruffly, releasing Mary, who quickly moved up against the wall again, her face turned from them, repeating the words. Naomi started toward her, but O'Hara restrained her, dragging her from the room, despite her resistance. Barney followed, lost in his own thoughts.

"You've got to be punished for this," Naomi said.

"Yeah. Maybe Father Glory will do that."

"I'm glad she's resisting you. I'm proud of her."

O'Hara turned away, his expression of exasperation clear. She reveled in his frustration.

Jack sat stiffly on the couch, his head in his hands, as if the raw brutality of this reality was too much to bear. O'Hara paced the room nervously. Barney leaned against the wall, impassive, inert.

Naomi's eyes drifted to the outside door. "Locked," Roy said, noting her interest. Then he put his arm around the forlorn Jack.

"It's okay, man," he said. "Just like coming out of a deep sleep."

"I can't believe it," Jack mumbled. "The things I did. And that girl." He shuddered.

"You didn't know what you were doing. You're not responsible."

Naomi looked at him, confused yet still unconvinced. Roy's solicitousness bothered her as well, so out of character with his previous indifference and brutality. He must have sensed her questioning.

"This kid needs a lot of loving care now. Like coming out of the womb. He's been on a real heavy trip."

"I can't believe he did that ... that awful thing," she mumbled.

She felt herself wavering, unable to comprehend, feeling a compulsion to know, to be certain. Had they put that idea into his head? She thought of Mary, so cruelly brutalized. The horror of it transcended revulsion.

"Leave it be," Roy said to her gently. "No point now." He squeezed the young man affectionately. "You hungry now, man?"

Jack looked up, showing the full extent of his remorse. He shook his head.

"Gotta eat, man. Gotta keep your strength up."

Slapping his thighs, Roy got up and went into the kitchen, clattering pans. Ignoring him, she continued to look at the young man. She sat beside him on the couch.

"Is it true?" she asked. "It's important that I know. I don't understand any of this." When he didn't answer, she spoke again: "Is it true?"

Roy, watching her shrugged and went about the business of cooking.

Jack nodded his head in the affirmative, then put his hands over his face, as if in shame.

"But why?"

"I told you," Roy shouted from the kitchen. "Leave him be on that. Talk to him about other things." Barney looked up from his notebook. So he had taken refuge in that, she thought, with odd contempt.

"He understands now," O'Hara said. He had been sitting at the table, brooding. "The problem is getting people to realize it." There was no doubt whom he meant.

"You'll be okay, kid. You got relatives. Parents. We've got to get you home. Where is it?"

"Steubenville, Ohio."

His hands went up to his face again. "How terrible I've been. I never went to Dad's funeral. I gave them all the money he left me. Mom said she would never speak to me again."

"She will," O'Hara said. "They all do. When we get to a phone, I'll call. Do you remember the number?"

Removing his hands again, the young man showed the struggle with his memory.

"That's okay, Jack," O'Hara said. "I know your real name. I'll find it."

He turned to Naomi.

"Hell, don't believe what you've seen and heard? Rationalize it."

She did not respond, feeling her uncertainty.

"And the other . . . ?" Roy asked from the kitchen.

"A problem. We need more time is all." O'Hara looked at his watch. "Damn. No sense kidding myself. She needs a good week."

"A week?"

"They've got her good." He got up from the chair and began to pace the room, running his fingers through his hair. Barney now sat down at the table, put his notebook before him and began to write.

"Without her confirmation," O'Hara said, "we're between the devil and the deep blue sea." The cliché angered her, but she kept it hidden, thinking of Mary and her promise. Impossible to keep now. And Barney. He was lost in himself, still investing his passion in the long monologue of his notebook. She felt beyond fatigue, her mind stalled.

Roy opened the shutters. Faint daylight filtered through the screens. A sunless morning was creeping in. He doused the lights, bathing their faces in a floury whiteness. Then he brought in piles of griddle cakes, grits and bacon, placing steaming plates on the wooden table.

Jack had stretched out on the couch, asleep in the fetal position. Roy lifted him and carried him into the room where he had been.

"Poor bastard. He'll sleep for weeks now," O'Hara said. "He's got a new nightmare to face. Reality." He sat down at the table. Roy sat down beside him. Naomi could not bring herself to join them. Barney was busy with his notebook, lost in himself.

"Won't hurt to eat," O'Hara said to her with a look of rebuke.

"Not until she does," Naomi said, gesturing toward the door where Mary was kept. No sound penetrated now.

"Never learn," O'Hara muttered, pouring gobs of syrup over the griddle cakes, cutting into them angrily with his fork, stuffing his mouth.

What she had witnessed, she realized, had only strengthened her alliance with the girl, despite the boy's confession. She stood up.

"Can I go in and stay with her?"

"Hell no," O'Hara said with a full mouth. "Next thing you know, we'll have to worry about you."

"Don't worry about me," she snapped. Shaking his head, he pointed a fork at her.

"I won't."

She sat down again.

"We're both being held here against our will."

"You came by choice, remember?"

"They killed Charlotte, Nay." It was Barney's voice, fluttering into her consciousness.

"I'm not ready to accept that," she said prissily. She had witnessed the violence of these men. Be suspicious always of people who claim doing good by being bad. The old caveat. She felt her strength returning, the recent guilt diluted. Her motives had been honest, she assured herself. If Barney hadn't come for his wife,

Charlotte would still be alive. All she did was exercise an act of conscience.

O'Hara, eyes narrowed, watched her and she was certain he read her thoughts clearly.

"You think we put the thought there ... in Jack's mind?"

"I think it's possible," she said, cautioning herself.

Roy shook his head as he wiped his plate clean with a shred of griddle cake.

"All come out in the wash anyhow," he said, lifting the dripping shred. "Don't waste your breath."

It was true the mind could be reshaped, she conceded, but the moral spirit was inviolate. Without that, the integrity of self, humanity dies. They were highfalutin concepts, but she held to them with tenacious purpose. To change an idea, however hateful or illogical, one could never resort to kidnapping, imprisonment, isolation, coercion. Not physical force. That was patently wrong.

What she had seen in the Glory camp were people captured by an idea, but she had seen no barbed wire, no guns, no cages, none of the visible the trappings of real oppression, the kind she fought against in other countries. The loftiness of her ideas bolstered her resolve. These were angry men, failed, frustrated men, seared by the terrible flame of defeat. They had not had their way in life. Now others must suffer for it. Oppression was endemic in this place. Locks were everywhere, keys in the hands of the masters.

O'Hara slapped his thighs and stood up.

"Back to the drawing board," he said. "But I don't think I can break her." He looked at his watch. "We've got till noon."

"And that will end it?" Barney stood up, fists clenched, menacing.

"I'm doing my best. I'm not a magician."

"I thought that was your claim," Naomi interjected.

"We still got the other one," Roy said.

"But you said yourself it's not enough," Barney snapped. "Why can't we get out of here? Go someplace else. Take more time."

"We could be buying trouble for the rest of our lives," O'Hara said. For the first time, Naomi detected a faltering confidence.

"I've already bought that concept," Barney said, glaring at them.

"It's not going to bring her back," O'Hara said, with surprising gentleness. His eyes were heavy with fatigue.

"But him ..." His head tilted toward the room in which Jack was sleeping. "He's confessed."

In the moment of tense silence, another sound intruded. A motor coughing in the distance. Roy jumped toward the door, fishing for his key, while O'Hara quickly spun the combination lock on the broom closet where they kept the guns, opening it, removing the submachine guns. He threw one to Barney.

"You stay," he commanded Naomi holding her arm as O'Hara and Roy rushed out the door.

"Sorry, Nay," Barney muttered. She remained silent.

Through the window grating, she saw the two men running, crouching, using the trees that edged the road as cover. Barney watched them from another window. A car's motor angrily sputtered and whined, pushing a vehicle up the sloping washboard road.

In the harsh gray light, the men seemed like bad actors in a melodrama, striking poses for some impending staged bloodbath, the kind of painless, sanitary killing one saw in western movies. Another game, she thought, feeling no sense of personal danger.

The sheriff's car came into view. She saw the upper part of his torso, fighting the wheel as the car bounced, halting finally in a copse beside the house. The two men revealed themselves now, O'Hara holding his pistol. Roy slung the submachine gun to his shoulder. The sheriff moved out of the car, his face ashen, his features troubled.

The three men talked in hushed whispers, grimacing, kicking the ground like impatient horses. In the way they held themselves, despite their differences in stance and carriage, she observed their tension. At one point in their conversation, O'Hara looked up, squinting toward the house. His companions followed his gaze. Then they moved out of view, angling toward the side of the house.

She forced herself to consider alternatives. The door was not locked. She could run for cover, perhaps lose herself in the thick forest. Then what? She rejected that possibility. Perhaps if the sheriff knew that she was no longer a party to it, they might desist, knowing that she would be a hostile witness. But even that possibility was anathema to her.

She had no desire to hurt these men, certainly not Barney, who had been through more than enough pain. No! She would agree to forget the entire episode, walk away from it, providing they left everything status quo and returned the girl to the camp and, if Amos or Jack, after due reflection, decided upon that course as well, to let him go back freely. Or home to Ohio if he so chose. If that displayed her naiveté, so be it. She would not be a party to this sham of imprisonment and coercion. Barney would hate her, of course, but she had to accept that, as he had to accept Charlotte's death. She would also have to make peace with herself. It was time to act. To vote her conscience with her feet.

Committed, she walked out of the cabin, and headed toward the men beside the house. They looked up, startled, but did not move to meet her. She noted that the faces of the three men seemed troubled and uncertain.

"I've had quite enough ..." she began.

"That's not the issue anymore," O'Hara said. She had expected some form of physical intervention, and was fully prepared for it. It puzzled her when they made no move to approach her.

"Why don't you go back in the house?" the sheriff said. He looked desperately tired. His voice was reasonable, gentle.

"Not until you tell me this is ended."

The men exchanged glances.

"It is," O'Hara said with an air of utter defeat.

"It's the only way," the sheriff said, talking to O'Hara. O'Hara's response had represented a kind of consent.

"I feel bad about him. Jack."

"Can't be helped," the sheriff said.

"It's a bitch," Roy said.

"We're taking them back to the camp. Both of them," the sheriff said.

"Amos ..." She hesitated, not understanding. Nor could she quite make up her mind as to what to call him. "Jack," she said balancing it in her mind.

"There's no way out of this," O'Hara said. "They beat us." He muttered under his breath. "Bastards."

"Why not put it to him?" she heard herself say.

"I'm afraid it's not his choice," the sheriff said. "After, he can do what he likes."

"He's finished," O'Hara said. "They'll have him locked up in less than a day." He kicked his toe into the ground in frustration. "Shit."

She was not sure what was happening. The men started to walk toward the house. At the door, they paused and O'Hara said: "I hate to be the one to tell him."

"My job," the sheriff's said. "Goes with the territory."

"Tell who? What?" she asked. It seemed a game of riddles.

O'Hara turned to her, his eyes blinking in swollen chalky pouches, his cheeks gaunt under a grime of beard and despair. The macho posturing had lost all its power.

"They've taken Harrigan's child," he shouted, showering her with specks of saliva, as if it were a deliberate spray of venom.

"Kevin?" His name sputtered out of her. Her body whirled in a moment of dizziness, as if she had risen quickly. Roy's arms buttressed her, preventing her fall. O'Hara's words rose in a flame of anger.

"What will it take for you people to understand? They're the most vicious corruption of humanity on the face of the earth. Yes, they've taken Kevin and they won't give him back until we give them back those two in there. It's you, self-righteous fools, the good people, the great moral people that make it happen by your ..." He turned away, banging the flat of his hand against the house, repeating the gesture, his own rant of frustration. The sound thumped in her head, like a pulse beat. She looked at the sheriff, who averted his eyes.

"It's ..." she began impotently.

"Kidnapping," O'Hara raged, his hands balled into tight fists, flaying the air. "That's what it is. Ruthless. You and your moral self-righteousness. Like what you think we did to them. An eye for an eye. Who do you think you're dealing with, Little Red Riding Hood? It's the wolf, stupid."

Naomi felt the disintegration of her persona. All her conceptions were suddenly undermined. The sheriff moved ahead toward the door with a purposeful stride.

They crowded into the main room, Naomi following. The sheriff ushered Barney into the kitchen. Roy put his submachine back in the closet.

They waited for the eruption. The sheriff returned to the big room, shaking his head. After a few moments of calm, Barney appeared. He had unslung the submachine gun and was carrying it in ready mode.

"Make way," he said. "Take this seriously. I intend to use it if I have to."

"Now that is stupid," the sheriff said. In the steadiness of the weapon's barrel, there was no mistaking Barney's resolve. He was calm, his eyes alert and clear. Roy took a single step, floorboards creaking. The gun barrel moved perceptibly and Roy stopped, assessing him.

"I know how to use it," Barney said with conviction. "Don't make me."

Roy froze.

"Don't do this," Naomi said, a sob catching in her throat.

Barney looked at her, then shook his head. He looked hard, focused, mean. It was obvious that he was in the grip of a single obsession. Vengeance!

"We'll get him back, Harrigan," O'Hara said. "It's all arranged." He looked toward the sheriff. Rings of sweat had soaked the underarms of his uniform.

"He's at the camp," the sheriff said. "We'll bring the others back and get him. That's all they want. They don't really want the boy. Don't complicate matters."

"There's no need for this, Harrigan," O'Hara said.

She could sense O'Hara's mind thrashing, searching for a solution.

"Haven't you used the boy enough?" He had fastened on guilt, always a potent weapon. It made no dent in Barney's resolve.

"Now here's what I want you to do," Barney said. She could see that his mind was made up, that nothing could sway him. That was a lesson learned years ago, even when his aspirations seemed so ordinary.

"I want the keys to the van."

"You're crazy, man," Roy said.

"It's overkill, son," the sheriff said. "I tell you it's all arranged."

"The keys, please," Barney said, thrusting the gun forward.

"Give it to him, Roy," O'Hara said. Roy reached slowly into his pocket, fishing out the keys, starting to move forward. Then he flung the keys on the floor. They rattled as they hit the wooden boards. Barney was alert to the gesture. He lifted the barrel and let off a brief burst. The men looked at each other. Fear infected the room. He spoke to Naomi.

"Now pick it up, Nay."

"Barney, please."

"Just pick it up, Nay."

Her knees shook as she bent, retrieved the keys, then stood, moving cautiously toward him, the keys held out, two fingers clutching the metal ring as if to avoid some contagion of his flesh. Reaching out, he took it quickly.

"Into that room." He jerked his head toward the room where Jack slept, oblivious to the fate others had concocted for him.

"Look, Harrigan. I know how you feel," O'Hara said. "But whatever you have in mind, think it out. The issue here is your boy, getting him out free and safe. You don't know those people as I do. I've been there. I know them."

He was trying another tack, but she saw that, too, was hopeless.

"In there." Barney waved the gun in the direction of the room where Jack slept.

"It's insanity, son," the sheriff said.

"You'll be hurting all of us, Harrigan," O'Hara said. "Her as well."

"She goes with me," Barney said calmly. The three men moved into the room. She did not protest. It would be futile. She was well aware that no arguments existed outside of Barney's mind, a walled city now. Still, she felt fear but no sense of panic. He moved the planks into place, locking the doors. He held the gun with one hand now, his finger still crooked around the trigger. In his other hand, he held the notebook.

"I need you with me, Nay," he said quietly, signaling with his gun, moving behind her. She felt words form, but they did not come. Outside, the air was still, frozen in the flat grayness of the overcast. He grasped her upper arm, not roughly, nudging her forward, opening the driver's side of the van.

Climbing upward, she felt the pressure of his help, more as a gentlemanly act than coercion. He got in beside her.

The motor sputtered, coughed, then sprang to life. He backed the van out of its space beside the house, his eyes on the side mirror. Pointing it toward the road, he started to accelerate, then slammed the brakes. She braced herself against the windshield. The van moved back and pulled up a few yards from the rear of the sheriff's car.

Opening the door, he slid out, unslung the gun and shifted it into firing position. Sparks spewed from the barrel, giving the sheriff's car an eerie life as bullets tore into the tires, settling it onto the hard packed dirt. Then he walked to its side and shot out the radio. Starting back on a run to the van, he paused a moment, almost as an afterthought, then sprayed bullets into the gas tank. The sheriff's car exploded in a plume of flame, vibrating the van.

He was back in the driver's seat quickly. Soon the van was bouncing over the washboard road.

Only when they hit the main road, the van riding smoothly, Barney's eyes squinting ahead, his body stiff beside her, did her mind tell her that she had better feel danger, that he was beyond reason.

19

Locked in the secure room, O'Hara, Roy and the sheriff had immediately concentrated on how to break out of it. Jack, awakening, watched them, frightened, squatting on the mattress.

At first, they had tried to break down the door, but the two-by-eights that barred it from the outside held, resisting their joint efforts.

"Built it too good," Roy muttered in frustration. The sheriff rubbed his shoulder, easing the pain. The sound of an explosion rattled the room, confusing them. They heard the crunch of the van's movement.

"Your car, probably," O'Hara said glancing at the sheriff.

"We got troubles," the sheriff said. "Big time."

Above all, his own stupidity was his most dominant rebuke, more powerful than fear. He had been stupid in the first instance, reacting wrongly, setting all of them loose. No way to keep the peace, he sighed. It offended his innate sense of caution and security. Like his car, he saw his whole life blown up. Earlier, he had seen the full measure of his failed strategy in Gladys' face, in her anguish.

She had faced him, uncomprehending, explaining what had happened, like a child recounting a nightmare. She had heard noises coming from where the boy was sleeping in the room that had once belonged to their oldest son. The room was on the ground floor. She had put on her robe and slippers, not rushing, thinking it was only the boy growing restless. But if he was awake, she wanted to be ready to comfort him. She had stopped in the kitchen to get a cookie and some milk. She had remembered hearing the hum of a moving car outside. It had been close to the house. Might be Tee coming, she had thought at first, except that the car was going. She berated herself for not acting sooner.

These were things that had happened in the twilight of afterthought, pulled from her memory. How could these sounds have set off fear? No one would dare burglarize the sheriff's house, no less kidnap a boy under his care.

"Did I do wrong, Tee?" she had asked. One of the caveats of her existence was that he did not bring fear home. What she knew of violence was sanitized.

"What was there to do?" he said, embracing her.

"It was them, wasn't it?"

He knew it had to be, but he let it lie there unsaid. It told him, too, that they no longer trusted him, that he was finished as far as their support was concerned. They knew that he would not report it, set no arm of the law in motion. Even when Gladys' anguished phone call had come, he had told no one, rushing back to see for himself, as they knew he would. He was as much their prisoner as the boy.

"I'll get him back, Glad," he assured her, getting her to take two Valiums, knowing the horror she had faced in the empty room, the boy gone. She had told him earlier how great it was to have a little boy around the house again.

He knew what had to be done. The ball was in his court. All the risks would have to be his. Taking Gladys' Ford, he drove to a pay phone on the edge of a deserted road and dialed Jeremiah's number. He feared calling from his phone at home.

It was nearly four a.m. He knew Jeremiah would be waiting. As expected, he answered on the first ring.

"About that matter," the sheriff said flatly, offering no potential recorded evidence, still clinging to a sliver of possibility that he might regain their goodwill and his job, a prospect that did little for his self-esteem.

"Yes. That matter," Jeremiah said with an air of sarcasm.

"We should meet about it."

"Yes, we should."

Beads of sweat had begun to hang on the sheriff's chin and the instrument felt moist in his hand. He was being diddled and dangled now, and he detested his powerlessness.

"When and where?"

"Here," Jeremiah said. "I think we can discuss it amicably. I'll have my ..." He knew the man was seeking just the right euphemism. "... material on the premises." Appropriate, the sheriff thought sadly. That's what humans were to them. Material. Inanimate and malleable. "Can you bring yours?"

It was no longer a test. They knew. They had flushed him out. How could they know he could deliver his ... materials? His heart and will urged him to resist. They had broken his sword finally and completely.

"Yes," he answered, surrendering.

"Say about seven?"

"All right. Seven."

"A.M."

"A.M.?"

He looked at his watch. Less than three hours. He thought about protesting. Futile, he decided. Better go along.

They would be gathered in front of the camp mess hall under one roof, ready to be marched out as spectators to view their victory, a celebration of Father Glory's power. Jeremiah would interpret it to them as divine intervention, Satan's defeat, showing them how Father Glory's hand can reach out and pluck his children from harm's way, proving that his divine power was greater than the mere law. The sheriff felt a churning in his gut. The psychic pain was worse.

After the call, he drove back to the house. Tiptoeing into their bedroom, he bent over Gladys' frightened face.

"Don't worry," he whispered.

"They're bad, Tee."

In her good heart lay the spark of their mutual dreams. From her body had come their treasures. No matter what, he would always have that. Being sheriff wasn't everything. Trying to outfox them was the worst mistake he'd ever made. Can't teach a hillbilly nothin'.

The black man and O'Hara were making a racket in the bathroom that adjoined the room, hammering with their shoes against the faucet of the sink. Amid the clanging, their curses rang in the room.

Roy came out with the faucet handle in his palm, setting to work digging away at the nailed planks that covered the window.

"What are you doing?" the young man whispered from the bed.

Roy ignored the question, knowing it might lead to others. He did not want to think about the boy and his fleeting breath of freedom.

After awhile, he managed to dig a finger hold under one of the planks that covered one of the windows. Pulling in unison, they strained to remove it. Slowly it came away from the wall. They huffed and sweated. The sheriff's fingers and wrists ached.

Finally the plank came away from the wall and they were able to get more leverage by putting their hands in the recess of the window. Soon they had ripped the planks from the wall.

"Stand back," Roy ordered. He stood on the mattress and punched out the window with a karate kick, hoisting himself over the sill and out. The others followed quickly. Rushing into the house, they removed the planks from the door of the room where they kept the girl and kicked it open.

She showed no fright, sensing her own victory. Seeing her nakedness, the sheriff turned away in embarrassment. O'Hara threw her clothes and she dressed in front of them without shame.

"Where are we going?" the young man asked when they had come back in the room, the girl in tow. His panic was rising.

"Am I going home?" he asked. He had not yet learned to fully exercise his own will, and what little showed was fragile. The girl sensed what was happening, her tight smile broadening as she saw their gloomy faces.

"It's all going to be all right, Amos."

"Amos?" He looked around him like a trapped animal. "My name is Jack."

"Shit," Roy said, turning away, as the girl locked her arm in Amos'.

"Where are we going?" he asked lamely.

"Back to Father Glory," the girl said.

Outside, they saw the still burning hulk of the sheriff's car. He led the way down the washboard road, O'Hara behind him, followed by Mary and Jack. Roy brought up the rear.

Hurrying down the sloping road, stubbing a toe occasionally on the mud-dried ridges, the sheriff forced his mind to consider alternatives. Each was as bleak as the other. To be loyal to his badge and the honor of his office, he would have to plug into the official apparatus, call his office and bring an armed force of his men to the camp. That, he knew, would open the vein finally, bleed him to death. A quick end. The exposure of his part in it would be inevitable, his world torpedoed.

On the other hand, Harrigan might coerce them into giving him his son without either conditions or bloodshed. They could strike a bargain. If he got there in time, he might tip the scales, negotiate a peaceful conclusion. All's well that ends well. The Glories, too, had a great deal to lose by exposure. But they had the money and power to weather any storm. In the end, the law would be their most potent weapon and he would be dead three times over.

"I won't go."

It was the young man's voice. He sat down beside the road. Mary kneeled in front of him, her eyes already locked into his. As Roy came up, Jack tore his gaze from Mary.

"Not back there, please."

"Don't listen to her, Jack. Don't even look at the bitch," Roy said angrily.

"I want to go home," the young man whined, his gaze drifting back to Mary.

"We love you, Amos," the girl said. Roy tugged at her hair, forcing her to rise, unlocking their eyes.

"Don't make no trouble. Not now," he said to the girl. "You just move." O'Hara and the sheriff had stopped their descent, looking back.

"Won't make any difference," O'Hara muttered.

"I want to go home," the young man persisted.

"Resist the devil," the girl shouted.

"Oh shit," Roy said, forcing the struggling girl to the road's edge, grasping her in a hammerlock, putting a palm over her mouth. She struggled intermittently. "We're taking you back, bitch," he said. "Leave him be. He's going with you."

She seemed to understand, casting a long look at the forlorn young man, squatting on his heels beside the road.

"You'll have him back. Just keep moving."

Smiling, she turned. Roy held her by the upper arm and started leading her down the road. He looked back at Jack and waved him forward as the sheriff and O'Hara continued their descent.

"Come on, man," Roy shouted. "You're gonna be fine."

"No one is gonna be fine," O'Hara whispered, his eyes lowered to the road, scuffing dust as he walked. "Harrigan's out there with a lethal weapon. No saying what the bastard will do."

"He wants his boy is all," the sheriff said. "We give them ours, that should end it." Whistling in the cemetery, he thought, hating this operation.

They reached a steep part of the road. The sheriff picked his way down cautiously.

"Maybe he'll get the kid out before we get there," the sheriff said, pausing, then moving forward. He was grasping at straws. Jeremiah wouldn't resist a determined man with a submachine gun. "At least, that's what I'm hoping."

"And if he don't?"

"I don't want to think about it."

"He's got one good head start," O'Hara said.

"If you're smart, you'll do the same," the sheriff said. "But in the other direction."

They were getting closer to the sound of cars moving along the main highway.

"Jack." It was the black man's voice echoing in the hills. They heard Roy call his name again, then come crashing down the road, the girl in tow.

"He come this way?"

"No."

"Damn. He flew the coop," Roy said.

"You deliberately let him go," the young woman said, glaring at Roy.

"He was scared shitless," Roy said. "Can you blame him?"

"Not my day," the sheriff said.

They all called his name and got no response.

"He couldn't have gone far," Roy suggested, leaving the girl and heading back up the road. They waited, the sheriff called out.

"He's up there."

For a long time there was no response. Then Roy came running back down the road.

"Nowhere in sight."

"He's hiding somewhere," the sheriff said.

He was thinking: they would have to take half a loaf. Hell, the girl would be a consolation prize. He wanted to laugh, but couldn't. All this cloak-and-dagger hocus-pocus was a pain. He'd made the fatal mistake: getting emotionally involved.

"Jack can't be far," Roy said. "Probably holed up. Doesn't know what to do."

"Let the poor bastard be," the sheriff said. "Won't matter much anyway. Harrigan and his son might be long gone once we get there." He knew he was trying to convince himself. Nothing had gone right from the beginning. Good riddance, he thought. Out-of-town troublemakers. Maybe he would survive this yet. He'd show them his good faith by not calling in his men. He wouldn't even call Jeremiah to warn him. Let the fucker look down the muzzle of that gun. Maybe all of them, parents, brothers, sisters, cousins, should descend on them armed to the teeth. Give them back their loved ones, or else. Bam! Maybe Harrigan was right. It might be the only way. If it was his Gladys or the boys, he'd do the same.

"I'll explain to Jeremiah about Amos," the sheriff said.

"I'd like another crack at that one," O'Hara said, looking at Mary. "Some day."

The road flattened. They could see the highway just ahead. He'd flag down a car. It was just light enough for them to see his uniform.

"You fellas better hang back. I'll take the woman."

"I think maybe we better go with you," O'Hara said. Roy, his face shiny with sweat, nodded.

"That's not wise," the sheriff said, although he was secretly comforted.

"We're in it, too," O'Hara said. "Up to our ass. They know we were doing them?"

The sheriff nodded.

"Hell, maybe we can talk Harrigan down," O'Hara said. "Besides, we're with the law."

Roy snickered and the sheriff shook his head and spat on the ground.

"Some law," he muttered.

They reached the highway. The sheriff waved his arms at an approaching car.

"Suit yourself," he said.

He was tired of making decisions for other people, tired of making decisions for himself. He looked at Mary. She was smiling, her eyes vague, inner-directed, her face turned toward him. She was zonked.

Lucky lady, he thought. At that moment, he felt the old latent regret. He should never have left West Virginia.

He stood at the edge of the highway looking for an SUV to flag down. He'd have to drop off the driver and give him a receipt.

20

In the opaque gray light, Naomi could see the camp gate, the low wooden buildings and neat, carefully tended paths.

The van was impossible to miss as it chugged and rattled up the sloping road. Beside her, Barney squinted ahead, lips tight, a total stranger now. Earlier, she had tried to penetrate his concentration, giving up finally. What frightened her most was that he appeared cool, deliberate. No hysteria. No panic.

"This is madness, Barney." It had been her first attempt to persuade him to retreat. He had ignored it. She tried others. Finally, she stopped trying. Yet she felt obliged to say something as he braked the van, paused, and surveyed the camp. Lifting the gun, he checked the clip.

"There's still time to stop this, Barney," she said. Jeremiah had emerged from the headquarters building, Holmes beside him. The camp, aside from the two men, seemed eerily deserted. They looked toward the van. Smoke curled from the chimney of the dining hall.

"You can't . . ." she began.

"Yes, I can."

"You could hurt Kevin."

"Kevin's been hurt."

He was extraordinarily calm. The memory of what he had done to the sheriff's car lingered. He had been calm then as well. Nothing she had ever observed in his character had prepared her for this.

He did not open the door of the van. He just sat there, peering out, waiting. She was certain he had calculated it all beforehand, had written it down in his notebook, an event waiting for its cue. When it would come, he would be fully prepared.

Jeremiah moved forward from the headquarters building, Holmes followed a few paces behind. They moved hesitantly, obviously trying to determine who was in the van. As they came toward them, Barney lowered the barrel of the gun below the dashboard so that it was hidden from their view.

His breathing was steady. He looked relaxed, cool, steady. Her heart was pounding in her chest. She felt on the verge of hysteria.

Halfway toward them, Jeremiah stopped suddenly. Then he turned toward the mess hall and raised his hand. From the building's entrance, Glories spilled out, one by one, in single file, stepping in cadence.

They seemed to have rehearsed the procession. She had the urge to count them, life-size toy soldiers with remarkably similar faces, broadly smiling, eyes vacant. They kept coming, forming a long line from one end of the camp to the other, end to end, facing the camp gate. When Jeremiah lifted his hand again, the line stopped all movement. It was an impressive illustration of perfect discipline.

Then Jeremiah lifted his hand again and a huge banner rolled down from the top of the mess hall, a giant photograph of Father Glory, smiling and benign, eyes angled upward into a burst of light.

That done, Jeremiah waited, peering ahead. Barney sat calmly in the driver's seat. The ceremonial aspect of the performance seemed quite clear. It was a welcoming committee for Amos and Mary. Jeremiah must have thought they were in the van. Naomi felt an urge to cry out a warning but held back. They would see the gun soon enough. Nothing must set him off, she decided.

From one of the nearby cabins, she saw a woman emerge holding Kevin's small hand. The boy was pale and confused, rubbing his eyes, as if he had just awakened from sleep. Her heart leaped with fear.

"There's the boy," Jeremiah said. "See, he's fine."

Barney had already seen him, but he made no move.

"Put the gun away," she begged. "There's still time. Reason with them."

"Reason?" He turned slowly, facing her. "There is no reason here."

"Maybe if I explained ..."

"Poor Nay." He shook his head. "How far apart we always are."

"Think of Kevin. Don't foreclose on him," she pleaded.

"I am thinking of him," he said, but his response seemed cryptic, mystical. They were on two different planets.

"Damn it, Barney. It's wrong."

He shrugged and turned away.

Watching the van, the long line of Glories behind him, Jeremiah turned to Holmes and they spoke together. Then Jeremiah began to come forward. Naomi saw Barney's grip tighten on the gun, knuckles whitening. Jeremiah came forward confidently, smiling. His expression was not vacant like the others, but mocking and arrogant. A few yards from the van, Jeremiah stopped. From his vantage, she realized, the light slanting against the glass was preventing him from seeing clearly who was inside. He said nothing, looking back at the line of Glories.

A quartet of men with guitars stood stiffly, also smiling. So they will have music too, she thought, feeling a thumping begin in her head, a tightening in her chest. Was it fear? Confusion? Surely this was a dramatic abstraction. Images jumbled in her mind. This was pageant. Spectacle. A waking dream. A giggle erupted inside of her, never quite emerging.

Then Jeremiah was moving again, coming closer.

"Are our people in the van?" he asked, reaching the open window of the driver's side.

Barney lifted the barrel of the gun, now fully visible. Jeremiah looked at it dumbly, his features twisting in surprise.

"Bring me my son," Barney said softly. Jeremiah's features blurred.

"Where are Amos and Mary?"

"I want my son," Barney persisted, calm but firm. He shot a look that seemed to say, See how reasonable I am.

Jeremiah turned to the line of Glories, then back to face Barney.

"Not until we have Amos and Mary."

"For God's sake," Naomi cried. "Give him the boy."

Barney lifted the gun, the barrel pointing out of the window, directly at his head. Still Jeremiah showed no fear. Did he feel protected by some divine force? It's real, she wanted to shout at him.

"We are not the least bit afraid of that," he said arrogantly.

"And I'm not afraid of you," Barney said with quiet resolve. Their conversation seemed almost casual, like a chance encounter in which they might be discussing the weather.

"You have the gun," Jeremiah said.

"And you have ..." He shifted the gun toward the line of Glories. "... them."

"They have more power than your gun," Jeremiah said, smiling.

"You don't seem to understand," Naomi said, adopting the reasonable tone employed by the two men. "He will use it."

"I know."

Looking at Barney, she expected some sign of frustration. Then it occurred to her. He had made peace with himself, an assumption that made him even more dangerous. The men looked at each other, like prizefighters on their stools at opposite sides of the ring.

"So you will not give me my child?" Barney asked, displaying what seemed more like infinite patience.

"Not until we get back Amos and Mary."

"You can't be serious," Naomi interjected.

"Oh, he's serious," Barney shrugged, opening the van door, getting out with almost delicate deliberation, poking the barrel of the gun directly at Jeremiah's midsection, a bare millimeter from his shirt. Naomi, fearing a reaction from the line of Glories, was shocked to find no change in their ranks. They were still smiling dolls, scrubbed and polished, waiting. Only Holmes had moved, taken a single step. The movement had called him to Naomi's attention.

"Make him give Barney the boy, for God's sake," she cried out to the lawyer as she followed Barney out of the van. Holmes started to move again, obviously uncertain and confused. Then he halted, watching them. She surveyed the frozen tableau of standing Glories in perfect formation, their eyes staring, but unseeing, as if they were blind.

"You don't understand," Jeremiah said softly.

"I'm afraid not," Barney said.

Only then did she see the nerve palpitate in his jaw, a tangible sign of his beginning agitation.

"There's no point to this," she began, forcing upon herself a calm reasonableness. She turned to Barney. "I'm sure there are other ways to handle this." She found herself trying to smile, searching for ways to be persuasive, ingratiating. "You're grown men. Be rational."

"Poor Naomi," Barney sighed, his glance darting toward her for a moment, then back to Jeremiah, whose features remained impassive. "What will it take for her to understand?" It seemed a question delivered directly to Jeremiah. Barney did not wait for an answer.

"I'm going to get my son now," he said slowly, backing away, still pointing the gun at Jeremiah's midsection. Naomi looked toward the boy. The woman still his hand, smiling and indifferent.

"Daddy," Kevin cried, his voice carrying in the silence. He squirmed in the woman's arms, but could not break free.

"Come with me, Nay," Barney said. It was more of a plea than a command. He spun around, taking a single step, moving the gun in an arc. She was conscious of making the choice but not of the process as she moved ahead of him.

He spun again, stepped backward, slowly, then spun again in a circle, covering both sides of the Glory line, his eyes alert. Step by step, Barney moved backward in the direction of the cabin in front of which the woman clutched the boy's hand, his eyes shifting, the barrel of the gun circling as he spun, like a dancer in a carefully choreographed ballet.

They passed Holmes. She saw his ashen face, the expression tense and frightened.

"Can't you make them stop this?" she begged, but he averted his eyes and she knew he was as powerless as she.

She moved in tandem with Barney, stepping backward, watching the smiling faces of the Glories, empty and indifferent, like carved figures resembling people, but hardly human. Halfway to the boy, Jeremiah raised his hand again. When she turned again the boy and the woman had disappeared. The boy's cry, muffled and angry, came from the interior of the cabin.

Barney spun, gyrating, his eyes calm and alert, although the nerve continued to palpitate in his jaw and a rim of perspiration glistened on his cheeks and forehead. As she moved, she tried to fix her mind on some future moment in time. Sooner or later the sheriff must come.

Considering the tension and the stubbornness of the protagonists, he had better hurry. Even the air seemed devoid of movement, a calm so empty and inert that it could only spring to life again explosively. They were teasing her. It was just a movie, the stuff of melodrama. Rescue, as always, would come in the nick of time. Only the gun in Barney's hands seemed alien to the script. Surely they were not real bullets.

They reached the steps of the building. She stood beside him, the muzzle of the gun roaming the air, like a telescope observing the silent row of Glories. Oddly, she felt no kinship of humanity. They did not resemble real people, people of flesh and blood, her own kind.

That this might be some aberration of the subconscious occurred to her. Not a waking dream but something that transcended even fantasy. Like they were ghosts of once living people and she had simply stumbled into their world. Pardon me, she spoke silently, as if she might have burst in upon some foreign family in some secret place, an alien, like E.T. And they were watching her, uncomprehending, as if she was not of their species, but not quite knowing how to react.

"The door."

Barney had barked the order. But his voice, too, sounded alien as if another species had invaded him, transformed him. Even his body seemed different. Not the Barney Harrigan of her reality. Certainly he was not the Barney of her old longing, the lost man who had made her dead baby.

Yet she knew what he meant. She bounded up the three wooden steps, confronting the door. She turned the knob, found it locked, struggled against it, then banged on it with the heel of her hand. She felt the dam of emotion break inside of her, the hysteria begin.

Her fists banged impotently against the wooden door, vibrating her body. Turning, she saw Barney still poised, the barrel arcing like a pendulum. From inside, she heard Kevin's pleading voice.

"Daddy."

"Step aside," Barney said softly. His body braced. Shifting his weight, he aimed a running kick at the door with his foot. It swung open. Still, the waxwork army remained motionless.

"Inside," he ordered. She obeyed instantly. She saw the boy. He rushed into his father's arms. His body shook with sobs as he clung to his neck. The young woman who had been with him stood in the corner smiling, eyes as glazed and vague as the others.

"We love him," she said. Like the others, there was no sign of fear. Love! The word hung in the air, leaden, without any meaning that she could understand. As Barney moved in, stepping backward, Naomi saw the woman disappear, withdrawing through the door in a quiet breeze of motion, like an apparition fading.

"It's all right, son," Barney said, patting the boy with his free hand.

Through the partially open door, still on its hinges, Naomi saw the first movement begin outside. As a reflex, she fell against the door, pushing it closed, bracing it with her back, facing the barrel of the gun, now poised at the level of her breasts. Kevin still clung to his father's waist. He had stopped crying and his moist eyes searched her face, uncomprehending.

"Barney, please. Think."

"I am," he said, holding the barrel steady.

"They won't let you leave. You saw them. They're not in control. They don't know what they're doing. It's not their fault."

"Whose, then?"

"I don't know," she pleaded, her thoughts confused. "Just wait. The sheriff will come. He'll bring Amos and Mary. That's all they want. Then we can go home. Think of Kevin. His life."

"And Charlotte? You want me to forget her?"

His eyes probed her.

"You've had a terrible shock, Barney. I'm sorry if I did anything to cause you pain. But you'll only hurt Kevin. Ruin everything. Please, Barney. Nothing will bring Charlotte back. It's just hysteria. It will go away."

The barrel wavered, giving her courage. She hesitated, unable to find words, watching the moisture rise in his eyes, tears spilling over his lids. His lips trembled.

"I need to make them understand," he said, blinking through the tears.

"Leave it alone, Barney. Don't ..."

Outside she heard chanting begin.

"Satan. Satan. Satan."

The sound rolled toward them, filling the room.

"Satan. Satan. Satan."

The barrel rose against her chest, and she saw his knuckles whiten as he held the gun's grip.

"Don't listen to it," she cried, above the quickening din.

"Satan. Satan. Satan."

The sound came in rising waves, echoing and re-echoing triggering her panic. This cannot, could not, be reality, she told herself. These are images on television, crowds in Muslim countries, chanting slogans, raising fists, burning effigies. Not here. Not in America.

Turning, she opened the door a crack. The Glories were lined up in a circle surrounding the building. There were four layers of them. They held hands, blocking the way out. They continued to chant.

"Satan. Satan. Satan."

It was maddening, relentless, obviously designed to keep them bonded, enhance their fanaticism, focus their energy and terrorize any observers.

"Stop it," she screamed. "Stop it."

Her words were drowned out by the chorus of voices, vehement, emphatic, repetitive. As if on cue, the Glories raised their connected arms, pumping them up and down, like some giant centipede caught on its back, squirming. Beyond the circles she saw Jeremiah, smiling a broad, taunting smile, as if her proudly reveling in his omnipotence.

Suddenly, she felt herself shunted to one side, feeling the cold hardness of the gun barrel. Barney stood beside her now, feet planted apart, the muzzle of the gun steady. Even his ominous presence made no difference to the Glories. They were oblivious to the danger.

"Satan. Satan. Satan."

The sound bounced against the nearby hills, echoed back, as if the hills themselves were crying out, alive with hate. She stood there, screaming out her rage. "Stop it. Stop it." She put her palms over ears.

Jeremiah signaled and silence came again. Except for her own voice, pleading and impotent. Then, she, too, was silent.

From somewhere in the shadows of her mind, another voice stirred, not her own. O'Hara's. "They have been brainwashed. They have lost their will." Hyperbole, she remembered thinking, an angry fool voicing his personal obsession for vengeance. In her heart, she had protested the possibility. In her mind, she had rejected it. It flew in the face of her values, her beliefs, her concept of human behavior. She was having second thoughts now.

"You cannot take the boy until they give us Amos and Mary."

It was Jeremiah speaking. A bullhorn had materialized in his hand, covering the lower part of his face. His voice sounded calm, reasonable, despite the treble amplification.

"We will let you have the boy after they give us Amos and Mary, our brother and sister." The words floated toward them, deep and resonant.

Kevin stood beside his father, his fingers looped in his belt, frightened and bewildered. She wondered if he was experiencing an adult fear, the same urgent sense of impending doom that assailed her now like a giant wind beating against her face. She fought against it, railed against it, invoked every resource, focusing whatever energy existed inside of her to resist it.

"Are you people blind?" she shouted, conscious of the high-pitched shrewishness of her voice, so tiny and ineffectual against the rich timber of the bullhorn. "He has a machine gun. He could kill many of you." The redundancy inflamed her anger and again O'Hara's words rumbled back at her: "If people like you continue not to understand, we've lost."

People like me? What would reasonable comprehension be if it were she in that line with a working mind, a living, human organism with all senses operating? What would register? A man with a submachine gun? A confused child, doomed to a lifetime of trauma because of these events? A desperate woman on the precipice of hysteria? Why don't they understand?

Barney stirred beside her. Was he reconsidering? The idea offered the tiniest glimmer of hope, but he was merely unclasping the boy's fingers, edging the boy toward her.

"Hold Kevin," he ordered, casting a determined glance her way. "We're getting out of here." In the mini-second of hesitation, it struck her that she might catch him off guard, wrest the gun from his hands. Perhaps even the struggle might burst the bubble, force his reevaluation of their dilemma. Another illusion, she thought, imagining the impending struggle, accepting the sensible reality of his superior physical strength. The thought told her that at least her mind was purring. The instinct for survival was alive, goading a search for alternatives.

"They won't let you," she said.

"Not my problem," he muttered. "They want paradise. I'll send them there."

"They're not in control of their actions, Barney. Their minds are not their own."

Was this her talking, she wondered? What had happened to her moral posture, the idea of free choice? She felt a growing hollowness in the pit of her stomach. Is this me? Was she finally, grudgingly, reluctantly accepting O'Hara's thesis? No, please, she told herself. But she was beyond resistance.

"You can't fight mindlessness. Barney, please. They don't believe they're ordinary people." Ordinary? "They're convinced they are immortal. They don't recognize the integrity of their living bodies."

Barney looked at her and shook his head.

"Too bad, then," he muttered.

Jeremiah raised his arm again, recharging the chant.

"Satan. Satan. Satan."

Waves of sound rolled over them, counterpointed by the deep bass of the bullhorn as Jeremiah joined in. Kevin buried his head against her belly and she pressed her palms against his ears. His little body shook with terror. Or was it her own?

Beside her, the gun's barrel spit fire. But he had raised the muzzle, firing rounds above their heads. The chant did not falter, as if the discharged weapon did not exist. Lowering the muzzle, he fired more rounds in a circle above their heads. Still, the chant continued. Her nose caught the acrid smell of gunpowder and hot metal. The boy huddled against her body and sobbed. She patted his head for comfort. Again, Jeremiah raised his hands and the chanting stopped.

"What is your bullets' sting against Father Glory's promise?" the bullhorn boomed. She saw Holmes backing away from his position behind Jeremiah. He kept moving, taking cover finally behind the wall of the mess hall.

"It's no use," she said, trying to remain calm. "They'll never let us out of here." She looked toward the road, searching for dust clouds from any approaching vehicles. Nothing!

"It's pointless, Barney. Let's wait."

He glanced at her and smiled ruefully. His face was moist with perspiration and the nerve continued to palpitate in his jaw.

"The sheriff will come soon," she pleaded. "Look at Kevin. He's scared out of his wits. Think of him, Barney. In the name of God ..." It sounded ludicrous, invoking the deity, a concept so distorted in this place. "We'll go home, fight this thing. This is not the way. We'll work together. We'll organize resistance. We'll tell the world. We can beat them. But not this way."

He turned toward her, shaking his head. There was no mistaking his contempt.

"Fight them? Look at them. How?"

"Give us the boy," Jeremiah raged through the bullhorn. "Father Glory will not give you the boy until you give us Amos and Mary."

Suddenly the gun barked. Barney had raised the barrel, pointing it in the direction of the banner with the likeness of Father Glory. The shots shredded his face, punched out his eyes, obliterating it with smoke and flame. The shots did not stop until the trigger's empty staccato click showed that the magazine was empty. Thank God, Naomi sighed. When the sound had died, the bullhorn, like some disembodied cosmic voice, spoke again.

"Give us the boy. We will give him back when we have Amos and Mary." the bullhorn roared.

"Raise your hands," the bullhorn commanded.

Responding to the command, the Glories all raised their hands. Four rows in a circle.

The bullhorn cracked again.

"Don't let them through".

Barney viewed the tight circles of Glories. He raised the muzzle of the submachine gun. Then he shook his head.

"Not enough bullets to kill them all," he sighed. "I wish."

Moving backward, they returned to the cabin's interior and locked the door. Naomi hugged Kevin. His body was shaking.

"Sons of bitches," Barney muttered, leaning against the wall. He dropped to his haunches, putting the gun aside. He put his hands to his face and sobbed.

Soon the chanting began again, then stopped abruptly. In the silence that followed, Naomi heard the sound of a car coming toward the camp. Then she remembered that Barney had destroyed the sheriff's car.

Miracles happen, she thought, although she was quickly losing hope.

21

It's not that, the sheriff's mind assured him as the commandeered van turned into the camp road, tires gripping the hard dirt ground. O'Hara sat beside the sheriff. Roy sat in the rear with the girl. As they moved forward, they heard a burst of gunfire.

"Shit," the sheriff muttered. Then hopefully, "Could be a backfire."

"No way," Roy said. Mary, beside him, giggled.

When another burst came the sheriff could not deny it to himself. Then another. He pressed the accelerator. The car bumped and jogged, flinging them upward. The crown of his hat flattened.

Any expectation that his world might miraculously right itself faded with the unmistakable sound of gunfire, leaving him only with the reflex of his professionalism. He was the sheriff of this county, and his official turf had been badly abused. Yet he couldn't seem to fire up his enthusiasm. If that were true, he'd have called in his men, done the job as prescribed by his official duties.

On his chest, his badge felt heavy and redundant. Perhaps, as a final gesture, he might be accorded some ceremonial disgrace, like the ripping off of epaulets on the uniforms of military officers who had violated their trust. No such luck, he shrugged. Not now. Not ever. He had no right to lead this pack of avengers. Again the burst of gunfire reached his ears.

"It's the submachine gun," O'Hara said.

"No answering fire," Roy said.

Were they moving toward a goddamned slaughter? He pressed the accelerator, warning those in the car to brace themselves against the ceiling. Another burst exploded in their ears, closer now.

"Sounds bad," O'Hara said.

"Real bad," Roy said.

Mary was silent, smiling.

The sheriff did not need his thoughts echoed. Whatever was ahead was certainly bad. The worst! But the bastard had destroyed his car with the radio. It was a pretty lame excuse for not calling in his men. He should have stopped, made the call. Worse, his mobile had been in the car and he had earlier confiscated theirs.

As the car rattled forward, they saw a man running toward them. It was Holmes, his face bleached like flour in the gray light, his features twisted in anguish. Waving his hands, he thrust himself in the car's path. The sheriff slammed down on the brakes. None too soon. Holmes slumped over the grill, gasping for breath. He groped toward the window on the driver's side.

"They've gone crazy." Spittle fell from his lips.

"They?"

"Jeremiah and Harrigan." He shook his head, eyes blinking. He was sobbing with fear. Really rattled your cage, scumbag, the sheriff thought. He felt his gut burn. The man was offensive, a toady. The sheriff pushed him free of the car, watching him stagger back and fall.

"Son of a bitch," O'Hara said. "They help create it. Then they run."

The sheriff braked the car abruptly. He had hoped that his experienced professional eye would observe the situation with cool circumspection. It didn't. They saw the circles of Glories surrounding the building.

"He's in there," Holmes gasped, pulling himself to his feet. "Armed and dangerous."

"Has he killed anyone yet?"

Holmes shook his head.

"Not all bad, then," the sheriff said. He turned to Roy in the back of the car. "Stay here with the girl."

O'Hara and the sheriff got out of the car and walked toward Jeremiah. The sheriff drew his pistol. His legs felt stiff as he moved forward. Behind him, O'Hara was following. Jeremiah, who had lowered the bullhorn, watched them coming, his face serene.

Jeremiah, holding the bullhorn, watched them approach.

"Have you brought Amos and Mary?"

The sheriff ignored the question.

"Harrigan in there?" he asked instead, motioning with his chin toward the building that Holmes had indicated. Jeremiah nodded.

"Get your people out of there," the sheriff ordered.

"He has the boy. There is a woman with him. I will see that they are released as soon as you hand over Amos and Mary."

"First get your people moving. The man is armed and dangerous."

"We're not afraid."

"Maybe you're not. But what about these kids?"

Jeremiah shrugged.

"We'll disperse and let them go when you give us Amos and Mary," Jeremiah said with flat determination, calm and reasoned. He showed no untoward emotion, appearing exactly the same as before. O'Hara had stopped a few yards from Jeremiah and watched them. Jeremiah ignored his presence.

"We have Mary," the Sheriff said.

"Not Amos?"

"He ran," the sheriff said, censoring himself. He had nearly said "escaped."

"No deal then," Jeremiah said.

"Are you mad? Have you any idea what you're doing?" the sheriff asked. "Harrigan is obviously desperate. He will kill some of your people."

"Our position was quite clear," Jeremiah pressed, his fingers toying with the pendant likeness of Father Glory, which hung, beside his whistle, outside his shirt. "The boy in exchange for Amos and Mary."

"Are you serious?" the sheriff said, searching for some common reality. "I told you. Amos is gone. He ran away."

"Find him, then."

He had often dealt with people who had "lost touch." There was a procedure that one followed—feign entry into the confused mental world, try to find a way into the distorted thinking, the twisted logic. Unfortunately, he had never been confronted with two madmen before with directly opposing aberrations. Easy, he cautioned himself, watching Jeremiah, surveying the circles of disciplined, smiling Glories.

"He'll slaughter them. He has a submachine gun," the sheriff said softly. "Can't you see?"

"Doesn't matter. These are Father Glory's children. If they have to, they'll go home to the spirit world."

"Go home? Have you lost your mind?"

"Death is nothing," Jeremiah said, dismissing it as if it were a bad cold.

"Nothing?" Death nothing? All right for him to say. He felt his own discipline begin to disintegrate, the dam of caution break. The sheriff raised his armed hand, pointing the pistol at Jeremiah's chest. Suddenly he felt a pressure on his forearm.

"Don't," O'Hara said, tightening his grip. "It doesn't end with him."

"But if he controls them ..." the sheriff began, confused.

"They're programmed to go if he goes. All of them." O'Hara looked at Jeremiah, who smiled back at him.

"Tell them, Judas," Jeremiah said.

"I don't understand," the sheriff said.

"You never did," Jeremiah said.

"Armageddon," O'Hara explained. "Their ultimate weapon."

"What the hell are you talking about?"

"That liquid in there." He pointed to the amulet around Jeremiah's neck. "Cyanide. This is a death cult, sheriff. Like most. They believe that the whole purpose of this world is preparation for the other. That's what it's all about. "

"Right on," Jeremiah said.

The sheriff looked around him, observed the Glories, like robots, poised, blissed out.

"My God!"

He hadn't known or had been in denial. Or both. He felt foolish, utterly incompetent.

"Our God," Jeremiah said as if it were a cue. He looked toward the shattered poster of Father Glory. "Father Glory has arranged for our salvation."

"You wouldn't."

"Yes, they would," O'Hara said.

"You're all crazy," the sheriff mumbled.

"Trouble with you, sheriff," Jeremiah said, "you don't understand the power of faith. Tell him, Judas."

"Faith!" O'Hara spat on the ground.

"What about him?" the sheriff said, pointing to Father Glory's picture. Know what you're dealing with, he urged himself, the first rule of a professional. He thought he knew. Now he confronted his own ignorance.

"He'll deny he ordered it. But he'll have his martyrs and the illustration of his power. Grist for the mill," O'Hara said.

"But these are human beings."

"Grist for the mill," O'Hara repeated. "No one ever comes back to prove him wrong. Or right."

The sheriff groped for alternatives. "I'm going to have to call in the troops." There was little choice left on that score. It had gotten totally out of hand. He'd have to get to a phone.

"It won't stop anything. He's perfectly capable of ordering Armageddon if you send in your boys. What they want is Amos and Mary. Both. Not just one."

"Listen to him, sheriff," Jeremiah said.

Between a rock and a hard place, the sheriff thought. How the hell could he give them Amos? Or was it Jack?

The sheriff looked toward the cabin surrounded by rows of Glories. He admitted to himself his total confusion and disorientation. Stupid hillbilly, he berated himself.

"The deal was quite clear," Jeremiah said.

O'Hara caught the sheriff's eye. He read the signal and turned to Jeremiah.

"Will you excuse us a moment?" The words sounded ridiculous.

"Take your time," Jeremiah said.

They moved out of earshot. The sheriff had the sensation of participating in a conversation between the pitcher and the coach at a crucial baseball game.

"They won't budge," O'Hara said, his toe kicking a rock on the ground. "Roy will have to go back and look for the kid."

"Suppose he doesn't find him?"

"We'll have to tell Harrigan what's up."

"Think he'll sit still?"

"He hasn't killed anyone yet."

"Not yet."

He looked deeply into O'Hara's eyes.

"You think Jeremiah will be crazy enough … ?"

O'Hara lowered his voice.

"Look at them, all glassy-eyed robots, holding hands. You tell me."

"And if we touch Jeremiah, they'll all do it? Drink that shit? All of them?"

His eyes darted to the transparent pendants, likenesses of Father Glory hanging around the necks of all the Glories. He wished he was back in West Virginia.

"Name of the game," O'Hara said. "Paradise awaits."

He shook his head, wanting to disbelieve.

"They'll commit suicide. Just like that."

"Jonestown, Waco, Al Qaeda. On and on. How much more proof do you need?"

"So it's stalemate."

"For the moment."

O'Hara shrugged.

"Shit happens," he muttered.

"I got to telephone."

"They won't let you."

"Then what the hell am I supposed to do?"

"One option. Roy has got to find Jack. Bottom line."

They take that shit, there was no way to keep it under wraps. It was a worldwide event, a featured attraction in the theater of terror. They'd all come barreling in, the FBI, the National Guard. Maybe even the CIA and the Marines. And all those hard-assed media people with their cameras. Horror gets eyeballs. Name of the game.

The sheriff looked at the circles of Glories, faceless young men and women. Somebody's children. He thought of his own boys, the love and sacrifices he and Gladys had made for them. Those in the line represented the hopes and dreams of other parents, torn from their progeny by these ruthless, greedy men. It wasn't fair, wasn't natural.

"So what happens now?" The sheriff felt helpless, inert. It was more than just the nightmare of the eyes. What had O'Hara called it—Armageddon? It was some kind of a Greek thing, the end of the world.

"Make one wrong move and bingo," O'Hara said. He looked over the lines of Glories. "Maybe five, six hundred out there."

"They're just young people. Just kids," the sheriff sighed.

"Yeah. Just kids."

"We could call his boss. Get him on the phone. Something. Anything." The more he speculated openly, the more he felt his impotence.

"Hell, you think he's a humanitarian? Dammit, he wants this. He likes this. Those kids don't mean anything to him. Think of it from his point of view. How many people are willing to die for you, sheriff? Think of the mythology created here."

"It's beyond my responsibility," the sheriff said. He wished the ground would open and swallow him up.

"Yeah. Beyond everybody's responsibility. That's the problem. Well then, sheriff. Let it happen. Maybe the good people of America will get the message." He paused and balled his fists. "Hell, they didn't get it at Jonestown or Waco. And this Jap cult. Then came the big banana, the World Trade Center. Fact is there are hundreds of cults out there ..."

"Fuck the propaganda, O'Hara. We got a situation here." Something had to be salvaged out of this.

"It's reality, sheriff. Not propaganda."

"We have to send Roy back. With luck, he'll find the kid. He's probably just wandering around in a cloud. He couldn't have gone far."

"Then what?"

"We make the trade. It's over."

"No other choice," the sheriff sighed. "We just sit here with our fingers up our ass."

"'Fraid so."

It annoyed the sheriff to solicit the man's consent. Who the hell was O'Hara? Another fanatic. And he hadn't delivered on his end. A rim of sweat had formed around his hatband. Droplets ran down his cheeks. He chewed over his thoughts. Jeremiah watched them. The circle of Glories barely stirred. How had he come to this? he wondered. He had wandered too far from home.

"Let's go," the sheriff said.

O'Hara waved toward the car and Roy came out with the girl.

"We'll give him one and promise him the other," the sheriff said. He started to move toward Jeremiah. At that moment, the girl broke loose from Roy's grip and ran toward the line of Glories. Roy started to follow.

"Let her go, Roy," O'Hara shouted. Roy stopped in his tracks.

"Just stay, Roy. We got a problem here," O'Hara said.

"No shit."

"We gotta go back and look for Jack."

"Fuck."

"They won't deal with one. They want 'em both."

Mary had got in the circle with the other Glories. The sheriff watched her and shrugged.

"You mean just leave everything in place?" Roy asked.

"Looks like it."

"Get to a telephone, Roy," the sheriff whispered. "Call my office. Tell them."

"Better not, Roy," O'Hara said. "People come up here, Jeremiah will give the order."

"Order?"

"Armageddon."

"Suppose I don't find him?" Roy asked.

"Then we go to Plan B," O'Hara said.

"What's that?"

"There is no Plan B," O'Hara said.

"We have to tell him now what's happening," O'Hara said pointing with his chin to the cabin, scratching his beard. Looking at his feet, the sheriff listened. The truth was that any idea would have been acceptable, that his own will had faltered, that his mind was empty of ideas. He could see why people turned themselves in, deliberately imprisoned their will, gave up their freedom to others. Too many unknown factors interfered with objective execution. They could be in instant danger. What the hell? In the end, he nodded consent. O'Hara nodded and Roy got in the car and headed out of the camp.

"I'll go," O'Hara said when the car had disappeared down the road.

The sheriff nodded then moved toward Jeremiah again.

"You win," he said. "He'll look for Amos and bring him here."

"And no one else."

"That's the deal."

Jeremiah's smile broadened. The sheriff controlled his urge to put a bullet in the man's brain, end it once and for all. Good idea, he thought. Armageddon. Get rid of the problem once and for all.

"Now we have to talk to him. Tell him what's going on," the sheriff said cautiously with a glance toward the building. He looked at O'Hara who nodded and started toward the building.

Jeremiah continued to smile. What was disconcerting to the sheriff was that Jeremiah seemed so ordinary, so human, a man like him. It was a trick of disguise, he decided, a pose. He felt the handicap of his own humanity, his fallibility and limitations. The person he faced seemed so sure of everything. The sheriff was sure of nothing.

"He'll try to get him to hand over his gun, then we can make the exchange when Roy comes back with Jack, just as we agreed."

"Jack?"

"I mean Amos."

Jeremiah nodded, but the sheriff knew he had given something away. Again, he cursed his incompetence.

"That's the deal. Amos and Mary for the boy. And oh, yes, we will have him back."

His remark was cryptic, but not totally puzzling. Yes, the sheriff knew, they would get him back, return him to his mental prison.

Unfortunately, returning Amos, or Jack, would change nothing. Kevin would return east with his father. The Forman woman would go back to Washington. O'Hara and the black man would continue to be itinerant deprogrammers unless the law got to them finally, and life would be the same. Nor would it end his nightmare of the eyes. It's time to go home, he told himself, back to his own people, back to his roots. Pack up Gladys. Time for us hillbillies to get back to the hills.

He watched as O'Hara moved to the cabin.

"Make way," Jeremiah said through the bullhorn. The circles broke for him to pass.

"Harrigan ..." O'Hara's voice was clear, echoing in the silence. He called again, then again. Finally the door opened and O'Hara disappeared inside.

A light drizzle began, the mist obscuring his vision: A chill had crept inside the sheriff. His bones felt like cold metal, despite the perspiration that poured down his sides and back. He forced his gaze along the circle of Glories. They, too, looked human. Yet not alive. Oblivious to what was going on around them.

He watched the door of the cabin, regretting the quick decision he had made. Well, he shrugged, just one more regret to join all the others.

22

Naomi sat on the floor, her back against the wall. In her arms, Kevin slept fitfully. When a spasm shook him, she soothed him with a reassuring word, kissing his forehead.

Barney leaned against the far wall, the submachine gun beside him. He was writing in his notebook, bearing witness as he called it. From time to time, his eyes drifted toward hers, glanced at her briefly, then back to his notebook.

She supposed she should be thankful. He had not shot anyone. Not yet. Through the window of the house, she had seen the sheriff and O'Hara talking with Jeremiah. The sight had calmed her. She assumed they had been negotiating, making a deal for them to go and take the boy.

From time to time, Kevin spasmed in his sleep.

"It's been terrible for him."

He mumbled an answer that she did not understand.

"You should never have got him involved," she whispered. "It wasn't fair."

He looked up briefly.

"So you are still on fair?" He sighed showing a measure of exasperation.

"Fair is everything," she said. "Without fair we are uncivilized."

He shook his head and let out a sigh.

"Poor Nay. Look at these people out there. You think they will be fair to us, let us leave with Kevin? Wouldn't that be fair?"

She did not answer. This was no time for a debate. Was she clinging to old ideas? She let it pass. Not now. Not until this horror played itself out.

Suddenly they heard movement outside.

"Harrigan!"

O'Hara's voice. Barney was instantly alert. He lifted the gun and stood up.

"Harrigan! It's me, O'Hara!"

Naomi and Barney exchanged glances. The boy continued to sleep, stirring briefly, then slipping back into slumber. He was obviously exhausted.

"I'm coming in," O'Hara said. "Is it okay?"

Barney hesitated, then moved closer to the window. Nodding, he moved to the door and pushed it open. The lock was broken but the hinges still worked. O'Hara came in and Barney pushed the door shut.

"You all okay?" he asked, nodding to Naomi.

"Yeah. We're okay. We want out of here."

"I know. We're taking steps."

O'Hara looked exhausted. There were deep circles under his eyes.

"Steps?"

He glanced from Naomi to Barney and bit his lip.

"Got a problem," he said, his nostrils flaring.

"I'm listening," Barney said.

"They want the two, the two we tried to break back there."

"I thought you broke the boy," Barney said, puzzled.

"He ran. Roy is out looking for him. We did bring the girl."

"Who gives a shit?"

O'Hara swallowed hard, moved to the window and looked out.

"You see what's out there."

"Yeah, we know what's out there. I'd kill them all if I had enough bullets." He patted the magazine. "That's all there is. Not enough. They won't let us through. I could knock off, maybe 20,30. They'd never let us out. These people ..." He paused. "Are they people, O'Hara? These aren't real people. They don't feel a fucking thing."

"The deal is," O'Hara said. "We bring them Jack ... Amos. Whatever. They let you leave with the boy." He glanced toward Naomi. "And her."

"You so sure Roy can find him?"

O'Hara shook his head.

"I don't believe this," Barney said.

"Believe it."

"I want out of here, O'Hara. And I'm going out one way or another."

"Don't do anything stupid." O'Hara shook his head. "This was probably not a good idea, coming in here with that."

"They took my son. And killed my wife, remember? What was I supposed to do? Okay. I should never have got him involved. I thought, well, I thought that it might trigger Charlotte's maternal instinct. Anyway, they wouldn't let it happen. I was wrong. Everything I did was wrong."

"Be patient, Barney. I know what you've been through."

"Why doesn't the sheriff act?" Naomi blurted.

"He's sort of on the horns of a dilemma," O'Hara acknowledged. "Its too fucking complicated. I'm here to tell you to cool it, is all. Wait it out. Jack is disoriented. He's probably just roaming the hills, maybe afraid to make contact with the outside world. It happens like that ..."

"What the fuck do you know?" Barney sneered. "So high and mighty. You couldn't break her."

"What can I say? You play the odds in this game."

"You fucked up."

"More or less," O'Hara admitted glancing toward Naomi.

Barney stiffened and raised the barrel of the gun, pointing it at O'Hara.

"Don't," Naomi cried. In her arms, the boy stirred again, then fell back to sleep.

"We're getting out of here," Barney said.

"Don't be a damned fool. They'll ..."

He never finished the sentence. Barney upended the gun and hit O'Hara a glancing blow to the head with the butt. O'Hara staggered backward and fell to the floor.

"Let's go," Barney said.

"I'm not ..." Naomi began.

"Just come. No bullshit. Enough, Nay. Enough."

Frightened, she rose unsteadily, shaking the boy awake. Barney moved cautiously, opening the door. The three rows of Glories, hands locked, stood impassively, smiling, robotic. Barney, his gun circling, moved toward the inner circle, Naomi following holding the boy's hand. He was too sleepy to know what was happening. She was petrified. It took an effort to force her legs to move.

Suddenly the chant began again

"Satan Satan Satan."

Waves of sound rolled over them.

"Satan. Satan. Satan."

Barney moved to the edge of the first circle. Pointing the gun down, he let off a few rounds on the ground. The noise was deafening, but the circle of Glories held their ground.

"These fucks aren't human," he screamed.

In the distance she heard the sheriff's voice.

"Don't, Harrigan. Don't."

With the butt of his gun, he hit the joined hands of two Glories in the front row. The force of the blow broke them apart, and he moved to the next row, followed by Naomi and the boy. The Glories, ignoring the pain, joined hands behind him.

"This is madness, Barney," Naomi cried. Kevin began to cry. "Don't worry darling." She told him. "Everything will be all right."

As they moved, the chanting continued: "Satan. Satan. Satan."

Suddenly the sound of the bullhorn boomed into the air. The chanting, as if on cue, was silenced.

"Stop this at once, Harrigan," the voice on the bullhorn cried. Go back to the cabin. Do you read me? Go back to the cabin."

"Fuck you," Barney cried, slamming the butt down on two locked hands in the second row of Glories.

Naomi looked at their faces. Their expressions were empty, devoid of emotion, their eyes glazed, their lips posed in a robotic smile. She noted, too, that as soon as they passed through the circle, the hands were rejoined again. Didn't they have any feeling? she wondered. Didn't they feel pain? Despite her galloping sense of panic, her mind could not grasp the reality of their reaction.

Kevin continued to whimper.

"It will be okay," she said, kissing the boy's forehead.

"Go back," the bullhorn blared again.

"Listen to him," the sheriff cried, his voice an impotent bleat next to the sound of the bullhorn.

Behind them, they heard O'Hara's voice. Looking back, she saw him staggering as he tried to negotiate the stairs. Suddenly he fell, slipping on the hard ground.

"Don't," he cried. "Listen to them."

"For Chrissakes, Harrigan."

It was the sheriff's panicked voice. She saw him running toward them. Again, Barney lifted the butt of the submachine gun and slammed it down on the hands of two Glories in the third circle. Then he moved to the last circle.

They broke free just as the bullhorn sounded again. This time there was no voice, only three whistling sounds. She could see the sheriff stop dead in his tracks. She watched him as he stood staring at something going on behind them. She turned and followed the direction of his eyes. Barney, too, looked behind him.

"Oh my God," he cried.

What she saw came to her as if in a dream. In the dead silence, the Glories were sinking to the ground en masse. She heard gurgling sounds, some groans, a few brief whines, then silence, utter, complete, devastating silence. Her mind could not process what her eyes were seeing. The four rows of Glories, a few hundred young people, were stretched along the ground, like scattered cordwood. She placed her hand over Kevin's eyes.

"You must not look," she said, while she stared at the sight, mesmerized and disbelieving.

Shots rang out. They turned. The sheriff was shooting Jeremiah although he was already on the ground. He had emptied his pistol. Turning again, she saw O'Hara stagger over the line of bodies to where they were standing.

"Off to paradise," he whispered. "I tried to explain." He shook his head and tears brimmed over his eyes.

"They've …" Naomi tried to speak. "All these young people. Why?"

"Because," O'Hara said, then could not go on. He dropped to his knees and began to sob hysterically.

At that moment, they heard the sound of a car coming up the road. The car came to a halt and Roy came out, dragging Jack along.

They both stopped abruptly, surveying the scene.

23

In the eerie silence of the camp, the sheriff stood frozen, barely comprehending, as he watched the living come forward. There were four adults and the boy. Five, counting Holmes, who sat on the ground with his head in his hands. On the ground, not far from the group, was the dead Jeremiah, the bullhorn at his side.

Jack lay on the ground, sobbing quietly. For a long time, neither of them spoke as they silently observed the grisly scene before them.

"Shouldn't surprise us," O'Hara said, his voice hoarse but calm. He seemed to have recovered from the shock. The sheriff was still not there. He had acted by instinct. Unfortunately, he had been too late. Too late, all around. He had seen it happening, had been part of it. It was even too late to blame himself. He continued to observe the scene in silence, his sense of action paralyzed.

"Sorry," he managed to say. "I wish I knew ..."

What he wanted to say was that he wished he knew what to do now, what to say, how to explain it. In a little while, as soon as he found his voice, he would have to do what sheriffs do. He would have to call people, bring them here, talk to them. He knew in his gut that they would not understand. No way. They would look at him like deer caught in the headlights, without any comprehension.

Of course, the evidence of the suicides were there for all to see. Sniff the burnt almond. It permeated the air. They had all drunk liquefied cyanide. Killed themselves instantly. But no one would truly understand. Even the big bastard himself, Father Fucking

Glory, would offer his version, which few would comprehend. He might even distance himself from the deed, babble something about valuing life or some such platitude. He was, after all, just another two-bit preacher with a thirst for power and another dumb idea about immortality, eternity and paradise. Fuck paradise, the sheriff shouted inside himself looking at the bodies strewn around the camp.

He felt shame. His badge lay heavy on his chest, leaden. Sheriff? That was a laugh. He was just a dumb hillbilly with a silly little badge on his chest, charged to protect the citizens of his county. He looked at the bodies strewn around the camp. Some stupid fucking lousy little sheriff. He knew he couldn't hide behind this badge any more.

Worse, he told himself, people will forget. The Glories will benefit, have their martyrs. His mind embellished the idea. People who give their life for a cause are often declared heroes. The Glories would create posthumous medals, even monuments and special songs. They had the money and the apparatus to promote things like that. The media would make it look like it was his fault, a slaughter aided and abetted by a corrupt sheriff who took the law into his own hands.

In anger, he tore the sheriff's badge from his chest and threw it on the ground. Yet even through his sense of abandonment and abdication, he knew he would have to see it through. The coming ordeal might give him his own salvation. He relished the idea, feeling his courage bounce back, the old pure sweet feeling.

They would use every trick, every legal maneuver that lawyers could concoct, twist the truth, make him the real culprit. They would find him guilty of malfeasance in office. He would taste public disgrace, humiliation. Maybe even go to jail. It didn't matter. In the end, he would be free of them, free of the nightmare of the eyes. Cleansed. One thing he knew, he'd go down kicking and screaming. He was on the side of the angels now. And he still had Gladys and his boys. They would understand.

"Hey, sheriff," Barney said, as if sensing what was going through his mind. "It's not your fault."

"Whose then?"

"I'll take some of that. Maybe I overreacted. I should have known after I saw what they did to Charlotte. We're all vulnerable,

I'm afraid, all victims." He pulled out the notebook he had stuffed behind his belt. "I've written it all down. Everything I did. Everything we went through. I'll get the word out."

"You don't look very concerned, Harrigan," the sheriff said.

"Tell you the truth, I'm not."

He glanced toward Naomi, who turned her eyes away and looked at the ground.

"I don't know what to say," Naomi said. "It's awful."

"Yes, awful," O'Hara said. "I know. Morality. Free choice. Civil rights. All the goodies of a civilized society. These people once owned all these things you cherish. Somebody deliberately stole them, absconded with their minds. Look at them now. Do you think they're in paradise? Explain it to me, Naomi. I'd like to hear your views."

"I can't," Naomi said, whimpering.

"Shit happens," Roy said.

"As good an explanation as any," O'Hara said.

"Better make my call," the sheriff said. He started toward the administration building, then he remembered that Jeremiah had a mobile strapped to his belt. He bent over his body and pulled it off.

"Who really gets the blame for this one?" he muttered to no one in particular. He looked at the bodies laying in their supine circles. Then his eyes drifted to the shattered poster of Father Glory. "Fuck you," he cried. "You evil son of a bitch."

24

Naomi sat in the back of the van. Kevin lay asleep, his head on her lap. She had sat there through the night, observing the parade of stretchers through the open doors. The mess hall has been converted into a makeshift morgue. Hundreds of workers, many in uniforms, had churned the once neat walkways and lawns into a muddy mess. The media, too, had descended with their strobes and cameras, like an invading army. Hordes of curious onlookers stood behind barricades. Ghouls, watching the ghastly proceedings.

The mass suicide had already become a worldwide event with the usual overblown commentary with sidebars about suicide bombers, terrorists worldwide, the World Trade Center horror, Jonestown, the Japanese cult that tried to poison the Tokyo subway system and on and on. Of course, by then, she realized, they were all related, united by the process of brainwashing. She could no longer continue her denial. She had seen it in action with her own eyes.

They had little to say. They had been interrogated ad infinitum. They were talked out, released now on their own recognizance, witnesses to horror. They would be telling their stories to the authorities for months, maybe years. They had, so far, avoided the media, but they held out little hope that such isolation would continue.

Roy had parked the van on a high knoll, nestled in a stand of trees. For some reason, they had all agreed on one last look. They all got out of the van and observed the scene. The morning sun threw shadows across the camp. They could see the sheriff moving in the crowd. He looked like a supervisor in a meat factory.

Naomi had no desire to sleep. Nor did she have to force her alertness. In her mind, she had spent the long night sifting images, cataloging her thoughts, challenging conceptions, opening figurative doors and possibilities, probing to the depths of her knowledge. She forced away the intrusion of emotion, guilt, terror, panic, hysteria, fantasy, illusion, testing her intuition against these uncommon events, searching for the truth of it.

She could not, she knew, will herself into a state of pure thought. For the first time in her life, she was beginning to question the values that had sustained her. She had bet all the chips of her convictions on man's inherent goodness, on the ultimate power of his compassion, on the irreducible bedrock of his loving nature. How then could we have come this far, built civilizations, created moral standards, revered life? It was, she knew now, half-made concepts, a charade of sorts. It skirted the central issue of mankind. In the mind was life's real center. And the mind was malleable, able to be manipulated. It could direct man against himself and all his carefully contrived values.

"We are driven by our ignorance," she thought, sighing, wondering if mankind would ever find ways to leach out the evils that plagued it.

It surprised her to think in these terms. Barney had accused her of politicizing everything, and she agreed. Her cause had always been man's right to political freedom, to equality under the law, to equality of opportunity, to the creation of a system everywhere that would ensure man's reaching his greatest potential whatever it might be, to the actualizing of his personal aspirations to the full limits of his talent. She had never dreamed that the mind carried with it the chemistry of its own destruction. Although she had bore witness, she vowed to remain questioning. There was no scientific evidence, only the evidence of what she had seen. For the moment, she would have to accept that.

To know how to use this chemistry, to ruthlessly exploit it, seemed now more terrible than any of the traditional enemies of humanity. Like the atomic bomb or nerve gas or bacterial warfare. Its use went far beyond the moral pale. Those other weapons killed the organism outright. But this weapon preserved the organism, yet put its control outside itself. It was also less tangible. It could hide behind a mask of freedom, or the scrim of law. It could pose as a religious or political order. It could disguise itself with the old values—love, goodness, dedication, fervor, zeal. It could lurk behind a smile, hide behind a saucer of benign eyes. The monsters had found the secret tunnel into our psyche and were turning our decency against us.

Had those sad young people been conscious of the enormity of their deed, abdicating life? But was it life, really? She would never stop wrestling with that. Everything these cults touch they corrupt, O'Hara had told her. That was true of all evil. It begets itself. The thought revolted her. Life was also hope, and she had seen the process reversed. So now she had a new enemy with which to do battle.

It seemed strange to her that after such traumatic events, she could face the morning with such clarity, as if she were peering through a window wiped clean of dust. It was important to her to assess and summarize. The memory of what she had seen, what she now saw, would be with her for a lifetime, a piece of herself, as tangible as human tissue. Living life, for her, had always been a series of moral choices. Now, she sensed, she was on the cutting edge of the most important moral choice she would ever make.

Choices. She mulled the word in her mind, felt it disintegrate like a dissolving clot in the bloodstream that fed her brain. In the end, that was what a human being was, an instrument for choices. That was the point of it, the point of life. Whether created by God or evolution, man must choose in the private soul of himself, unfettered, unmanipulated, his will free.

She felt the thrill of insight, wondering how long its power would last. After awhile, they started to return to the van. Then, as one, they stopped and the four of them with, Kevin beside them, suddenly reached out and embraced. They stood like this for a long moment, feeling the heartbeats of one another, the shared warmth, the sense of joined humanity.

Then they separated and got into the van, and soon they were heading down the highway.

The complete works of Warren Adler are now available in both trade paperback and hardcover. All titles are also available in all formats of e-books at all online retailers.

Mainstream Novels

The War of the Roses

The Roses thought they had a perfect marriage, but discover that their relationship is barely skin deep. This is the acclaimed and best-selling novel that became the classic divorce movie starring Michael Douglas and Kathleen Turner.

Random Hearts

Two survivors of a tragic plane crash discover their dead spouses' infidelity. This best-selling novel of love, passion and forgiveness became a major motion picture with Harrison Ford.

Trans-Siberian Express

American doctor Alex Cousins knows a dark and dangerous secret, and the Soviet Union will stop at nothing to keep him in Siberia on the world's longest and most exotic train ride to prevent him from revealing it.

Mourning Glory

A down on her luck 38-year-old single mother with a dysfunctional teenage daughter snares a rich widower in Palm Beach. But her cynical scheme unravels and she finds herself enmeshed in a self-spun web of deception and danger that threatens to rob her of everything she holds dear.

Cult
A novel of brainwashing and death

The suspenseful story of a man's increasingly desperate attempt to rescue his brainwashed wife from a religious death cult. A thriller with a chilling climax that shows how the power of sinister forces using mind control techniques can turn innocent people into weapons of destruction.

The Casanova Embrace

In this explicit and erotic thriller, a charismatic Latin diplomat cynically seduces three lonely women and uses them as pawns in international terrorism. Discovering his ruthless manipulation and betrayal, they plot every woman's revenge fantasy.

Blood Ties

During a family reunion at their ancestral castle, the famed Von Kassel family—arms dealers for over a hundred years—suddenly find themselves in possession of stolen plutonium capable of creating the most destructive weapon on earth. Secret revelations erupt into violence as the family is torn apart by their acquisition's deadly potential.

Natural Enemies

Pursued by human predators, a young urban couple becomes lost in the Colorado wilderness and is forced to confront the chilling and impersonal wrath of nature in this taut and acclaimed novel.

Banquet Before Dawn

After serving his Brooklyn district for many years, an Irish Congressman is challenged by a youthful and more liberal opponent. In this remarkable novel full of unforgettable characters, the last hurrah becomes a poignant and seething masterwork.

The Housewife Blues

An innocent and naïve young woman marries to escape from her small mid-western town. But her controlling husband moves her to an apartment in New York City and keeps her a virtual prisoner. Her journey of self-discovery from naiveté through disenchantment and eventual wisdom makes for a suspenseful story with explosive consequences.

Madeline s Miracles

A young family falls prey to a woman who convinces them that she is a psychic and can foresee their future in this critically acclaimed and chilling bestseller about brainwashing and superstition.

We Are Holding the President Hostage

When terrorists capture the daughter and grandson of a Mafia Don in Egypt, the angry Godfather insinuates himself into the White House and teaches the President some lessons of the mob. This classic confrontation between two men on utterly opposite sides of the law is laced with humor and illustrates how fierce paternal love can motivate even the most ruthless of gangsters into reckless acts of courage and bravery.

Private Lies

Two Manhattan couples are caught in a complex and emotional web of adultery, sexual obsession and deception that turns deadly on an African safari.

Twilight Child

Readers Digest originally published this acclaimed, heart wrenching novel about the visitation rights of grandparents and the terrible ordeal that ensues between generations locked in a bitter struggle for a child's love.

The Henderson Equation

The people who run the influential newspaper the *Washington Chronicle* have just brought down a President through their damning investigative reports. Now they want to create their own choice for Chief Executive! The power of the press to manipulate comes under the microscope in this tense exploration of the media and the thirst for power.

Undertow

After the beautiful black aide and lover of a womanizing married Senator accidentally drowns, the Senator mounts a massive cover-up of cynical lies designed to deflect the potential damage to his career in this suspenseful tale of adultery, media manipulation, and political chicanery.

Short Stories

The Sunset Gang

With time running short, the retired residents of Sunset Village in Florida continue to thirst for life, love and happiness. In the process, they teach us all a lot about living—a subject on which they are, after all, experts. These critically acclaimed short stories were adapted into a PBS trilogy that won worldwide recognition for its wonderful insights into the aging process.

Never Too Late for Love

The intrepid crew from Sunset Village is back! With sensitivity and humor, these brilliant stories depict the lives, loves, conflicts and trials of the modern senior citizen. This is the complete collection of the classic *Sunset Gang* stories.

Jackson Hole, Uneasy Eden

These acclaimed stories capture the truth, warts and all, of how modern life can both corrupt and enhance a traditional environment. Based on the author's experience as a long-time resident of this pristine valley in Wyoming nestled in the heart of the Grand Tetons, America's most beautiful mountain range.

The Fiona FitzGerald Mysteries

American Quartet

This is the first book in the popular Fiona FitzGerald mystery series. Fiona is a senator's daughter turned Washington, D.C. homicide detective. Four seemingly unconnected murders stimulate Fiona's sense of history as she delves into our country's dark past. In her effort to solve the crimes, she uncovers the twisted sexual and homicidal obsessions of a socially prominent but failed Washington politician. Named by the *New York Times* as one of the top ten crime novels of the year.

American Sextet

Fiona takes us behind the scenes of power and unravels a massive political sex scandal that shakes the Washington establishment to its core. As Fiona investigates, she uncovers a conspiracy involving six men from the highest offices in the country—a great American Sextet!

Senator Love

A seductive and philandering Senator is the prime suspect when bodies begin turning up buried in an upscale Washington neighborhood. Besides solving the mystery, will Fiona submit to the powerful sexual charm of "Senator Love?"

Immaculate Deception

The clock is ticking both figuratively and biologically. During Fiona's pursuit to conceive a child, a powerful female pro-life Senator is found dead. The case gets even more baffling when one shocking clue contradicts the entire investigation.

The Ties That Bind

The daughter of a prominent lawyer is found murdered, and a Supreme Court Justice with a sadomasochistic fetish is the target of Fiona's investigation. This is a case that truly brings Fiona to the dark side of the Washington scene.

The Witch of Watergate

When an infamous and unpopular *Washington Post* reporter whose poison pen has destroyed many careers is found hanging in her Watergate apartment, suicide is the logical explanation. But Fiona won't stop investigating until she uncovers the truth, even as it leads to the corridors of power on Capitol Hill.

DISCARDED